WITHDRAWN

# OLEANNA

# Oleanna

## Julie K. Rose

Second edition: August 2012

ISBN 978-1-105-36141-8

Image credit: Sogne Fjord, Norway by Adelsteen Normann (1848-1918)
Private Collection/ Photo © Bonhams, London, UK/ The Bridgeman Art Library
Nationality / copyright status: Norwegian / out of copyright

Printed in the United States of America
Set in Adobe Caslon

For Janis Terry Hunt Nelson

# CHAPTER ONE

Lake Jølster, Sunnfjord, Norway
May 1905

OLEANNA TOLLEFSDATTER MYKLEBOST was beset by ghosts: winter ice in her veins, chill and stiff even during the long summer days of the midnight sun. *Always winter with us,* she thought. *Severina, Anton, father, mama, Anna: all gone. Everyone gone. And now, John too.*

The waves of grief, held mostly at bay over the long, cold, dark winter by sheer will and the numbing properties of ice and hard work threatened now to overcome her. She gritted her teeth and forced herself to press on. She had not ventured to their summer meadows and cabin—their ancient sæter—since the previous autumn, when the skies were leaden and the winter only a breath away.

Oleanna stepped onto the cabin's narrow wooden porch and stamped her feet, dislodging mud and chunks of ice and snow. She looked down into the deep valley, the lake sparkling and blue below. And next to it, the farm, her home: a brush of green and brown on the southern bank, nearly lost among the newly verdant fields and dark evergreens, visible only if you were searching for it.

The tiny farm clinging to the side of the mountain, scrabbling away from the cold lake, was surrounded by towering dark pine trees and tall, graceful birches. And though there were farms dotting the shoreline all around the long, thin lake, none were as old as the Myklebost farm.

The store house and the farmhouse, the barn and the fields, all were touched by the dusty hand of age, despite the bright flowers spilling from the window boxes during the long days of the short summer. The crops came in well enough, against all odds in the small, rocky plot just beyond the store house. No rambling split-rail fences were necessary to mark their land; everyone, even their animals, knew their lives were bounded by the dark trees and the deep, cold lake.

"Who's there?" a voice called from within the cabin.

Oleanna sighed, then pushed open the door and leaned against the doorframe. After a few moments, she said, "So this is where you're hiding."

"Go away," the voice croaked, its owner buried under the covers piled high on the bed.

Oleanna set her pack down on the clean pine floor. "Why can't I get a moment's peace?" she muttered, shutting the door.

Her sister Elisabeth shifted under the covers. "What are you doing here?"

"Making sure it's ready for the summer."

"John's already done that."

"Oh." Oleanna hesitated, looking around the small cabin.

"It's cold now," Elisabeth said. "You've brought in all of the ice."

Oleanna scowled and turned to tend the fire, bending down and warming her hands. "How long are you going to stay up here?" she asked, pulling a hewn chair to the fireside.

"I don't know."

Oleanna could hear Elisabeth shifting around in the bed behind her. "Hiding up here like a child isn't going to make John change his mind," Oleanna said, pulling off her boots and socks. "You can't stay up here forever."

"Of course I can."

"I can't run the farm by myself. We'll starve." Oleanna warmed her tingling toes at the fire and, after a few moments, looked over at

Elisabeth, who had thrown off the covers and was sitting up, resting her chin in her hands.

"I can't do it," Elisabeth whispered.

Oleanna walked over and stood next to the bed. "Of course you—"

"I don't want to do it."

"You have ten generations of Jølster farm blood running through your veins. Don't be an ass."

"Mama wouldn't—"

"Don't talk about her," Oleanna said. She glanced around the cabin and shivered.

"I'll talk about her if I damn well please."

Oleanna shuddered. "Stop it."

Elisabeth sprang forward and grabbed her sister's wrist. "You're not the only one who misses her," she hissed. "You're not the only one who's lonely. Stop being so selfish." She squeezed Oleanna's wrist and then shoved her away.

Scowling and rubbing her wrist, Oleanna retreated to the fireside. Elisabeth crossed her arms and glared, imperious as a queen. Finally, with some effort, Oleanna said, "I need your help."

Elisabeth threw herself back on the bed, covering her eyes with her arm. "John is a bastard," she muttered finally.

"Don't blame him. You'd do the same if you could." Oleanna looked out the window of the cabin, toward the far mountains and deep waters of the Sognefjord. "So would I."

Elisabeth huffed and pulled the covers over her face.

Oleanna watched the outline of her sister for a few moments, until a long list of chores wailed in her brain like an insistent toddler. She pulled on her still-damp socks and boots, then paused at the door. "I'm not going to take care of Torjus all day and all night again," she said, pulling open the door. A rush of chill spring air filled the room. "Stop pouting, come home, and look after your son."

"I'm not pouting."

"Just come home," Oleanna sighed.

She stepped out onto the cabin's small porch and pulled the door closed behind her. The lake sparkled in the mid-day sunshine, fragrant pine trees swayed in the breeze, high clouds scudded across a pale blue sky, and intrepid wildflowers poked their heads out of the grass near the protected cabin wall. But Oleanna noticed only the squelching coldness in her boots and the ache of her shoulders and heart. "John is a bastard," Oleanna whispered.

# CHAPTER TWO

Lake Jølster, Sunnfjord, Norway
May 1905

THE NEXT MORNING, AFTER LONG HOURS OF TOIL and quarrels with both of her siblings, Oleanna pulled herself out of sleep, every limb complaining and groaning. Next to her, Elisabeth turned over. "Stop thrashing around," Elisabeth grumbled. "Go back to sleep."

The small farmhouse was still in the gray dawn, save for John's contented snores in the other box bed across the room. She was momentarily tempted to lie back down; the bed was warm and the room dim and quiet. But the pounding of the chore list recommenced, and Oleanna sighed. She heaved off the heavy sheepskin coverlet, gasping as the cold hit her bare hands and feet.

"Where are you going?" Elisabeth mumbled.

Oleanna leaned down and kissed her nephew on the forehead as he slept between them. "To the barn. Break the ice on the troughs. It's your turn next time," she whispered, climbing over her sister. The rough wood floor was icy and Oleanna gasped with the cold. She stumbled into her loom in the corner and gritted her teeth on an oath, squeezing her eyes closed against the pain in her toe.

Fumbling around next to the door, she found her heavy coat and pulled it on over her chemise, then slid her bare feet into her boots, hand-me-downs from John. They were too big and in tatters, but she loved them and refused to give them up, despite their decrepit state. She paused and listened for the gentle snuffling that told her Elisabeth had gone back to sleep.

Oleanna pulled the door open a fraction and slipped through. Though the air was icy she breathed deeply, gazing at the dawn unfolding slowly above the mountaintops. She bent down and laced up her boots properly, then stood and buttoned up her long overcoat. Shoving her hands deep into the pockets, she rounded the corner of the main house and headed past the store house toward the turf-roofed barn.

She pushed open the door; the sharp smell of new grass and a long winter mingled with the fresher scents of the animals. The fjord pony and newly shorn sheep huddled together with the goats in a far corner of the barn, while the chickens rested quietly in their cages under blankets.

Terna whinnied softly as she approached. "Good morning, my love," Oleanna whispered. She patted his flank and wandered toward the troughs. A thin layer of ice coated the water and she cracked it easily with her heavy boot, swirling the fragments, watching the patterns form and disperse.

After a few moments, she shook herself from her sleepy reverie. "I'll be back later," she whispered, running her hand along Terna's strange, short mane, taking comfort in his steady warmth. She patted him one last time and ventured out into the cold morning.

The gray dawn was giving way to clouds touched with pink and gold. Oleanna smiled; there was still time for a ramble before her round of chores began. She turned toward the mountain and struck the thread of a trail, wandering under the trees and around the sturdy boulders.

Though it was early, the echo of a fiddle being tuned floated up to her on their hillside above the lake. She caught the melody and hummed along under her breath as she walked; the song shared space, as it always did, with the questions and worries crowding her mind: had she brewed the beer properly, had she darned the hole in her second-best socks, had she made everything perfect for John's last Constitution Day at home?

She strolled, as she always did, without regard for direction or distance. She knew every inch of her mountainside and lakeside, and she let them direct her where they would. When she looked up again, she was again near the water's edge. The lake was losing its steely sheen and growing blue in the coming sunrise.

On clear days, she thought she might be able to throw a rock and hit the storm-weathered farmhouses clinging to the steep mountainsides across the lake. Her father had told her it was the Årdal farm, a half-day's ride away. She had never seen it up close; she would not row across the lake, preferring to cling close to the banks. She had rowed as far east as Sandvika, nearly six kilometers away, and west only to near Sanddal. But that was last spring. She had not been on the lake since.

A soft splash startled her and she noticed, belatedly, a dark-haired man sitting on a boulder near the shore, throwing pebbles into the water. Oh no, she thought. It is too early to be civil. She started to back away, to melt silently into her woods, when the man turned around quickly, heavy eyebrows knitted.

"Pardon me, Anders Samuelsson," she said. "I didn't mean to intrude." She backed into the cover of the evergreen trees and pulled her coat more closely around her, then stepped back into the forest and the hillside trail.

"You're not intruding. This is your farm, after all."

Oleanna stopped and turned reluctantly toward the lake. "My family's farm," she corrected.

Anders shrugged and looked at the water.

She watched him toss pebbles into the lake, his rhythmic movements soothing, keeping time with the fiddler's song in the distance. After a few moments, the chatter in her mind began again, and she had half-turned to go home, when suddenly she spun around and was walking down out of the woods to sit on the rock next to him. He made room.

She looked at him, mostly to avoid looking at the water so close to her feet. His face was like a mountainside, rocky and jagged: his nose was too large, his jaw too square, his lips too full. His eyes, a deep gray-blue, were like the lake when the first fingers of frost grasped the shoreline. And yet his arms, his hands, were delicate and gentle as a birch.

He looked over at her and held her gaze, but said nothing.

Finally shaking herself, she asked, "Are you going to the party today?"

"Yes. Of course. Why wouldn't I?"

"Oh—well..." She shrugged.

"What?"

"You're always keeping yourself to yourself."

"There's a lot to do on my little farm."

"Of course. Well, you're always welcome—"

"Yes, I know. I like the quiet. You don't get much quiet in that house," he said, looking out at the lake.

"Even so. We should have welcomed you properly. It's been two months?"

"Four."

"We should have been better neighbors."

"I expect I was the least of your worries."

Oleanna flinched.

Anders shrugged and looked back out at the lake. "It's no crime to break off an engagement. Even with Pastor Søren."

Oleanna breathed a short, mirthless laugh. "You *are* new here, aren't you?"

He looked over at her and smiled, then looked back out at the lake. She sighed and picked at her ragged nails. "I'm sorry," she said finally. "It was—"

"You don't have to explain it to me."

Oleanna looked up at him and smiled, an uncomfortable thing tight from neglect. "Thank you," she said.

He tossed another pebble, and they watched the ripples course along the surface of the still water.

After a few minutes of quietly watching water and sky, she picked up a slender birch branch from the rocky shore and twirled it between her hands.

"And why aren't you married?" she asked.

"You mean because I'm so old?"

"No—well," she said, testing out her smile again. "Yes."

"I'm an old man," he said, stilling her hands with his delicate fingers and taking the branch. "Nearly forty."

Oleanna whistled. "I'll call you grandfather," she said. "Though I suppose I'm not so far behind."

Anders smiled, watching her openly again. Oleanna suppressed the urge to turn away, and held his gaze.

"It's true," he said finally, twirling the branch between his fingers.

"What?"

"What they say about you."

"Go on," she sighed. "I've heard it all."

"That you're the forest wife," he whispered, narrowing his eyes. "You lure men deep into the woods and—"

Oleanna blinked, and then raised an eyebrow. "I think you've spent too much time by yourself over here," she said. "It's addling your mind."

Anders laughed, a short bark of a sound, and stood.

Oleanna watched him, assessing, then stood and said quietly, "You shouldn't tease an old maid like that."

His smile faded and his face clouded over. He bowed slightly and backed away. "Good morning, Oleanna Tollefsdatter," he said. He turned and walked along the lakeshore to his small cotter's hut without a backward glance.

"We're taking the wagon over to the party just after breakfast if you would like to join us."

"I prefer to walk."

She watched him disappear into his home, a confused half-smile on her face; the door clicked shut and she sighed. Maybe I am a forest wife, she thought. Hollow like an old log.

Turning away, she stretched, raising her arms high above her head. She abruptly stopped and dropped her arms, looking down at herself. "Sitting out here in the cold in my chemise and a coat," she tutted. The list of chores returned, insistent, to the forefront of her mind. She folded her arms and hurried back into the woods.

Their farmhouse was too small for a proper loft, so clothing and dowry chests and baskets ready for the spring wool were all stacked in a corner of the turf-roofed store house. The room was small, but the pitched roof and dim light sneaking in through the smoke hole gave it the feel of a great stone cathedral. Generations of wood smoke hung about the rafters, along with the ghosts of her father's family: sturdy, hardworking, and rooted.

She set about gathering their best clothes from their hiding places in the neatly packed trunks and untidy piles. Shaking the dust and winter stuffiness from the clothes, she paused when the memory of another quiet Constitution Day struck her, like a blow to her chest.

"Your mother was practically useless when we were married," her father had said, stone faced and stern. "You'd think she had been living in the forest her whole life, instead of on a proper farm in Skei."

Oleanna clutched the blouse to her chest, hands shaking. Her mother's face, small and delicate like Elisabeth's, came yet again to her mind's eye: lovely and wild around the eyes, her strange half-smile tugging at her small mouth. And then, her mother changed, ageing, lines growing, hair graying, shoulders bending, eyes dulling. Staring, expressionless, from under her burial coverlet, family and neighbors gathered around the bed...

Oleanna shivered and opened her eyes; her hands still gripped the blouse, fingers white and ghostly. With a steadying breath, she set her jaw and walked over to the last trunk against the wall.

She knelt before the large case. It was dark with age and many years in the dim store house; the intricate acanthus leaf rosemal painting was beginning to fade. Along the smooth top of the trunk, she ran her hand, tracing out the letters *Brita Johannesdtr 1874*: the year her mother had married her father and come to live on the edge of the water, deep in the fold of his family's history.

Oleanna unlatched the trunk and pushed the top open, the musty scent of old wool and ageing pine heady. She knew exactly where to look for her mother's intricate sølje brooch, protection from wraiths in the form of delicate steel and a waterfall of mirrored gold.

She had dug through her mother's dowry chest many times: furtively as a child, hidden in the dark corner of the store house when she should have been driving the sheep to the summer sæter, kneeling on the cool earthen floor, breath coming in short bursts. Gently, reverently as a young woman, searching for the hidden keys to unlock the mysteries and meanings of her strange wild mother.

Then she had searched, openly, as an adult, digging through the layers of her mother's life, clearing away the topsoil and clutching roots, until she found it: her mother's christening coverlet in the square-weave diamond pattern of Sogn. She had left the trunk in disarray, racing back to the farmhouse to cover her mother and Anna before the mourners arrived.

The round brooch, glittering silver and gold, still lay on the top of the untidy pile of clothing and linens. She laid it flat on her calloused palm, angling it to catch the scant light in the store house. She stood, closing the trunk carefully, and slipped silently out into the chill. Oleanna leaned against the weather roughened wall of the store house. In the golden light of morning, the brooch sparked and glowed with beauty and the untold stories of her mother's life.

# CHAPTER THREE

Lake Jølster, Sunnfjord, Norway
May 1905

HOURS LATER, THE OLD WAGON and reluctant pony were decorated with wildflowers and garlands of birch and pine. "I knew you you'd look fine and handsome," Oleanna said, patting Terna's flank; he stamped and whinnied in annoyance. She chuckled and looked back at the farmhouse. "Are you ready?" she called, leaning to see round to the front door. "We're going to be late."

"Yes, yes, we're coming," Elisabeth replied. She emerged, John close behind with Torjus in tow.

"Are you ready?" Oleanna asked.

Elisabeth grinned and spun around, her pleated black skirt swirling around her ankles, the red and white embroidery on the bottom edge a blur. "It's a shame we only dress up for special occasions," she said, pausing to run her fingers over the fine work on her green vest.

"Speak for yourself," John muttered, nervously smoothing down his red woolen jacket, burnishing the gold buttons down the front with his sleeve.

Oleanna shuddered, smoothing her own identical green vest and black skirt. "Imagine all the washing and mending," she said.

Elisabeth huffed. "Must you always be so—"

"Are you ready?" John interrupted, settling Torjus on the bench. "We're going to be late."

Oleanna moved to step into the back of the wagon when Torjus suddenly jumped off the bench and sprinted back toward the house.

"What are you doing?" Elisabeth called.

"I forgot my horse!"

Oleanna stepped down and Elisabeth and John joined her, kicking at the pebbly grass. Standing together, the three looked like a group of strangers, passing the time, talking about the doings of the parish or the great changes afoot in the country.

Looking at her siblings, Oleanna's heart constricted. John. Tall and thin, with straw-blond hair and ice blue eyes, the spitting image of their father, but so different in temperament. And Elisabeth, beautiful Elisabeth, with her brown curls and pale green eyes, so much like their mother, and Anna. The only thing that marked the three as siblings was the stubborn set of their jaws and their wide, thin lips: John's set in concentration, Elisabeth's in frustration, Oleanna's in resignation.

Oleanna turned away. Don't think about it, she thought, today of all days. Be merry. Don't think about—

Torjus returned in a whirlwind of noise and dust, clutching his carved wooden horse. John settled him again on the bench. "Mama?" Torjus said, swinging his feet and kicking the front of the wagon. "Come sit with me, please?"

Elisabeth sighed. "Yes, of course," she said, walking around the wagon and stepping up onto the board.

John climbed onto the bench and took the reins, while Oleanna scrambled into the back. They finally rumbled and creaked their way out of the farmyard and toward the parish church.

After half an hour of Torjus' chattering, Elisabeth's remonstrances, and John's muttered peacemaking, they finally rounded the last arm of land along the lake, and the church and the celebration came into view.

The small wooden church boasted two large flags: one scarlet with a deep blue cross, cutting through the red like a fjord, the proper Norwegian flag; the other marred in the corner by the yellow herald of the generations-old union with Sweden.

Oleanna raised her eyebrows at the impertinence of the proper flag, then smiled at the scene: fluttering banners, laughing children, matrons and grandmothers gossiping under the eaves of the church. Even the lake was sparkling especially for the occasion. She did not notice who handed her down from the wagon.

"Green suits you," a deep voice fluttered in her ear. "Like the trees in the forest."

Startled out of her reverie, she glanced up to see Anders looking at her over his shoulder, a strange smile on his full lips. He walked around the wagon and offered his hand to Elisabeth, who grinned and shot a quick look at Oleanna, then laughed like a Hardanger fiddle, droning and full, yet slightly out of tune. Elisabeth picked up her skirts and ran past him, toward the edge of the lake and a group of laughing men.

Torjus bounced up and down on the wagon's seat, squirming and struggling to get down, like an oversized four-year-old trout.

"John—" Oleanna pleaded.

In one swift motion John grabbed his nephew, swinging him through the air, and set him down right in the path of the fiddler leading the children down to the shore. Torjus looked up at Oleanna, eyes wide. She nodded, and he fell into line with the other children, dancing and capering to the fiddler's tune leading them away.

On a small stage near the church, festooned with more of the proper pre-union flags, a very round man with a startlingly loud voice was declaiming on the subject of independence from Sweden to a small audience of young farmers, including Anders; local government officials and their families watched from a respectable distance, looking uneasy. The children's fiddler tried his best to drown out the political speech, as he did every year, though Oleanna knew the speeches would outlast the fiddler, especially as the long day wore on and the food and drink ran out.

"Looks like they've already started in on the beer," John said, nodding toward a stout old man sniffing at the bottles of beer lined up on a makeshift table near the lakeshore.

"Go have a good time," she said. "It's your last time."

John hesitated, and she took the opportunity to pile their own bottles into John's arms. "Go," she said, giving him a shove.

He gave her a sad half-smile. "I will miss this," he said, then walked away.

Then don't go, she thought. Oleanna walked up the hillside to the eaves of the church, the cacophony of the party trailing behind her. She leaned against a thick wooden pillar on the porch, suppressing the pang of relief and guilt that she did not see Søren at the festivities spread along the lakeside.

"Too proud, and too proper," Elisabeth had always said about him.

"So what does that make us?" Oleanna had asked.

"Too good for him by half, that's what."

Oleanna smiled at the memory, and the jolly scene before her. Families from nine or ten farms chatted, waved their flags, admired each other's finery. She spotted Anders again easily, chatting with a slight, bookish man near the temporarily empty stage. The children broke away from the fiddler and pulled off their black buckled shoes and stockings and dipped their toes into the cold waters of the lake, much to the dismay of their mothers. Musicians tuned up on the far side of the church. A group of men, led by her brother, laughed boisterously over their beer. She closed her eyes and let the sounds collect and combine, a soothing buzz, like insects in the summer grass. Nowhere to go, nothing to do.

The speeches started up again, and Oleanna was surprised to see, on the stage, the slight young man to whom Anders had been speaking. Even from her perch, she could see him shaking, white as a sheet on a summer's line. And yet he pressed on, growing more passionate as he spoke about a separate consular service, and equality for Norway, and freedom after 600 years. She closed her eyes and felt a thrill of excitement along her arms and neck as the small crowd cheered him on.

A few minutes later, a voice broke the spell. "Oleanna?"

She opened her eyes. Standing at the bottom step was a young man with a shock of blond hair, tall and thin, ruddy already from sun and hard work. He smiled and walked up the stairs to stand next to her.

"A good turnout this year," he said.

She nodded. "Hello Jakob."

"I'm glad to see you all here, after..."

She shifted back and forth on her feet; he chewed on his thumbnail.

Finally, he asked, "How is Lisbet?"

"She's well."

He turned to look at her. "Oh, come on, Lea," he whispered. "How is she?"

"Fine."

"Lea—"

"She is fine."

"Has she told Torjus—"

Torjus at that moment ran up toward the church, feet covered in lake mud, grinning wildly, his sun-blond hair tousled by wind and water. "Lea, Lea," he yelled. "Come play in the water!"

Jakob grinned.

"No, you fiend," she said. "Go find your mama. I'm sure she'll..."

"No!" Torjus wailed. "She won't play with me, I already asked her."

"I'll come," Jakob said.

"No, you can't," Oleanna whispered, grabbing his arm.

Jakob shook off her hand. "I won't say anything," he hissed. "My God, just let me play with him, for a few minutes."

Torjus looked up at Oleanna.

"Yes, it's alright," she nodded. She scanned the crowd for Elisabeth's dark head and found it near the men with the beer, her back to the lake where the children played.

Oleanna watched Torjus and Jakob run off in the other direction. Jakob picked Torjus up and spun him around, laughing, then set him down at the water's edge and knelt at his side.

Oleanna looked back to find her sister laughing and angling herself so the men could not see her taking four bottles for herself.

Oleanna chuckled and shook her head: for many years, liberating as much beer as possible had been their private Constitution Day tradition. At that moment, Elisabeth looked up at her and flashed a wicked grin. Oleanna smiled, then turned and pushed open the door to the dark, empty church.

She shut the door behind her and slid into the back pew. The architects, not so many years ago, she thought, wanted the congregation to focus on the sermon, so only put windows on the hill-side of the church. No sparkling blue lake or spread of green to distract honest parishioners from the word of God. "What a shame," Oleanna whispered, sighing.

The door clattered open and slammed shut, and Elisabeth slid into the pew next to Oleanna.

"How many?"

"Four this time. I didn't think you'd come in here."

"Shhh."

"He's not here, is he?" Elisabeth whispered.

"No," Oleanna said. "I don't think so."

"Good. He was no good for you."

Oleanna sighed. "I know."

"In any case, you have your eye on someone else," Elisabeth said.

"No, I—"

"You do!" Elisabeth said, laughing. "I knew it!"

"Lisbet, hush," Oleanna said, looking around. "Already into the beer?"

"Maybe a little," Elisabeth said, while waving the suggestion away. "Honestly, just smile at them and—"

"Well, don't keep it all to yourself," Oleanna said, taking the bottle from her. A little of the beer sloshed onto her hand and she licked it off.

A sound near the altar, like a snapping twig in the forest, startled them, and Oleanna sloshed more beer, now onto her pleated black skirt.

"I thought we were alone?" Elisabeth whispered.

Oleanna nodded, furiously rubbing at her skirt. "I thought so, too," she whispered.

"Come on," Elisabeth said, grabbing Oleanna's wrist.

"No, I should—"

"Come on," Elisabeth said, pulling her out of the church, spilling more of the precious, and strongly brewed, celebration beer in the process. They hurried around to the side of the church, and up into the dark wood which was never very far away.

Elisabeth led them deeper into the forest and they settled with their backs against a fallen log. After a few moments, Oleanna took a long drink; the beer wasn't theirs—sharp with too much new grass—but she swallowed nearly half the bottle at one go, and then quickly dispatched the second.

Elisabeth finished off her own bottles and set them on the ground. They sat together quietly, feeling the beer work its magic, listening to the chatter of the crowds just beyond the curtain of trees.

Stretching, content as a cat, Elisabeth leaned into Oleanna. "What did Jakob want?" she whispered.

"What he always wants," she whispered.

"I can't."

"I know."

After a moment, Elisabeth looked up at Oleanna and grinned. "He is beautiful, though, isn't he?"

Oleanna stretched and smiled. "Yes, he is."

"I'll go find him," Elisabeth said, standing up a bit unsteadily, smoothing down the front of her skirt.

"And do what?" Oleanna asked.

"Just say hello," Elisabeth shrugged.

"Don't be cruel. He worships you."

Elisabeth scowled and stumbled down the gentle hillside, then regained her footing, setting her shoulders and walking away. When she reached the edge of the forest she turned around. "I worship him, too," she shrugged. She settled her face into a merry smile and walked back out into the crowds.

Oleanna rested her head against the log and closed her eyes, and dreamt not of the next pile of washing, or shearing the sheep, or making the lefse, but of high mountaintops and rowing, rowing around the lake, close to the shore, towing her mother and Anna behind.

Later she awoke, curled into a ball and covered dirt and twigs, to find it quiet and cool under the trees. If she stayed very still, she could just see a red fox melting into the hillside, hear a marsh tit calling to its mate. She sat up, yawning, and realized that the din of the crowd had lessened and if she concentrated, she could pick out different conversations—a gaggle of matrons next to the church, a couple high on the hillside above her, a group just beyond the trees below.

"Why can't you be happy for me?"

She recognized John's voice and picked her way down the hillside, brushing twigs off of her skirt. She peeked through the trees and saw John talking with Elisabeth and Anders; Elisabeth had her small hand closed on Anders' arm. Oleanna stepped back into the cover of the trees; she could no longer see them.

"You won't let him leave, will you?" Elisabeth asked.

"It's not my place," Anders replied.

"What on earth do you mean by that?" she demanded.

Oleanna smiled, imagining her sister with hands on hips.

"What he means," John said, "is he couldn't stop me, even if he tried." She could hear the laughter in her brother's voice.

"Could I?" Elisabeth said, more quietly.

"Could you what?"

"Could I stop you? If I tried?"

After a moment, John replied. "No. No, I have to go. I can't stay...If you could understand, Lisbet. Lisbet—"

"Let her go," Anders said.

After a few moments, she could hear her brother sigh. "She hates to be left behind," John said quietly.

"So take her with you."

"She would hate to go."

Oleanna closed her eyes. "Don't leave us," she whispered.

The long winter, cold and dark despite the constant drifting of white snow, came back to her: the long winter after Anton had left. Only three years ago, she marveled, looking up at the green canopy, which then had been only sharp spikes of dark against the whiteness and ice.

Anton and her mother had quarreled: so soon after father had died. He promised to send money from the farm he hoped to establish, promised to write every week. Her mother sat stone-faced as John waited on the wagon's bench, Anton saying his goodbyes. He'd kissed their mother's cheek as she stared out at the lake. When John had returned from taking Anton to the ferry in Vadheim, their mother extracted a promise from him that he would never leave.

John was the only thing that kept them together, Oleanna thought. The only thing that kept them sane, during the last long dark winter, just after mama and Anna died. Steady and sure, reliable and strong. And now that the spring has finally come, he has thawed, and he'll be gone, too.

"You missed the children's parade."

Oleanna gasped. She opened her eyes and spun around. Anders leaned against a tall birch, hands in the pockets of his trousers.

She gathered herself. "Anders Samuelsson," she said.

He smiled at her formality. "Sleeping it off, were you?"

"Sleeping what off?" she demanded.

"The beer."

"Oh. No. Just tired."

He stepped away from the tree and walked up the hillside to stand next to her. "Why did she do it?"

"Do what?"

"Steal the beer. You've been drinking it since you were a child, why steal it?"

Oleanna blushed, then straightened her back. "Oh, that," she said. "The old men stand there, making all the rules, like they get to decide who drinks and who doesn't, and there we are, having to ask nicely and politely, just for a stupid bottle of beer. I hate it. So we take turns stealing as much as we can every year."

He laughed, that short, strange bark. "Very sensible," he smiled.

She narrowed her eyes, bristling. "You've never had to go begging for beer."

"How do you know?"

Oleanna shrugged. "You're a man. You don't have to beg for anything."

He grew serious. "Men may not have to work for their beer, there are things we do have to work for."

"Name one."

"Freedom."

Oleanna looked sidelong at him. "Was it you that put up the proper flag?"

Anders smiled, a warm blush of excitement spreading across his cheeks. "No, not me. Though I'm glad they did."

Oleanna cocked her head. "Was it the young man? The one who spoke so well earlier?"

"Yes."

"Who is he?"

"He's from across the lake, near Årdal. He's been working in Førde and Bergen, and has contacts in the capital."

"Did you ask him to come?"

"Me? Oh, no," he said, looking down at her. "But I was very happy to make his acquaintance. He seems to think change is coming, and quickly."

She caught his excitement and laughed. "I'm glad to hear it."

They stood in the forest, the sunlight dappled around them, smiling at each other. After a moment, she grabbed his arm. "How did you know we took the beer?"

He smiled broadly, eyes sparkling. "Green suits you," he said.

She paused, taken aback, then raised an eyebrow. "Red suits you," she said, squeezing his jacketed arm.

His eyes widened momentarily, and then his grin softened into a fond smile. "You are a wild thing," he whispered, squeezing her hand gently before removing it from his arm.

"No more than you." She looked him in the eye.

He stared down at her, smiling, then abruptly turned and walked out of the forest.

Oleanna's eyes narrowed. "Oh no," she whispered after a few moments. "I can't do this again." And even so, Oleanna leaned against a birch tree, smiling, her face flushed and heart pounding.

"Lea?" Elisabeth's voice floated from beyond the veil of trees. "Are you still up here?"

Oleanna pushed away from the tree and smoothed down her hair.

"There you are," Elisabeth huffed, wandering up the hillside and sitting down on a fallen tree. "I've been looking everywhere for you. John says it's time to leave," she said, fanning herself with her hand.

Oleanna turned her flaming face away and began to walk down the hill without a word.

"Wait—Lea, wait," Elisabeth said, chasing after her. "Wait."

Oleanna stopped just at the forest's edge. "What?" she asked, adjusting their mother's brooch at her neck, avoiding Elisabeth's eyes.

"Did I see Anders Samuelsson come out of the forest a few seconds ago?" Elisabeth asked.

"Yes."

"It's not time for Midsummer games yet," Elisabeth leered. "Bit chilly still."

Oleanna looked at her sister, eyes wide. "I—we—"

"You don't have to explain to me. I have Torjus, remember?" she laughed.

Face flaming, and yet suppressing a grin, Oleanna shook her head and walked away, blinking in the bright light of the lakeside. She shielded her eyes with her hand and saw her brother turning the pony and their wagon in the direction of the farm. She lifted her skirts and ran down the grassy hill, Elisabeth close behind.

When Oleanna reached the wagon and climbed in the back, John lifted Torjus, red-faced and wailing like a myling alone in the forest, onto the bench.

"Lisbet," Oleanna said, "get up there."

Elisabeth groaned and took her son in her arms, who lay like a dead weight, tears streaming down his face. Elisabeth leaned down and cooed in his ear, and received a crack in the forehead for her trouble as he flailed in her arms.

John urged the pony on. The wagon trundled along the rocky lakeside, back toward the lonely farm.

A voice from the crowd called out. "We'll see you at Midsummer, John!"

"No, you won't," Oleanna said, under her breath. "You'll never see him again."

# CHAPTER FOUR

Lake Jølster, Sunnfjord, Norway
June 1905

A PERSISTENT HOWLING RACED DOWN from the mountaintops like the icy wind in a winter's storm and pierced Oleanna's dreaming.

After a few confused moments, she opened her eyes. The sky was still an indeterminate gray, teetering on the edge of gold.

"Get up! Get up!" Torjus' shrill voice bounced around the small farmhouse, echoing off the bare pine walls.

"Torjus," Oleanna whispered. "Hush. Go back to sleep."

"No!" he squealed, tugging on Oleanna's hand. "Get up!"

"Lisbet," Oleanna muttered, nudging her sister with her elbow.

Elisabeth groaned.

Oleanna sighed and sat up.

"Hooray!" Torjus screeched. "Lea, let's go feed the ponies."

"Shh," Oleanna hissed. "Be quiet, and I'll take you—"

John wandered over, fully dressed, and picked Torjus up, throwing him over his shoulder. "Go back to sleep," he whispered.

Oleanna nodded gratefully and fell back onto her pillow, asleep within moments.

When she woke next, the smell of coffee suffused the farmhouse. She sat up on her elbows, blowing wisps of hair out of her face. "Good lord, what time is it?" she muttered.

"Nearly four," John said from across the room.

Elisabeth struggled to a sitting position next to Oleanna; they leaned into each other. "Where's Torjus?" Elisabeth croaked.

"Running in circles outside."

"Good," Elisabeth said, climbing out of bed. "What's for breakfast?"

"What do you think?" John asked over his shoulder.

"Mmmm, porridge," Oleanna said, climbing out of bed and shuffling over to the fireside.

John poked at the fire with the copper tip of the bellows, pushing the kindling around, sharp jabs at the crumbling wood. They all sat together quietly for long minutes, Oleanna and Elisabeth trying desperately to wake up, John lost in thought.

Elisabeth and Oleanna sat side by side in their straight-backed chairs; both had pulled their bare feet up and were hugging their knees. John looked up from the fire a few minutes later and laughed.

"What?" Elisabeth mumbled, yawning.

"It's as if you two hadn't grown up at all—still pale and sleepy little girls."

Elisabeth and Oleanna both smiled at him.

"I've already fed the ponies, though I haven't been up to the sæter to check on the sheep and goats," he said, pouring them both a cup. He handed the mugs over and folded his arms with a smile.

Oleanna shook her head. "You might as well let us do that," she said, blowing across her coffee.

He shrugged. "Just wanted to give you two one last lie-in," he said quietly.

"You're the one with the long journey ahead. You should be resting," Oleanna said.

Elisabeth remained quiet and still.

"I'm fine. I'll be fine. Listen, I want to go over everything again. I've written it all down," he said, picking up a small book with a tattered leather cover from the mantle. "Lisbet, make sure the last barley is brought in by early September, and not much later, or else it will get caught in the freeze. And Oleanna, the market at Skei will be a good place to sell any surplus during the autumn. You've planted enough onions and potatoes for an army."

"If we have any surplus," Oleanna muttered.

"John?" Elisabeth said suddenly, her voice still and icy around the edges.

"What?"

"You've told us this at least a hundred times," she said, voice rising. "We know."

"I just want to be sure—"

"John," Oleanna mumbled through a yawn. "Stop. Please. We'll manage."

"If you could find a farm hand—"

"It is far too early for this," Elisabeth said angrily, rubbing her eyes with the heels of her hands. "I've gone over the accounts, we can't afford it."

"But when I send back money—"

"If you send back money," Elisabeth said, standing and stretching, but giving him a pointed look.

"But—" John started.

Oleanna stood up, setting her chair out of the way against the wall. "Leave it," she said, looking at John and raising her eyebrow.

"We all know what the answer is to this," Elisabeth said, reaching for a comb and tugging the snarls out of her long, dark hair.

"Elisabeth," Oleanna said, turning to her sister. "Leave it."

Elisabeth looked at John. "You could stay. You don't have to go."

Oleanna sighed. "If you're going to fight, go do it outside. I don't want to hear it anymore."

"He's just being selfish," Elisabeth said, turning her back.

"Lisbet. Don't—"

"Then don't leave us! Don't leave us here!" she yelled, spinning back around and throwing the comb across the room.

John ducked and sighed. "You have to understand—"

"Fine," Oleanna said with a huff.

"I don't understand," Elisabeth said behind her, voice shaking. "I don't understand why you want to leave. Why do you get to leave?"

"Lisbet—" John said, warning in his voice.

"I am not a child, John," Elisabeth said.

"Are you sure about that?" Oleanna said, wriggling into her skirt and shirtwaist, and stepping into her boots.

"He has no right to be high and mighty with us now."

Oleanna turned back around, smoothing her blouse. "I'm going to the sæter," she said, pulling her hair into a hasty plait. "You two stay here and fight. I've had enough."

"Good. You leave too," Elisabeth spat.

"Lea—"

Oleanna shut the door on her brother's protestations. She headed quickly up the hill, toward the trail to the sæter, grumbling under her breath.

At the last moment, she veered off and made for the barn. She kicked open the door and Terna whinnied a greeting; Oleanna sighed. "Good morning," she said, patting Terna's flank. "I suppose we had better just get down to work."

Later, after mucking and feeding and tidying, Oleanna emerged from the barn. She stretched out her back and groaned with the pops. The list of chores for the day marched through her mind, and she straightened and turned toward the store house, then stopped. Did we invite Anders?

She walked toward the farmhouse; the door was open, and from inside she could still hear John and Elisabeth's sporadic bickering, tiny wildfires that could not be stamped out. "And when we have so much work to do for tonight," she muttered, shaking her head. Folding her arms tight across her chest, she hurried into the woods.

Every few steps, she glanced up, peering at the sky above the tall tree-tops, calculating how much time it would take to prepare John's going-away feast, and precisely how much time she was losing at that very moment. Why didn't I just send John? she thought. She quickened her pace, and within a few minutes the forest thinned and she could see Anders' cabin just over the last rise in the trail. She jogged over the last few meters and stopped just under the eaves of the forest.

"Good morning," she panted, wiping the sweat from her brow with the back of her hand.

Anders, kneeling in the dirt, looked up at her, over his shoulder. A slight smile crossed his lips. "Oleanna," he said, then returned to his digging.

She narrowed her eyes. Finally, she said, "I haven't seen you since the party."

Anders sat back on his heels, stretching his neck. "I've been tending my crops," he said, nodding at the squalid lines of ratty saplings.

She stepped forward. "What are they supposed to be?"

Anders stood, wiping dirt off of his hands and onto his trousers. "These," he said, pointing to a scraggly half-dead patch, "are oats. And that's rhubarb."

She raised her eyebrows. "And that?"

"Potatoes."

"And where are your sheep?"

He looked down, kicking at a clod of dirt. "I had to eat one—"

"What, already?"

He shrugged. "And the other ran away," he said, glancing toward the hillside.

"Oh dear," she said, suppressing a laugh. "I'm sure John could come and help—"

"John is leaving."

The grin disappeared from Oleanna's face. She composed herself and said, "He's written it all down—in a book, at home. For me and Lisbet. I could get it for you, if you'd like. I can show you where the cloudberries—"

"I don't need your help," he said, turning his back on her and kneeling back down among his ragged crop.

"I meant no offense. I just thought—"

"I'm sure you have some washing to see to," he replied, doggedly digging through the rocky soil.

Oleanna raised her eyebrow and folded her arms. "You have pretty manners. You may think I'm wild, but at least I know a friendly hand when I see it offered."

He dropped his head and after a few moments snorted a laugh. "Oleanna," he said standing and turning to face her. He extended his hand. "Please accept my apology," he said quietly with a strange half-smile.

She shook his hand, hard and brusque like she'd been taught by her father. "Apology accepted."

"Are we friends again?" he smiled, holding onto her hand.

"We'll see," she smiled, blushing.

With a squeeze, he let go her hand and folded his arms, looking down at her. "Thank you for your offer," he said. "I want to learn on my own. Succeed or fail on my own merits."

"But, that's—"

"—what I want to do."

"You weren't a farmer before you came here, were you?"

"I was a fisherman," he said, turning and looking out at the lake. "On Sognefjord."

"Oh," she said. "Why—"

"I'll tell you, one day," he smiled briefly.

They stood together, shoulder to shoulder, watching the morning sun dance and sparkle on the lake, a gentle breeze rippling the surface. In this light it could even look beautiful, she thought. After a few minutes standing silently together, she sighed. "I should get back," she said quietly.

"You'll be fine," he said, walking back to his crops and kneeling down in the dirt. "You're strong."

"I'll be fine because I have no choice."

Anders nodded.

"Did anyone invite you to dinner tonight?" she asked.

"Yes."

She cocked her head. "So are you coming?"

"Of course."

Oleanna turned back toward the forest. "Good. He'll be very glad to have you there."

"Will you?"

She slowed and looked back at him. After a moment, she said, "Let's see if you actually come, first."

He spun around to face her. "But I've been—"

"Yes, tending your crops. Keeping yourself to yourself. I know."

He stood and took a step toward her, then stopped. "I'll see you tonight."

"We'll see," she said, turning her back on him and walking into the forest. She walked along the narrow trail to the farm, humming under her breath, a small smile growing at the corners of her mouth.

When she returned to the farm, she found John leaning against the wall of the barn. His arms were folded and, she realized as she drew closer, his eyes were closed.

"Are you and Lisbet still quarreling?"

"I'm not," he shrugged, opening his eyes. "She is."

Oleanna leaned against the wall next to him. "You can't blame her."

John sighed. "I know."

"Why are you going? Why so soon?"

"Lea, I've told you—"

"Yes, I know. Oceans of wheat, as far as the eye can see."

"Yes."

"And what else?"

"Isn't that enough?"

"John," she said, pushing away from the wall to face him.

"I'll send you money from my farm," he said. "When I begin to make a profit. You won't have to worry."

"And what else?"

"I can't stay here anymore," he whispered finally, looking out at the lake and avoiding Oleanna's gaze.

"Why?"

He did not respond.

Oleanna grabbed his shoulder and shook it. "Why, John?"

He looked at her and sighed. "I'm a coward," he shrugged.

Oleanna dropped her hand. "You're the bravest man I know. Last winter…well. We would not have survived without you."

He shook his head.

She waved his protestation away with a flick of her hand. "And anyway. It takes courage to leave."

"If I were brave, I would stay."

"But you have a choice."

John opened his mouth, a question floating in the air, then snapped it shut.

"Besides," she said quietly. "Who would take care of Elisabeth? She can't take care of herself."

He laughed. "If that's what you'd like to believe."

"Will you ever come back?" she whispered.

"Lea, don't—"

"I'm never going to see you again, am I?"

John did not respond.

"Am I?"

He sighed.

She hugged her arms around her middle, shivering. "Just don't forget about us."

"How could I?" he half-laughed.

"How often do we get letters from Anton?"

"It won't be like that."

"Twice a year, if we're lucky."

"But he has a family now, his farm—"

She sighed. "And so will you."

"And so will you," he countered. "You'll forget all about me, soon enough."

She shifted and would not meet his eyes.

"Lea, I don't want to go. But I can't stay," he said, looking over his shoulder to the dark trees on the hillside. "The woods are too filled with ghosts."

"So you leave them to me, then?"

"I told you I was a coward," he whispered. He pushed away from the wall and without another word, walked away.

Oleanna watched him, silently, until he disappeared under the trees at the far edge of their land. She shuddered.

At that moment, the farmhouse door banged open and Torjus emerged with a toy boat in his hand, laughing and running full-out to avoid Elisabeth, who sagged against the doorframe.

"Little man," Oleanna called.

Torjus slowed.

"I need your help. Come here."

Elisabeth shook her head and disappeared back into the farmhouse, shutting the door behind her.

Torjus increased his speed and ran directly into Oleanna, nearly taking her out at the knees. "Are we going fishing?" he asked, breathless.

"No. We're starting John's feast."

"Oh," he said, pouting.

"Come help me dig potatoes," she smiled. "You'll like it."

She followed a dancing Torjus over to the vegetable patch between the farmhouse and the store house. "No, don't step there, you're crushing—" she groaned. "Torjus," she sighed, "over here." She knelt down, digging her hands into the cold earth.

He settled next to her in the dirt, resting his boat in the trough between the waves of dirt and leaves. "What are we doing?" he said.

"We're digging potatoes and onions. And later, you can gather eggs for me from the chicken coop."

"Oh."

"You don't like digging in the dirt? I thought all boys liked that."

"I like the water," he shrugged.

She nodded. "I used to like the water, too."

"Why don't you now?"

Oleanna looked up and across their small plot of land toward the lake. "I'll tell you someday," she said.

Torjus tugged on the sleeve of her jacket and she jumped slightly. "Where are the onions?" he said.

She looked down at him and smiled. "Right in front of you."

"Where?"

"Right here," she said, scrabbling in the rocky soil beneath a stand of tiny green shoots.

Torjus dug into the cold soil, shooting dirt in all directions, like a terrier going for a bone. Oleanna stood and smiled. "Be careful, now," she said. "Don't want to hurt the onions."

Torjus stopped abruptly and looked up at her, dirt already sprinkled liberally throughout his white-blond hair. "Can I go fishing?"

"Right now?"

"Yes."

"No."

"Please?"

"Later. I need you to catch me at least four big trout."

His eyes widened. "Four?"

"Do you think you can do it?" she smiled.

He nodded, puffing his small chest. "Yes."

"Good," she grinned. "I'm going to go check on Terna. I need you to find me six onions, yes?"

He nodded.

"Once you've found them, bring them to me in the store house. And don't go near the water," she said, shaking her finger at him. "Wait for John to come back."

He nodded and returned to his digging.

She turned and wandered up the hill toward the barn. When she'd nearly reached the barn doors, Torjus hollered, his voice echoing along the lakeside. "Lea?"

She turned around and put a finger to her lips, then walked back down the slope to the vegetable patch.

"Lea," he whispered.

"What is it?"

"When John's gone, am I going to live with my papa?"

Oleanna's heart constricted. "No, you're staying with us. With your mama and me."

"But I want to live with Jakob."

"Why?"

"Jakob not afraid of the water."

"But Jakob is not—" she began, but the protestation died on her lips. "No, Jakob is not afraid of the water. Now find those onions for me," she said, smoothing Torjus' hair down.

Oleanna walked back toward the barn. "How did he know about Jakob?" she wondered to herself, the thought trailing away as she pushed open the barn door and began in earnest the day's round of chores.

Hours later, Elisabeth found Oleanna in the store house. "Torjus is covered in mud," she said, rolling up her sleeves.

Oleanna laughed, a throaty sound that vibrated around the store house. "I told him to be careful. He's digging potatoes for me. Already found me more than enough onions," she said, nodding to the pile spilling from the table to the dirt floor.

Elisabeth cocked her head. "It's good to hear you laugh."

Oleanna sobered and shrugged. "I laugh."

They worked together in silence, Elisabeth picking up the onions from the ground and piling them in a bowl, Oleanna rhythmically kneading dough.

They worked together, chopping onions and kneading dough until their eyes stung and their hands ached. Finally, Elisabeth leaned against the table and looked around the store house, at the piles of wash and mending spilling off of the table and out of the tub, and groaned. "A whole lifetime of this," she muttered, shaking her head.

"Don't start," Oleanna said, blowing hair out of her eyes and applying herself to a new mound of dough.

Elisabeth was quiet for a moment, then said, "But a whole life—"

"Lisbet. Leave it."

Elisabeth grabbed Oleanna's arm. "There is more than the sæter and making the lefse and mending your second-best stockings every other week. There are things out there you can't imagine."

"Why do you do this to yourself?"

"What?"

She removed Elisabeth's hand from her arm. "We are trapped here. We will live here, and we will die here. Why torture yourself?"

Oleanna said, enunciating every word like a sentence of law.

"But don't you want to see it?" Elisabeth said, eyes wide and wild around the edges.

"It doesn't matter what I want."

"I know you want to go," Elisabeth said, her whispered voice urgent. "I can see it. We can go together! We can—"

Oleanna shook her head. "Lisbet, don't—"

"Together! It's an easy walk to Skei, we could sell some of the jewelry in mama's chest…"

"And then what?" Oleanna asked. "Honestly—"

"We can see the world!"

Oleanna smiled despite herself, tracing maps in her mind, a fresher breeze on her cheeks. She indulged in the soaring feeling for a few moments, then forced herself back to earth. "And what will we do for money?"

"We—we could find jobs," Elisabeth whispered. "We have skills—"

Oleanna sighed. "And what about Torjus?"

"And what about Anders?"

"What about him?"

"Nothing," Elisabeth said, reapplying herself to the dough she'd been kneading.

"Don't do that. Say what you have to say and stop being so dramatic," Oleanna snapped.

"Well, it's just when I was at his cabin a few days ago—"

"And why *have* you been going to Anders' cabin all these weeks?" Oleanna demanded.

"Does it matter?"

"What have you been doing?"

Elisabeth shrugged. "You'll see."

"You're avoiding my question. What about Torjus? Jakob? Would you leave them behind?"

Elisabeth flinched but did not reply. She gathered her dough and set it in a bowl, then covered it with a towel. She wiped off her hands on her apron, then leaned against the worktable, arms folded. "I saw you," Elisabeth said, looking at Oleanna sidelong.

Oleanna shook her head, brows knitted. "What are you talking about?"

"With Anders. I see how you look at him," she said evenly.

Oleanna blushed, the pink in her cheeks growing with the effort of not blushing. "And how is that?"

"Like he is the first red apple of summer," Elisabeth said, savoring the words.

"Lisbet—"

"You're a grown woman," Elisabeth shrugged. "You were engaged, for pity's sake. There's nothing wrong with wanting."

"So why are you teasing me?"

Elisabeth grinned. "Because—" she said, then stopped, shaking her head. She sobered. "Because you were never like this before."

"Well, wanting is all I can do," Oleanna snapped. "We're both tarnished now." She turned her back on Elisabeth and began peeling potatoes.

"That's ridiculous."

"We have work to do," Oleanna said quietly. "We'll never be done in time at this rate."

"Lea."

Oleanna continued peeling, her movements sharp and jagged.

Elisabeth sighed. "Fine. What do you want me to do?"

"We can't start on the gomme and lefse until later, and we can't make the fiskeboller until John takes Torjus to catch us some fish—"

"John's still gone."

"Oh," Oleanna sighed. "Well, can you take him?"

Elisabeth laughed. "You know I don't know how to fish."

"Maybe Jakob could take him," Oleanna said, looking over at her.

"Don't tease," Elisabeth whispered.

"Fair's fair."

"Lea."

"He knows," Oleanna said, wiping her hands on a towel.

"Who?"

"Torjus knows."

"But who—"

"I don't know," Oleanna said, walking toward the door. "Perhaps Jakob told him?"

"Damn," Elisabeth whispered, staring into space.

"Lisbet—"

"Damn."

Oleanna paused in the doorway of the store house, but Elisabeth said no more.

Hours later, Elisabeth and Oleanna emerged from the farmhouse in procession, carrying steaming bowls and heaping serving platters, enough to feed a dozen hungry farm hands. They set the feast on the table; a jar filled with wildflowers and a bottle of akevitt with three tumblers awaited them.

"John," Elisabeth called, rousing him from his ramble along the lakeside. "It's ready, come eat."

He nodded and walked up the hill with his hands in his pockets.

Elisabeth and Oleanna stood back, watching him expectantly. "Did you bring the flowers?" Oleanna asked as he approached.

"Yes," he nodded. "And the akevitt. Gifts from the Sanddal boys." He sat on the bench and sighed. "You've gone to too much trouble."

"It isn't the kind of feast you deserve," Oleanna said, settling onto the bench next to Elisabeth. "The boys from Sanddal should be here, and your friend from Årdal."

"Doesn't matter. It's perfect. And Samuelsson will be here, sometime," John said, smiling. "Pass the akevitt. I don't expect I'll have as good for a long time."

"I hope you meet a good Norwegian girl out there in your wilderness," Elisabeth said. "A proper cook."

John laughed. "Not like you then?"

Elisabeth reached across the table to swat at him, and he leaned back, nearly tumbling off his bench.

Oleanna laughed, but quickly sobered. "It should be more than just the three of us," she muttered.

"I miss Anna," Elisabeth said, sipping her akevitt. "And mama."

Oleanna sighed. "And Anton."

"Don't start this now," John said. "Please. Let's be merry."

Oleanna and Elisabeth nodded but said nothing, pushing food around on their plates, matching John in tumblers of akevitt.

They sat together silently at the table, the great feast Elisabeth and Oleanna had spent all day preparing going cold as the quiet minutes passed. Oleanna rested her chin in her hand, looking past John to the small log farmhouse, letting her eyes grow unfocused until the building was no more than another glacial boulder. Elisabeth drew patterns in the spilled stew on the tabletop, a map to an imagined life outside the mountains. John sighed, staring out at the lake, shimmering gold in the evening sun.

"Hallo?" a voice called from beyond the barn and store house.

Shaken from their reveries, Elisabeth and Oleanna turned to look behind them. "Who's there?" Oleanna called.

Anders emerged from the fence of the forest, face flushed. "It's just me," he called, bending over and resting his hands on his knees.

"There you are, Anders Samuelsson," Elisabeth chided, standing up from the table.

Oleanna looked at her sister.

Elisabeth flashed her a quick grin then picked up her skirts and ran up the hill to meet Anders. Oleanna stood up and hovered near the table, glancing back at John and shrugging her shoulders.

"Let me help you," Elisabeth said as Anders stood and adjusted a rope slung over his shoulder.

"No, I can manage, thank you," Anders said, gently shrugging off Elisabeth's hand. "It's just a few more yards."

Elisabeth grinned and skipped down the hillside, Anders moving cautiously behind her. She reached John and Oleanna and clapped her hands. "I thought I would burst!" she said, dropping onto the bench next to John, then leaping up again a moment later.

John and Oleanna looked again at each other. "What are you talking about?" Oleanna asked.

"You'll see," Elisabeth smiled slyly. "Oh, I wanted to tell you, but..."

Halfway down the hill, Anders looked up from his labors. "Oleanna," he smiled.

Oleanna's heart skipped; she grinned broadly. "Anders," she replied, taking a few steps toward him. "What do you have there?"

"A gift."

Anders pulled behind him, on a makeshift sled, a magnificent trunk: as large as their mother's dowry trunk, painted aqua blue, blue-green as the lake when spring gives way to summer. And all along the outside of the trunk, vines and acanthus leaves, swirling, liquid designs in white and red and ochre, like the forest when winter gives way to spring.

Oleanna gasped, kneeling next to the trunk. "Did you make this?" she breathed, holding her hands above the rounded top of the trunk, not quite touching it.

Anders stood back with his hands in his pockets. "Jakob, from the Logard farm made the trunk," he said. Oleanna glanced at Elisabeth.

"It's for John," Elisabeth said, smiling. "See, 'Johan Tollefson Myklebost 1905'," she said, tracing the name on the top of the case.

Oleanna looked at John, who remained at the table, his face pale, hands unmoving.

Anders opened the top of the case. Oleanna gasped again: the swirling vines and acanthus leaves adorned the inside of the trunk as well, blossoming in the bottom of the trunk in one bright rose.

Oleanna looked up at him, wide-eyed. "Who painted the rosemal?" she breathed.

"I did," Anders whispered, standing stone-still, holding her gaze.

She glanced at the trunk and then back at Anders. "It—" she whispered. "It is magnificent."

He closed his eyes, briefly, and relaxed his shoulders.

Oleanna looked eagerly back at the trunk. In one corner of the inside of the top of the case, Anders had painted a small Norwegian flag–the proper, old flag. In the other corner, two names, swirling in fancy white script: "Elisabeth Tollefsdttr" and "Oleanna Tollefsdttr". Oleanna stood and smiled uncertainly.

"So you'll be with him, every day," Anders whispered.

Heart pounding, she reached out and took Anders' delicate hand. "Thank you," she whispered.

He squeezed her hand gently. "It was my pleasure," he whispered, his gaze unwavering.

Oleanna's eyes fluttered closed. The pressure on her hand increased.

"I knew it!" Elisabeth laughed.

Oleanna opened her eyes and with a quick squeeze dropped Anders' hand. "What?" she asked.

"I knew you'd love it," Elisabeth said, pirouetting, casting Oleanna a sly grin over her shoulder. "Isn't it beautiful? I thought of it months ago."

"It's magnificent," Oleanna said, hugging her arms close, looking at Anders.

Elisabeth spun around again. "Well, what do you think, John?" she called over her shoulder.

They all turned to look at him, expectant.

Oleanna groaned. "John?"

John was slumped over the table.

"Akevitt?" Anders asked as they ran down to John's side.

"Yes, how—" Oleanna asked, shaking John gently.

"I've told him more than once," Anders said, shaking his head but smiling. "Here, take his other arm."

Anders and Oleanna struggled John off of the bench, grunting under his deadweight. "Lisbet, get the door," Oleanna gasped.

The farmhouse was dim, the tardy twilight finally shadowing the mountainsides beyond the open windows. Anders and Oleanna dragged John the short distance from the door to his box bed and dumped him unceremoniously near the head. John groaned and curled himself around his pillow.

Oleanna pushed a lock of matted hair away from John's damp forehead and sighed. Anders touched her arm and nodded toward the door. With a last look at John, and a confirmation that Torjus still slept, she turned and followed Anders.

"I'll be back for him after breakfast," Anders said quietly, pulling the door shut behind him.

"Thank you," Oleanna said, hesitating by the door. "This isn't exactly the send-off I'd hoped for," she said, looking toward the lake and mountains.

"It's the send-off I expected," he replied, wandering away toward the table.

"What do you mean?" Oleanna said, following and sitting on a bench, randomly tidying the forgotten feast left on the table.

Anders hovered but did not sit down. "He's been dreading this night for weeks."

"So have I."

"I'll miss him," Anders said, smiling tightly. After a few moments, he looked around, eyebrows furrowed. "Where did Elisabeth go?"

"Oh," Oleanna said, looking around. "I don't know. She's probably running up to the cabin. She thinks she's punishing John by going up there."

Anders chuckled.

"There is still plenty left, please, sit down and have some," she said briskly, waving at the serving bowls and plates on the table. "We didn't even start on the lefse and gomme, though I expect it's all cold now."

He smiled gently, a blanket of sunshine on the shadowed mountainside. "I have to get back and get ready for our trip."

"Yes, of course," she said, standing up and stacking plates and bowls, avoiding his gaze.

"I will be gone for a few days," he said quietly, taking the plates and bowls from her hands and setting them back on the table. He stepped close.

"Thank you for the trunk," she whispered, her face growing warm. "It is—"

"—my pleasure." He raised his hand to touch her face. Her breath caught; he dropped his hand and stepped back.

"I will see you tomorrow morning," he said quietly, turning and walking quickly up the hill, disappearing into the forest.

Oleanna watched him into the trees and stood gazing at the dark curtain of the wood for long minutes after he'd gone. Finally, she sighed, turning back to the table, clearing away the evidence of the half-eaten feast.

I can't do this again, can I? she thought.

# CHAPTER FIVE

Lake Jølster, Sunnfjord, Norway
May 1905

THE BRIEF DARKNESS THAT HAUNTED MIDNIGHT was giving way to a dawn so early even the animals had not yet arisen. Though she had slept for only a few hours, Oleanna was already awake and dressed, getting Torjus out of bed and out to feed the animals in the barn. "Don't forget the chickens this time," she whispered, swatting his behind as he stumbled, sleepy-eyed, out the door.

John groaned from his bed across the room.

"Good morning," Oleanna whispered. "I'll set some coffee—"

He groaned again. He sat up, stretching his neck and shoulders. "Why am I still dressed?"

"You passed out at the table," she said, opening the top of John's trunk. She spread a length of muslin along the bottom to protect the rosemaling, and began to set John's extra shoes in the trunk.

"Oh. Yes," he said, rubbing his temples.

"How do you feel?"

"Ha!" he laughed, then immediately stopped and held his head with both hands. "How did you get me in here?" he mumbled.

"Anders and I—"

John sighed. "I'm sorry about last night."

Oleanna shrugged. "I'd have been surprised if you didn't get drunk at your own dinner."

"I was an ass."

"Yes."

John rubbed his forehead. "Was I really?"

"Yes," she smiled. "We forgive you."

"Did you say something about coffee?"

"Yes, but you have to wash up in the meantime. You smell awful."

He groaned his way out of bed and shuffled past her out the door. Oleanna shook her head and turned back to the trunk and resumed packing, fighting down the sudden bottomless sense of loss clutching at her throat.

Half an hour later, Oleanna pushed open the door. "John, can you please find Torjus?" she called. "Breakfast is nearly ready."

"Yes," John's voice floated to her from up near the forest line.

"Do you see Elisabeth anywhere?" she hollered, bustling to finish boiling their second pot of coffee and lay out a plate of open-faced sandwiches.

"No."

"She's going to miss him," Oleanna muttered, piling breakfast onto a tray and kicking the door open wide. "I thought we could eat outside, since it's so fine this morning," she called.

John nodded, a wriggling Torjus tucked firmly under his arm. Oleanna set their breakfast out and poured herself a cup of coffee.

"Eat," she said, nodding at the table as John set Torjus on the bench next to him. "It will help your head."

He grimaced. "I'm not hungry."

Oleanna raised her eyebrow. "I don't care. Eat."

With a sigh, John reached instead for the coffee and found refuge from Oleanna's glare in his mug.

"Fine," she shrugged. "It's on you if your head is split open before you even pass Sanddal."

While Torjus chattered, making imaginary animals out of slices of cheese and choreographing dances to the songs in his head, Oleanna and John picked at their breakfasts in silence. After a few minutes, John stood up, extricating himself from Torjus' grasp. "I am going to finish packing," he said quietly.

She nodded and sipped her coffee, her breakfast, like his, going untouched. "Are you done with your breakfast?" she asked Torjus, who was spinning in dizzying circles on the grass.

"Yes–yes–yes—" he said, each time his spin brought him around to face her.

"Remind me not to let you nap all day again," she said, shaking her head.

"What–what–what—" he giggled, finally flopping on the ground.

"Torjus, get up," she said, standing up and organizing the dishes.

"The world is spinning, Lea," he giggled. "It's fuzzy."

"I know."

"Can I go fishing like this?"

"Not if you want to catch any fish."

"Oh."

"Torjus, get up and take these dishes to the store house—"

"Lea," he whined.

"Don't argue with me," she said. He stood unsteadily and walked over to the table. She placed a pile of dishes in his outstretched arms. "After you take these to the store house, I want you to go up to the sæter."

"Why?" he whined.

"Because your mama is up there, and she needs to come down before John leaves. Can you do that quickly for me?"

He nodded and sped off up the hill, the pile of dishes precariously balanced in his small arms. She watched him into the store house, wincing at the speed at which he raced back out. "We'll need a new serving platter now," she muttered.

Oleanna wandered back to the farmhouse. She pushed open the door and leaned against the frame. "Do you want any help?" she asked.

John looked up from where he knelt next to the trunk and shook his head.

"Do you have everything you need?" she asked, walking toward him.

"Yes, thanks to you."

"Good. How is your head?"

"It has felt better," he shrugged, smiling ruefully.

"I can imagine," she smiled.

His smile faltered. "No sign of Lisbet?"

"I sent Torjus to the cabin. She should be back by the time Anders gets here."

"Lea," he said. "Thank you for everything you've done."

Oleanna felt tears prickling and ruthlessly willed them away. "I don't have anything as nice as Elisabeth's trunk to give you. Just this," she said. She turned and pulled open the bottom drawer of the small chest next to her bed, pulling out a coverlet woven with the traditional geometric designs of Sunnfjord. "Maybe it will keep you warm on the ship."

"When did you do this?" he said, shaking it out.

"It was the one I did over the winter."

"I thought that was for Søren?"

She shrugged. "It's for you."

"Thank you," he whispered. He folded the coverlet carefully and, opening the lid of the trunk, set it on top of the pile of clothes and books. He closed the lid and turned back to Oleanna. "If I had asked, would you have come with me? To America?"

"Don't say that—"

"Hallo?" Anders' voice carried in through the open door.

Oleanna gasped. "I didn't realize how late it was."

John smiled tightly, adjusting his tie and high, stiff collar. "Time to go," he said, settling the black bowler—bought new for the occasion—on his fair head.

"You can't, not before Lisbet comes back," she said.

Anders leaned in the door. "Good morning," he said. "Are you ready?"

"Yes," John said briskly. "Will you help me settle the trunk in the wagon?"

"Of course—"

"No!" Oleanna cried.

"Oleanna—" John started.

She turned and pushed past Anders. She narrowed her watering eyes against the bright light and ran half-blind to the store house.

Oleanna pushed open the door and stood blinking, again, adjusting to the dark, the only light coming from the smoke-hole in the ceiling. She stumbled to the corner and pawed through piles of linen and winter clothes. After a few moments of desperate searching, she pulled out a long length of muslin and trailed it behind her as she ran to the door. She stooped to grab a skein of yarn and ran back out, down the hill, the muslin flying behind her like a kite.

"What are you doing?" John asked, standing with arms folded next to Anders at the front door of the farmhouse.

Oleanna pushed past them and into the farmhouse. She spread the muslin on the floor.

"Lea, what are you doing?" John asked again.

"Anders, please lift the trunk onto the cloth," she said, looking up over her shoulder.

He nodded and stepped in, lifting the trunk and placing it in the middle of the muslin. "Thank you," she said quietly. She folded the muslin up and around the trunk, then stood with her hands on her hips and her head cocked to the side.

"Why did you do that?" John asked.

"It's a work of art," Oleanna said, not looking at either one of them. "I didn't want it damaged on your trip."

"Ah," John said. "Yarn won't work, though. I'll go up to the barn and find some old leather."

"I'll harness Terna and the wagon in a moment," Anders said quietly as John hurried out the door. He turned to Oleanna. "It will be fine, you know. It's very sturdy."

"It's too precious," she said quietly, standing up and facing him. "I don't want a single scratch on it."

He smiled.

"Will you promise me something?" she whispered.

Anders nodded and leaned closer. "Of course."

She took a deep breath. "Tell me everything. When you come back, tell me everything."

He cocked his head to the side. "What do you mean?"

"Tell me about the road and Vadheim, and what the Sognefjord looks like in the morning and in the evening. Tell me what the women are wearing. Tell me what the steamboats sound like, and if the people speak differently in Sogn." She stepped forward and took hold of his wrist. "Please."

He narrowed his eyes. "Have you never left the farm?"

"No," she said, dropping her hand.

Anders caught her hand and held it lightly in his. "I'll be back in a few days," he said, stepping closer and holding her hand close to his chest. "I will tell you—"

"Found some leather," John said, pulling the door open wide.

Oleanna pulled her hand away and stepped back.

John furrowed his brows. "What—"

"I'll go get the wagon," Anders said, striding out.

"Lea—" John said.

"Let's see that leather, then," she said, holding her hand out, cheeks flaming.

"What was that?" John said.

"What?" Oleanna said, leaning down and lifting one side of the trunk, snaking the leather under it.

"He's not good for you, Lea," John said, handing her the other length of leather.

"I don't think that's your business anymore."

John sighed. "Here, let me do that," he said, kneeling down on the opposite side of the trunk. Oleanna stood up and watched him secure the leather around the trunk.

"You don't know anything about him."

"Leave it," Oleanna said quietly.

He stood up. "I wanted him to look in on you two, not—"

"John, I said leave it." She turned and walked past him, out into the yard where Anders was leading Terna and the wagon.

"Is he ready?" Anders asked quietly.

She nodded. "I think he'll need help with his trunk," she said, chewing the inside of her lip.

Anders smiled, squeezing her shoulder as he walked past and into the farmhouse. Oleanna could hear their voices but not their words, harsh whispers giving way to Anders' deep voice, soothing and conciliatory. A few minutes later, John and Anders emerged, each carrying an end of the heavy trunk. They set it in the back of the wagon, Anders jumping up to secure the trunk against the side.

John readjusted his hat and brushed the dust from the front of his black suit. "Well," he said.

Oleanna took a shaky breath. "Well."

"No sign of Lisbet?" he asked quietly.

Oleanna shook her head. "Torjus should be back with her any minute..."

"I can't wait much longer," he said, pulling out his pocket watch.

"Just give her a few—"

"Are you just going to leave?" Elisabeth called from the forest near the store house. "You're not going to wait to say goodbye?" She ran awkwardly down the hill, dark hair flying behind her, Torjus in her arms. Her face was red with exertion and tears.

"Lisbet—" John began.

"He was waiting for you," Oleanna said, catching Elisabeth as she stumbled. She took Torjus and set him down.

"I will write, every week—" John said, his face flushing.

"No you won't," Elisabeth replied.

"It's time, John," Anders interrupted, jumping down from the wagon. "Say your goodbyes. We need to get on the road." He squeezed Oleanna's hand, fleetingly, as he passed.

"Good luck," Oleanna said, putting her arm around Elisabeth and pulling her closer. "Think of us, once in a while."

"All the time," John said, his voice breaking. He leaned down and hugged Torjus, who burst into wailing tears.

"Name a town after us, out in those flat fields," Elisabeth said, sobbing and laughing.

John laughed, his shoulders relaxing. "I will." He reached out for Elisabeth and pulled her into a hug. "Be good to Torjus, Lisbet. He'll need you more, now."

She nodded and sniffled into his shoulder. He released her and reached for Oleanna. "Lea—" he started, but she shook her head.

"Be quiet for once, John." She looked into his face. "Be safe," she said.

"Of course I will."

"You had better get going," she said, nodding up at the wagon's bench.

"You know I have to go."

"Then go," she said.

John nodded, once. He placed one more kiss on Torjus' fair head, and squeezed Elisabeth and Oleanna's hands. He climbed up onto the bench next to Anders. Without a look back, Anders twitched the reins and Terna began his slow plod toward the western trail.

"Send us a note from Bergen," Elisabeth said, walking next to the wagon.

"And England," Oleanna said, walking with her sister.

"And America," Elisabeth laughed, jogging as the pony and wagon picked up speed down a small hill toward the lake.

John turned and smiled. "Yes, of course. Of course. Goodbye!"

Elisabeth walked behind the wagon, waving and laughing and crying. Then suddenly, they all disappeared around a bend near the lake, and were gone.

The lake. Forever taking what Oleanna loved.

"Just us, now," she whispered. She slowed and rested against the smooth bole of a birch, breathless and sweating. The sunlit morning, the light dancing on the lake and the green trees against the blue-washed sky, all dimmed, and Oleanna slid down the tree, shivering. She was floating. "Just us now," she muttered, and slipped away.

# CHAPTER SIX

Lake Jølster, Sunnfjord, Norway
September 1904

THE BOAT FLOATED, NOT ON THE STEELY WATER, but on a cloud of mist clutching at the banks of the lake. The autumn afternoon was grim and dark, presaging the cold, barren winter. Along the banks, the grass had grown brown and yellow; the only green, the only remembrance of the brief summer, was the mottled moss and lichen blanketing the glacial boulders at the water's edge.

Oleanna watched the boat float away, propelled not, it seemed, by her mother: the wake was smooth, the water glassy. She tossed the rock she'd been turning over and over into the cold gray water and watched the ripples flow out, out, until they disturbed the tail end of the boat's wake. With a sigh, she turned and walked into the forest.

The forest floor was littered with the remnants of the warmer days: vibrant green birch leaves that had gone yellow and now a shriveled brown; stands of lovely wild purple lilies and wood violets, withered like offerings on a lonely grave. She pulled her shawl over her head and folded her arms under it, shivering with the chill of the coming winter: its bite hovered just above the canopy of trees, waiting for the right moment to swoop down and nip at her ears and nose.

The long walk to the sæter and the cabin, over drying rivulets and rotting trees, up the steep mountainside to the wide, dying meadow in the view of the imperious glacier, served to warm her. Oleanna ran the final few meters over the crest of the hill and threw herself on the ground just before the cabin, panting with the effort.

The sky above was gray as dirty snow, the wind more chill on the unprotected mountaintop, and she shivered as the sweat under her hair dried. She laid back and pulled the shawl over her like a blanket; the warmth of the cabin and a crackling fire were only steps away, but today she preferred the rocky ground and glowering skies and wind-whipped treetops.

Oleanna often escaped to the solitary sæter, where the wind bowed the tops of the tall pines, and there was no bickering between her siblings and her mother, no well-meaning suggestions and questions from her fiancé Søren.

She felt the drops of icy rain first on her bare feet, then sprinkled in her unbound hair, and she stood quickly, casting a glance at a sky that had gone from merely morose to threatening. She heaving herself to her feet and brushed the dead grass from her skirt.

Hours later, she sat dreaming before the cabin's fire, an open book neglected in her lap. She tried to look out the broad windows, to see the moonrise, but all she could see was the reflection of her own pale face and the crackling flames. "How I'd love to leave," she whispered, marking the place in her book with length of yarn and setting it on the floor.

Oleanna stretched and leaned her forehead against the cool glass, and thought not of her fiancé and their spring wedding, but instead imagined the smell of fir trees in distant valleys, the crash of the ocean against high cliffs, the taste of the air under a different sky. With a sigh, she turned and bent down, picking up her book, a dog-eared atlas. She hid it behind a stack of Elisabeth's novels on the mantle.

A strange, booming sound made her heart jump, and she pulled her shawl more closely about her. She hurried across the room and pulled open the door.

Above, so close to her mountaintop, sheets of shimmering green light flickered across the sky. Oleanna reached her arms, smiling.

After a few awkward, halting steps, she spun circles, giggling and dizzy, joy bubbling up from a place she'd nearly forgotten after Anton left. The northern lights obliged her in the dance, swirling and swaying across the sky, shimmering green and yellow and blue, close as her breath and immeasurably far away. She stopped her spinning and gave into the spell, watching the show for what felt like hours, but was likely only minutes, smiling and content.

"Oleanna!" a man's voice called, echoing despite the gentle thunder rolling above.

She stopped and dropped her arms. The spell was broken.

"Oleanna, are you up there?" John crested the hill at a jog.

She sighed, picking up her shawl from where it had fallen in the middle of the meadow. "Yes, I'm here."

John ran full out to reach Oleanna and stumbled into her, despite the acres of space around them. "Thank God," he said, grabbing her roughly by the shoulders.

She shook him off and stepped back. "John—"

He shook his head, making to grab her arm again. "Lea, there's—you have to come back, now. Is there water in the cabin?" he asked, dropping his hand as she shifted further away.

"What? Yes, there's water in the cabin."

"Good." He turned and ran to the cabin.

"What on earth..." she muttered, following him through the door. She leaned against the frame, arms folded. "What are you doing?"

John pulled out the cork on a large jug and in one swift movement poured the water on the fire. It crackled and spluttered, and he stamped out the remaining flames at the edges with his heavy boot. The cozy room went dark, the only light the weird green glow of the aurora beyond the windows.

"John—I'll freeze up here tonight," Oleanna complained, stepping into the room. "Why—"

He turned back to her, face shadowed in the dim room. "There's been an accident."

"What?"

"There was an accident," he said slowly, looking down at the dark floor.

"No."

"They died. In the lake."

"No," she said, but in a nauseating moment, an image floated into her head: her mother and Anna, drifting slowly under ice-gray water.

Oleanna's head began to swim, and she swayed. "I—"

John caught her and settled her on the edge of the large bed. "They...mother took her out this afternoon..."

"Yes, I know," Oleanna said, squeezing her eyes shut. "I saw them go."

"I wondered why they were taking so long," John explained. "I went to find them a few hours ago."

Oleanna looked up at him.

"Anna," he said, sinking on to the bed next to her. "She's only nine."

Oleanna put her arm around his shoulder and pulled him against her.

"I found them," he shuddered. "Well, I found the boat. They were almost at the Sanddal farm. Mama's shawl was in the boat..."

"Did you ask the boys at the farm—"

John shook his head. "They said they didn't see anything, they'd been mucking the barn."

Oleanna's heart began to race. "How do you know they—maybe they ran away? You only found the boat. Maybe they ran into the forest. They'll be back by daybreak—"

"Lea," John whispered. "I found them. The Sanddal boys helped me—they're better swimmers than I am. They jumped into the water," he shuddered, "and found them. It's not very deep near the shoreline. It was freezing."

"But—how?"

John stood. "I don't know," he said, shoving his hands into his pockets. "They must have been standing in the boat. Maybe they were reaching for the branches. Neither one of them could swim well."

"John—"

"Why did they go out? Mother..." he growled, running his hands through his short hair. "She's so irresponsible. Why did she take Anna?" He dropped into the chair by the fireplace and covered his face with his hands.

Oleanna dropped her chin to her chest and did not speak.

"Poor Anna," he whispered.

The image resurfaced, Anna and their mother floating silently, wide-eyed, in the gray water. Oleanna groaned and pulled at her hair, as though the physical pain could release the images in her head.

"Lea?" John said, standing up and reaching a tentative hand toward her.

She stopped, dazed.

"Lea, come with me," he said, reaching to put an arm around her shoulder.

Oleanna stepped back and shook her head. "Do you realize what this means?" she asked, looking past his shoulder, out the window to the fading northern lights.

"What?"

"It's up to me now," she said, sinking to the floor, cross-legged.

"What are you talking about?" he said, kneeling down next to her.

She started laughing.

"What—"

"It's up to me now," she whispered.

John stood and folded his arms. "Lisbet will—"

"Elisabeth will do what she pleases and not what's necessary," Oleanna snapped, tears tumbling down her cheeks.

After a few moments, he sighed and nodded. "We have a lot of work to do," he said, offering her his hand. She closed her eyes and sighed. When she opened them, John's hand was still extended. She took it and he pulled her to her feet.

"What was she thinking?" Oleanna whispered, fists clenching again. "If she wanted to go...but why take Anna?"

"Did you ever understand why she did the things she did?"

"No."

"No. So we get on with it," he said, squaring his shoulders. He double-checked that the fire in the fireplace was out and strode to the cabin door. Oleanna watched him.

"Coming?" John asked.

"I'll be down, soon," she said quietly.

"Lea, please come with me. I need your help."

"I need to—I'll be down, soon. I promise."

"Don't be too long," he said, pushing the door open. "We can grieve later."

"Just a half an hour. Please?"

John nodded. "Half an hour."

He walked into the fading green light, leaving the door open behind him. The cabin was utterly silent, though Oleanna felt the refrain pounding in her mind might soon be audible: no chance to say goodbye. No chance to say...anything. The wave of grief rising in her was so powerful, she wanted to scream, or tear her hair, or destroy the cabin and everything in it, to shunt that grief away. Anything to keep it from lodging in her heart.

Instead, she stood in the dark, clenching and unclenching her fists. "Oh, Anna," she whispered, covering her face with trembling hands. As soon as she gave in, her hands dropped and she shook her head violently. "Not now," she whispered. "Not now."

She stepped out onto the porch and shut the door behind her with a soft click. Squaring her shoulders, she broke into a run, surefooted in the dark, shawl trailing behind her until it was caught in the bare branches of a young birch. She ran on without it, her straw-gold hair flashing in the dark, taking not the trail back to the farm, but a trail leading northwest.

After flying, leaping over the dying ground of the wood, she reached her destination: a tiny church, dark with age. The pointed roof reached past the forest's canopy with fierce-mouthed dragons, its wood shingles laid on like leaves. It was not so much a product of the hands of men, but a natural growth of the forest itself.

Panting and relieved, she threw herself down the last few meters and stumbled through the doors, skidding to a stop, surprised to see flickering candlelight near the altar. "Oh," she gasped, blinking in the light.

A graceful, delicate man sat in the first pew, turning and half-standing as Oleanna burst in.

"Oleanna?"

"Søren," she said, hands on her thighs, bent over and struggling for breath.

"What's wrong?" he asked, walking toward her.

She shook her head, overcome.

"What's wrong? Here, sit down," he said, guiding her to a nearby pew with a firm hand on her shoulder. The broad windows overlooking the lake were mirrors, reflecting only the flickering candlelight and the look of fear and wildness in her eyes.

He sat in the next row of pews and turned to look at her. "What's happened?" he asked quietly.

"Mama," she said.

"Has she finally left you?" he sniffed.

"No. She died. This afternoon."

Søren sat back, eyes wide. "What happened?"

"She took Anna out in the boat and–I don't know what happened, but they both..." She folded and unfolded her hands in her lap, then leaned toward him.

He nodded but did not reach out to comfort her. "Go on."

"That's all I know."

"Your mother has always been reckless." Søren stood and walked back toward the altar.

She watched him gather his Bible and personal effects from the altar, avoiding her gaze, stiff and unbending.

She took a shaky breath. "Søren—"

"I'll come tomorrow and discuss the arrangements with John," he said quietly. "Go home now, and help him."

She shivered from head to foot. "They'll be lying out—oh, Søren, they'll be lying in my bed," she whispered.

"Oleanna, go home. You'll find a way."

"I can't go home. How can I go home?"

Søren stopped and folded his hands before him. "You can't shirk your responsibilities. Not now."

"But, mama," she whispered. "Anna." She began to sob, wracking heaves that seemed to rattle the glass in the windows, shivering the candlelight.

He did not move and she cried until the discomfort of his embarrassed gaze shamed her into silence. She wiped her eyes with her sleeve and looked up at him, seeing not the leader of their church and parish, not her fiancé, but the awkward and quiet boy she'd known since childhood."

He smiled, a constricted thing that felt to her more like a grimace. "There will be time to cry later," he said.

She stood slowly. "I get no comfort from you, then?"

He glanced around the church and stiffened. "Here?"

Oleanna laughed, though it felt like icicles in her throat. "No, of course not." She pushed him out of the way and stalked toward the door. She paused, and said, "The engagement is off."

# CHAPTER SEVEN

Lake Jølster, Sunnfjord, Norway
May 1905

ACROSS THE WATER A SMALL VOICE rose and fell with the tops of the wind-driven waves. Oleanna tried to reach toward the dark lake, to take hold of that shimmering sound, but found her arms heavy as boughs under winter snow.

The voice was insistent, growing stronger as the wind grew from the north. Oleanna struggled to meet it, groaning.

"Lea! Lea! Wake up!"

Oleanna shuddered, but did not open her eyes.

"Mama, Lea won't wake up."

"What are you talking about?" Elisabeth's voice, high and impatient, cut through the heavy darkness.

"I shake her, but she won't wake up."

"Torjus, mama has a headache. This is not a time to play tricks."

"I'm not playing," he said, thumping Oleanna's arm with each word.

"Torjus," Oleanna groaned, opening her eyes and sitting up slowly. "Please."

"There you are," Elisabeth said. "She's awake. Now run along, it's time to feed the sheep."

"But—"

"Torjus."

"Yes, mama." He clambered to his feet and bounded away into the forest with a last look over his shoulder at Oleanna.

Oleanna pulled her legs under her and rested her elbows on her knees, cradling her face in her hands. "Where have you been?" she mumbled.

"I went to see the Sanddal boys."

Oleanna looked up. "What?"

Elisabeth shrugged.

"You stayed with the wagon all the way to Sanddal?"

"No. I followed them for a while, but after they disappeared, I carried on walking. It was nice to see new scenery."

"How is their mother?"

"Ill."

"Why didn't John tell us?"

"Didn't want us to worry, I expect."

Oleanna nodded, and sighing, climbed to her feet. "Suppose I should start the wash," she said.

"I'll do it."

"No, I will."

Elisabeth folded her arms. "Were you sleeping?"

"What?"

"Just now. Were you sleeping? Or did you faint?"

"I—" Oleanna started. She furrowed her brows. "I don't know. I think I dreamt of mama and Anna," she whispered. "They all leave, don't they? Everyone leaves and we're all alone." Oleanna swayed.

"Lea—" Elisabeth said, reaching out and grabbing her arm.

Oleanna turned to her, eyes wide. "When they disappeared around the bend—just there," she said, pointing. Elisabeth did not look. "It was like they disappeared for good. They no longer exist. They're just echoes now. All of them." Oleanna's breathing grew shallow and the world grew dark around the edges.

"Don't you dare faint," Elisabeth said, shaking her.

Oleanna gritted her teeth, willing away the wave of nausea, then took a deep breath. "We have work to do."

"Go rest for a little while, I'll look after the wash today."

"No," Oleanna said, squeezing her sister's arm. "I need the distraction."

"You haven't fainted since—"

"I'm fine. Bring down the linens from the cabin. They need a good wash. As a matter of fact," she said, rubbing her hands together, "why don't we wash all of the linens today? Start fresh."

"I don't think—"

"Lisbet," she said, dropping her hands and looking at her. "Please."

"Have you eaten today?"

Oleanna cast her mind back across the long hours of the morning. "No. I suppose not."

"Eat—even just a piece of bread."

"Yes, I will, later."

"Oleanna," Elisabeth said, raising her voice. "For once, please let's not argue. I will go to the cabin for the linens, you sit and eat."

Oleanna sighed, exhaustion again overtaking her. "Fine."

"Thank you," Elisabeth said, walking away toward the barn.

Oleanna stood still and silent, watching her crest the small hill.

"Lea," Elisabeth called, exasperated. "Go eat!"

Oleanna nodded slowly. After a moment, she called, "Do you dream about mama?"

Elisabeth stopped and turned back. "No. I can't."

With a sigh, Oleanna wandered across the short distance from the lakeside to the farmhouse door and pushed it open. She stood on the threshold, arms folded across her chest. The unmade beds, half-drunk mugs of coffee, the clothes left behind on the dusty pine floor next to John's bed, too bulky for the already overstuffed trunk: the remnants of her old life. Again.

With a shudder, she stepped over the threshold and quickly grabbed an end of bread from the small table near the fireplace, then darted back out into the late morning light. She shut the door behind her settled onto the bench at the table, her back to the shining lake.

It was so quiet, with everyone gone. She could be alone in the world, bound forever to the meager farm on the rocky shores of a mountain lake. "Everyone leaves," she whispered, staring past the store house to the dark wood beyond. She threw the crust away, choking down what was left.

Oleanna and Elisabeth worked silently, side by side, for long hours in their small field, planting new crops and tending to their garden. The repetition of digging, planting, moving to the next row kept their hands and minds occupied, and bickering to a minimum.

Late in the afternoon, a crash and wail from inside the farmhouse made them both jump. Oleanna left aside her shovel, running across the small plot. She wrenched open the door and stumbled in. Torjus had overturned the small kettle hanging above the ashes in the hearth, and was sitting on John's bed, holding his hand and crying.

"Torjus," Elisabeth said, sitting next to him on the bed. "What did you do?" She took his small hand and blew on it gently.

Oleanna righted the kettle and swept up the ashes. "You'll be fine," Oleanna said, pushing the ashes into an old newspaper.

Torjus continued to cry, burying his face in Elisabeth's chest. She wrapped her arms around him and rocked back and forth. "Do you miss John?" she whispered, looking up and catching Oleanna's eye.

"Yes," he sobbed.

Elisabeth stroked his hair. "So do I. So does Lea. Shhh," she whispered, picking him up and turning around to place him back on John's bed. Torjus curled into a ball around John's pillow and closed his eyes, sniffling. Elisabeth smoothed back his hair and Oleanna leaned down and kissed his cheek. She straightened and followed Elisabeth out the door and into the evening.

"Are you hungry?" Elisabeth asked, sighing as she leaned against the side of the farmhouse.

"No," Oleanna said.

"Please eat something."

"I ate."

Elisabeth narrowed her eyes. "Suit yourself," she said, disappearing into the house for a few moments, and reappearing with the rest of the morning's bread, the half-empty bottle of akevitt, and two tumblers. Without a word, she walked past Oleanna toward the lake. "Are you coming?" she said from the other side of the farmhouse.

Oleanna walked around to where Elisabeth had settled herself against the farmhouse, facing the darkening lake. She slid down the wall to sprawl, unladylike, next to her sister.

After a few moments, Elisabeth said, "He's not going to write, is he?"

Oleanna shrugged. "I don't know."

"Is he going to be safe?"

"I don't know."

Elisabeth tossed the last bit of bread across the small green verge and into the lake. The water rippled out and Oleanna watched it spread.

"Are you going to be like this for the rest of our lives?" Elisabeth asked finally. "Because if you are, I think I'm going to need a lot of this," she said, tipping back a shot of akevitt. "And so are you," she said, filling a tumbler and handing it to Oleanna.

Oleanna chanced a half-smile; it felt unnatural and tight on her face, but she took the tumbler and drained it, saluting her sister with the glass.

Elisabeth nodded. They looked out at the lake again, quiet as they watched the light slip away behind the mountains; the deep mountain valley darkened to a hazy blue. "At least Anders will be back in a few days," Elisabeth said. "We should invite him to supper. Maybe you can get a bite of that apple," she laughed.

Oleanna's heart jumped, but she tamped it down. "He's not coming back," she said, drinking another tumbler of akevitt in one go, setting the heavy glass on the cool grass beside her.

Elisabeth sighed. "And how do you know?"

"I just know," Oleanna said, closing her eyes again. "They're all gone. We are left alone." She could feel Elisabeth shudder next to her.

"Don't say that," Elisabeth whispered. "Drink some more akevitt and shut up."

They lingered outside, each lost in their own thoughts, trading yawn for yawn until Elisabeth nearly fell asleep sitting up. Oleanna stood creakily, yawning and stretching, her head swimming. "It's time for bed," Oleanna whispered, bending down and shaking Elisabeth's shoulder.

Elisabeth sighed and struggled to her feet. "Did we feed the chickens?" she muttered, rubbing her eyes.

"Yes. Nothing to do until morning," Oleanna said, walking around the house to the front door. She pushed it open, squinting in the relative dark. She shuffled in, careful not to stub her toe on her loom, her hands out before her like a blind woman.

Elisabeth huffed behind her. "Just light the lantern for pity's sake."

"Shhh. Don't wake Torjus," Oleanna whispered.

They pulled off their shirtwaists and stepped out of their skirts, leaving them strewn on the floor. Elisabeth pulled the covers back and crawled in, snuffling and yawning as she curled around her pillow. Oleanna stood, hesitating. She wrapped her arms around her middle against a shiver and, sighing, shut the door. She climbed into bed in the full dark and pulled the covers up to her chin.

As she settled into the darkness, the nightsounds of the room and the farm grew clear: a bird flitting from branch to branch outside the window, searching for a place to rest. Elisabeth shifting in her sleep, sheets scratching and rustling. A creature padding along the turf roof of the farmhouse. She listened hard for John's rasping snores, but heard only Torjus, in John's bed, breathing shallowly in his dream.

Oleanna shuddered. "I am the only person awake," she thought, pulling the covers tight. "The whole world has gone to sleep and has left me alone."

She lay in the dark, watching the outlines of the ceiling and the fireplace and the box beds become visible. The dark became less impenetrable, rendering the room more familiar, and even more empty. I can't stay in here, she thought.

Oleanna swung her feet off the bed and leaned down to the bottom drawer of the cupboard pushed up against the wall. She fumbled in the drawer and pulled out an old coverlet she'd woven under her mother's tutelage.

"Whareydoin?" Elisabeth mumbled.

Oleanna straightened and pulled open the farmhouse door. She walked out without a word, closing the door quietly behind her.

The edges of the twilight at midnight still clung to the tips of the mountains, though the forest was a dark veil of swaying leaves and trailing branches. She headed straight for that dark place, breaking into a run, slowing only when she was well beyond sight of the tiny farmhouse and broad silvery lake.

The nightsounds of the forest were friendlier than those of the farmhouse: small, darting things in the brush and the trees, stretching their arms, yawning before settling in for the night. She slowed, her breathing labored, until finally she settled with her back to a boulder, the sæter and cabin just visible beyond the forest's edge.

She leaned back, peering up to the darkening night sky, pulling the coverlet around her shoulders. Stars pinpricked above the swaying branches, and the tears streamed down the sides of her face, down her neck, into her chemise. It was growing cool; she drew her legs in and wrapped her arms around them, hiding her face in the fabric of her chemise, soaking it with her tears.

Only a few months before, when the forest was cold and quiet, she had run, full speed, from the store house back to the farmhouse, grasping her mother's glittering sølje brooch so tightly in her fist the pin punctured her palm. She did not feel it, and ran down the gentle slope, stumbling through the open farmhouse door. She leaned over her mother's silent, still body and hesitated: so unlike her wild and skittish mother in life, arrayed like a matron with her hair tucked under a headscarf.

"They're coming, Lea, hurry," John whispered.

She pinned the brooch to the cloth at her mother's neck and stood, stepping away, not daring to look at Anna's small form laid out next to their mother.

"Ready now?" John asked, laying a gentle hand on Oleanna's shoulder.

She nodded but said nothing.

John leaned out the door and nodded to someone Oleanna could not see, then stepped back into the farmhouse next to Oleanna. Elisabeth walked in, a tattered lace handkerchief over her mouth, Torjus trailing behind, clutching at her skirts. Søren followed moments later, stiff and disapproving in his vestments, and behind him, the boys from the Sanddal farm with their mother.

Oleanna and John stepped back and allowed them all to move forward to the bed. Elisabeth knelt next to the bed and clutched her mother's hand, sobs wracking her small frame. Torjus began to cry in sympathy and fear, but Elisabeth did not comfort him. When his wails continued, and the men in the room shifted uncomfortably, Oleanna stepped forward and took Torjus by the hand. "Come with me," she whispered.

He would not budge. "Mama," he wailed, stamping his foot.

With a sigh, Oleanna picked him up and carried him out the door and into the cold, damp morning. The gray sky of the day of her mother's death had not broken, and while threatening rain, never came through. The clouds were a heavy woolen blanket hanging low over the lake, obscuring the mountaintops. Torjus continued to wail, squirming to get out of her arms.

She reached the store house, edging the door open with her foot. "Shhh," she whispered, cradling him close.

"Mama," he whimpered.

"She's sitting with bestemor, who's gone to heaven."

"Is mama going with her?"

"To heaven?" Oleanna asked, setting him down near the dyeing table; he loved to spread out the herbs and flowers, making designs only he understood, ruining Oleanna's careful organization.

He nodded, sniffling.

"No, not yet. Not for a long time, I hope."

"Will bestemor be able to see us?"

"No, my love. I don't think so."

"Will she be lonely in heaven?"

"I expect not," she said, picking him up and settling him on a corner of the table. She pulled some dried purple heather toward them and gave him a handful. "I expect that bestemor will be running through the forest, picking flowers and dipping her toes into the cold river."

"Is that was heaven looks like?"

"I hope so," she said, smoothing his hair.

"What about Anna's heaven?"

"Hmmm?" she asked, arranging the heather and maple flower into alternating patterns, imagining the colors in her weaving. "I don't know, what do you think?"

He shrugged.

Oleanna nearly laughed; he looked so serious all of a sudden, a little man in a toddler's body. So much death already: first father, now mama and Anna.

"I don't think there will be a lake in her heaven," he said, sighing.

She shook her head. "No. I expect not."

"There will be dolls there," he said, nodding.

"I hope so."

He yawned. "Are they there already?" he whispered, leaning toward her with his arms spread.

She picked him up and settled him on some fresh hay in the corner, near the open dowry chest. "What do you think?"

"No, Lea, tell me," he whined.

"Shh, shh," she whispered, smoothing the hair away from his eyes. "They are always with us, and they are always in heaven, I think," she said, surprising herself.

"Are they wraiths?"

She shuddered. "In a way."

"I don't like wraiths."

"Nor me."

"I want them to stay in heaven."

"Yes," she said, leaning down and kissing his soft forehead. "Yes, they will stay in heaven. And in your heart, if you remember."

He nodded and closed his eyes, curling into a little ball in the dry summer hay. Oleanna stood, hands on her hips, and watched him fall asleep. After a minute, she turned and walked quietly back toward the store house door. "No," he murmured, and she stopped in her tracks. "I'm scared."

She sighed. "I'll be right here, by the door."

He mumbled something indistinct and fell right back asleep. Oleanna turned and sat next to the open door, watching the empty space between the store house and the farmhouse. She watched, but saw no movement: the communal grieving of her mother and sister continued without her.

After a quarter of an hour, she closed the store house door on a sharp pang of loneliness, and curled herself into a ball, like Torjus. The tears, however numbing, however close to the surface, would not come. Her mind spun along the same track, like a wooden toy train or a racing tin horse: trapped, trapped, trapped.

Minutes later, John pushed the door open and peered round the frame. "They've all gone," he said quietly.

"Shhh," Oleanna hissed, sitting up and nodding at Torjus' napping form.

John nodded and beckoned with his hand. Oleanna rubbed her itching eyes and stood creakily, following him out, the chill autumn air sharp after the warmth of the store house. "Jakob was here," John whispered, shutting the door.

"No," Oleanna said, surprised. "Did he come in?"

John shook his head. "No, he said he didn't want to disturb Lisbet."

"So why did he come?"

John shrugged. "I don't know."

"Is he still here?" she asked, looking around the farmyard, and up into the forest.

"I don't think so."

She continued to look up into the forest, steadfastly ignoring the broad, cold lake. "Did Lisbet put out the food?"

John shook his head. "No, I did. She disappeared before Søren even said a few words."

Oleanna sighed. "Are the Sanddal boys and their mother still here?"

"No, they've all just gone."

She sighed. "We'd better pack it away. No sense letting it go bad. We can eat it for supper tonight."

"Lea," John said, grabbing her shoulder.

She stopped and turned to look at him.

"We—I—" John stammered, face suddenly pale. He dropped his hand.

"What?" she asked.

"Never mind. I can do it myself."

"Do what?"

He took a deep breath. "Søren and the Sanddal boys left."

"Yes, you told me."

"Søren is not coming back."

Oleanna shook her head slowly, eyes narrowed. "What are you talking about?"

"I need your help. I can't dig both of them myself," he whispered.

The blood rushed from her face and she swayed.

John reached out again and took a firm grip on her shoulder. "Lea, I'm—never mind, I shouldn't have asked you. Here, sit down," he said, attempting to settle her on the grass next to the wall of the store house.

"He won't let us bury her in the churchyard," she said.

"No."

"Where?" she asked.

"Where?"

"Where should we bury them?"

"Lea, I shouldn't have asked."

"Where, John?"

After a moment he sighed. "Not next to father."

"No," she agreed. "The Sanddal boys aren't coming back?"

"No," John said, shaking his head. "They can't come back until day after tomorrow. We don't...we can't wait that long."

Oleanna pushed down the horror of what that statement meant and nodded. "We can't take them up to the sæter," she said, hugging her arms around her middle. "Though Anna would have liked that." She closed her eyes, and after a few moments said, "I think we should bury them at the elves' wood."

"The what?"

"The elves' wood," she said. "Don't you remember?"

He shook his head slowly, looking over her shoulder and into the past.

"Anton named it, when we were all little," she whispered, as John's eyes narrowed. "The stand of birches that always go golden first."

"North around the bend?"

"Yes. Near the long trail mama always used to get to the sæter."

"The leaves all go golden first," he whispered, "and stay golden after all the other leaves have dropped."

"Yes."

He looked at her; the emptiness in his eyes made her stagger. "How could I have forgotten the name?" he whispered.

Oleanna's heart constricted. "You're going to leave us."

"What?" he said.

"You—oceans of wheat—" she muttered. The gray autumn afternoon grew dark, darker, and she stumbled backwards, into the wall of the store house. "You're going to leave us."

"Lea, I'm not going anywhere. I'm not leaving. Where do you get these ideas?"

She took a deep breath and dropped her hands, squeezing them into fists. "I'm sorry."

"It's been a long few days," he said.

"Yes."

"Are you ready?"

"What about Torjus?"

"He'll be fine. We won't be long."

With a last look at her nephew, she followed John down the slope to the small, lonely farmhouse. He pushed open the door and they stepped quietly inside. The food for the viewing had hardly been touched, and Oleanna moved to begin gathering it, covering the bread with a linen towel.

"Lea," he said, holding her arm. "Later."

She nodded, her breath coming short and quick.

"Are you ready?"

Her heart thudded. "Yes," she whispered, still looking anywhere but the bed.

"We will have to take them separately," he said. "Take mama's feet, and I'll take her shoulders. I'll have to come back for Anna."

Oleanna nodded but did not say anything.

"1...2...3," he said. They lifted their mother's small, stiff body and Oleanna backed them out through the door and into the farmyard. Her mind was blank as they struggled over the hillside and around the bend, into the thick forest. The last of the south-heading birds cried overhead, gliding on the cool breeze, but she only remembered them afterwards, as if in a dream.

John spied the elves' wood first, still glowing gold and silver while the forest around it died. "Over there," he huffed, and Oleanna nodded, without really knowing what she was agreeing to. They stumbled over fallen branches and found a clear spot beneath the trees, lowering their mother's body to the ground. John stood and wiped his brow with the back of his hand; Oleanna leaned over, her hands on her thighs, panting.

After a few moments, John stood straight and took a deep breath. "Ready for Anna?"

"We can't leave her here," Oleanna said, still panting.

"She's not going anywhere."

Oleanna followed John as he again skirted the elves' wood and headed back toward their small farm. The return trip took only a few minutes and as they approached the farm, John pointed to the store house. "Go get two winding sheets. And a shovel."

She followed his orders, and in a half-dream walked up the short hill into the store house. Torjus was still sound asleep on the hay in the corner; she tiptoed past him to the linens, stacked in piles on a low shelf behind the dowry chests. She grabbed the first two sheets off the top, the rest falling to the floor of the store house in an untidy heap. She hurried out, the linens clutched close to her chest, and half-ran to the barn.

Oleanna pushed the door open and Terna whinnied at her quietly. Warmth returned to her limbs and her heart, and she nuzzled his nose with her own. "Now where did you put the shovel, my love?" she whispered. She spied it in the corner and with a last pat for the pony, picked it up in her free hand and stepped outside.

John stood in front of the farmhouse, Anna's impossibly small form stiff and unnatural in his arms. Oleanna broke into an awkward run to join him. When she got closer, she saw his face was pale and pinched. "Do you want me to—" she began, offering him the linens and shovel.

He shook his head, turning and again walking the path to the elves' wood. Oleanna gripped the linens tightly in one arm, clenching her jaw against the wail threatening to wrench her throat. After a few deep, unsteady breaths she followed her brother along the path.

They were a strange funeral procession: the tall blond man, solemn and rigid as a statue, his small dark-haired sister peaceful in his arms, his golden-haired sister struggling behind, linens caught like a sail in the autumn breeze.

John and Oleanna set their burdens down and retreated to opposite ends of the small wood. John stood, arms folded, looking up into the depths of the forest, face impassive. Oleanna leaned against a slender birch bole, panting. The breeze that had been following them throughout the afternoon grew stronger, swirling the leaves on the forest floor, the trees swaying gracefully in a dance. Oleanna raised her face to the wind, grateful for the cool against her heated skin.

"Are you ready?" John asked finally.

She opened her eyes and looked at him; her heart broke. "John, let me—" she began, bending to pick up the shovel.

"No!" he said, moving more quickly than she could have expected, taking the shovel away from her.

"I don't mind, John. Honestly. Sit down and rest."

"No," he said, stepping back and surveying the ground.

"John, you haven't stopped since you found them. Sit, and rest. I will do this."

He looked up at her. "This is my responsibility. You can't do it for me."

"Your—" she began, but stopped when he put a hand up.

"Please, Lea. Wrap them both in the winding sheets and I will get started."

She nodded and laid out the sheets on the rocky ground. She stepped over her mother's body and picked up Anna, awkwardly, and set her on the sheet. "How—" Oleanna began, looking up at John. "How did they do it for Severina?"

"It's a winding sheet, Lea. Roll her up in it."

"Oh," she said quietly. She leaned down and smoothed the wavy dark hair away from her sister's face. She moved to kiss Anna on the forehead, but stopped with a shudder at the last moment. She looked up at John, who had paused, resting his hands on top of the shovel, and he nodded. She rolled Anna's body in the winding sheet, tucking in extra fabric as she did. She found a small branch of golden birch and tucked it into the front of the sheet.

Oleanna stood, back creaking, and hesitated.

"Just leave her there," John said over his shoulder.

"That's the last time I'll see her face," she whispered. She steadied herself for the nausea, the tunnel vision, but none came: she had grown numb. "I'll need your help with mama," she said, stepping over her sister's body.

John nodded and set aside the shovel while Oleanna shook out the other sheet, fluttering in the breeze. The low gray sky was growing dark with the coming of the evening, and the breeze blew cold as the wind direction shifted, blowing at them from across the icy lake. "We should hurry," she muttered, holding down an edge of the sheet with her foot as she tried to maneuver her mother's shoulders onto the linen.

He only grunted in reply and they worked together to wrap their mother in the sheet. When they finished, John stood and walked back to his shovel, resuming his grueling task, while she remained and knelt at her mother's side. As with Anna, Oleanna smoothed the curling dark hair away from her mother's face. "Did mama ever tell you about her life? Before she met father?" she asked John, still looking down at her mother.

"No," he panted. "I asked her once, but she wouldn't tell me."

"I wonder why," Oleanna said, twisting an end of the winding sheet around her hand.

"Well, why did she—"

"—ever do the things she did? I don't know." Oleanna peered into her mother's face, gray as the lake mist, fragile and beautiful. For long minutes she tried to imagine her as a young woman, before marriage, and hard work on the farm, and six children had turned her brittle and strange. Who had she loved? What songs had she sung? What did she dream? A rush of shame reddened Oleanna's cheeks; she was only ever mama to her, source of comfort or frustration or shame. But she was Brita Johannesdatter, with her own dreams and stories. All gone.

Oleanna pushed down the sob in her throat and looked around the elves' wood. In a sheltered corner, behind a small rock, a final fragile stand of tiny glacier buttercup shivered in the breeze. She scrambled to her feet and, stepping over her mother's body, knelt next to the flowers, cupping them in her hands. "These shouldn't be here," she said, half to herself.

"What?" John said, halfway through digging the second grave.

"These flowers–they're still blooming," she said. "They should have died off in August, but...here they are."

"And the leaves should have dropped from these trees. It's the elves' wood, remember?" John said.

She looked over at him and he paused in his digging, looking up at her and smiling.

Gently, she uprooted the flowers and stood, cradling them in her hands. "Like summer in a cup," she muttered.

"What?"

"That's what mama always said about the beer she and I brewed. These flowers," she said, uncupping her hand for John to see, "look like summer."

Oleanna stepped back to her mother's side and tucked the bunch of flowers in a crease of the winding sheet. As she did, her hand touched something hard and metallic—the delicate sølje brooch she had fastened at her mother's throat only an hour or two before. She pulled aside the sheet and unfastened the brooch, hooking it to her own skirt for safekeeping.

She tucked the delicate flowers at her mother's throat, letting her hand rest on the cold marble skin. Closing her eyes, a rush of images flooded her, scenes she did not remember from her own childhood: a different farm on a different lake, a jolly dance, a broad, bright city and a handsome young man...

"I'm done," John said.

Oleanna jumped and opened her eyes, snatching her hand back. After a few steadying breaths, she looked up at him. "We should find Lisbet."

He shook his head. "She had her chance to say goodbye."

"John."

"She had her chance."

Oleanna nodded. She leaned in and kissed her mother's forehead, quickly, then covered her face with an end of the linen winding sheet, and stood. "You should rest for a few minutes," she said, watching John pant, his face ruddy.

"No," he said. "I don't want to draw this out."

Oleanna took the shovel from him and leaned it against a pine tree at the edge of the wood, then walked back and stood behind Anna's head. "Ready?"

He nodded and leaned down, and without speaking, they lifted their sister and settled her into her grave. They walked to their mother, and settled her into her own grave. Oleanna stepped back, hugging herself against a sudden chill. "Should we say something?"

John shrugged.

Oleanna took a deep breath, but found no words came. She squeezed her eyes closed tight, but her mind was blank, numb. She opened her eyes. "I don't know what to say," she whispered, tears starting.

"Me either."

She sighed and walked to her brother's side. "She always bewildered me in life," she said, "and here she does it from the grave. Almost the grave."

John put an arm around her shoulders and squeezed. "She loved you."

Oleanna snorted, half-laughing and half-crying. "If you say so."

"I do," he whispered, releasing her and walking over to retrieve the shovel. "Ready?"

She nodded, and he handed it to her. "Goodbye," she whispered, shoveling dirt onto her mother's grave. As she worked, her even strokes became erratic, and she rushed, moving furiously. John knelt next to Anna's grave, moving armfuls of dirt with his hands and arms, soiling his shirt and arms.

Finally they both stopped, panting, and looked at each other. Oleanna stood up and threw the shovel away, staggering back and wiping the sweat from her forehead with her dirt-covered hand. John's face was similarly smeared with sweat, and dirt, and tears.

He walked over and stood next to her, his arms folded.

After a few minutes, Oleanna rested her head on his shoulder. "It's just us now," she said. "Us, and Lisbet."

John nodded but did not reply.

Oleanna awoke as the first fingers of sun illuminated the tiny hilltop cabin. She had fallen asleep, curled under her coverlet, exhausted by toil and grief. She pushed herself up onto her elbow, and winced at the stiffness and pain in her neck. Shivering, she struggled to her feet, gingerly shaking the leaves and pine needles out of her coverlet. How am I going to get any work done today like this? she thought.

She rolled her head side to side, groaning, and walked to the open meadow of their sæter. The intransigent goat bleated at her sleepily in greeting and Oleanna patted her on the head. She continued on to the cabin and pushed open the door, grunting in disgust when she stepped into the small room: Elisabeth had left the place in a horrible state, bedclothes awry, ashes strewn across the floor before the hearth, books piled, open and closed, across the bed and on the floor.

Oleanna, righteous and angry, tidied the small cabin, channeling her grief and loss into duty and fevered activity. She stopped, in the midst of picking up a book. Was it only yesterday, while John prepared to leave, that Elisabeth had hidden here, believing that if she only stood apart from the action, the action would never come? Lisbet always felt that the world of the farm revolved around her, Oleanna thought, shaking her head. And yet, who carried on and who broke down, when the final blow came, when John disappeared forever?

Looking around the sæter, watching the morning creep into the deep valleys of the Sunnfjord and Sognefjord, she sighed: the first full day without John. The first full day without Anders. Nothing to do but work. Fate is strange, but somehow symmetrical, she thought: a loss for a loss, a loss for a loss.

# CHAPTER EIGHT

Lake Jølster, Sunnfjord, Norway
June 1905

THE NINTH DAY AFTER JOHN'S DEPARTURE was much the same as
the first eight: planting, harvesting, fishing, cleaning, cooking,
milking. John's bed remained unmade; Torjus spent much of his
time in it, sleeping to make up for the weeks on end that he hardly
slept before John's departure. Elisabeth continued to wonder where
John was in his journey—had the ship already left Bergen? When
would they reach England? Oleanna shrugged each time the
question was posed, and each night collapsed into her bed,
exhausted and heartsick. Though Anders had said he would return,
he had not, so she comforted herself in the way only grief can: I told
you so.

The ninth day was different in one respect. A rainstorm swept
in from the sea far off to the west, gathering moisture and chill from
the lake, gathering speed and power as it swept up the
mountainside, drenching Oleanna as she tended to the goat and
sheep at the sæter. She had been watching the gray clouds speeding
in from the west with only half a mind, focused instead on milking
the goat and running through her list of summer chores.

The deluge came just as she stood and stretched, hands in the
small of her back. The drops hit her forehead first and she opened
her eyes in surprise; she knelt down and protected her hard-won
bucket of goat's milk with the apron of her skirt, then trundled

toward the shelter of the cabin, hunched and stumbling like an ancient troll. She set the bucket inside the door, spilling only a bit of the contents, and raced back out into the sheeting rain, hounding the sheep and goat into the relative shelter near the cabin. Two lambs insisted on frolicking in the cool rain, and Oleanna chased them around the meadow until she was drenched from rain and effort. Nearly half an hour later, she trudged back to the cabin, the surprise storm showing no signs of letting up.

Oleanna stood on the threshold and shivered, looking hopefully into the grate, but finding no wood. She stuck her head out the door and found no wood piled next to the cabin. A breeze whipped her hair into her eyes and she hesitated: a long, wet run back to the farm, or wait out the storm in the cabin? The list of chores reverberated like drumbeats in her head, and with a longing look at the warm, soft bed, she sighed and retied her snarled, wet hair into a plait. Head down, she shut the door behind her and ran into the storm.

She stopped in the middle of the meadow, and turned and ran back to the cabin. With a heavy sigh, she poured the hard-won milk into the grass: it would not keep in the cabin, and it would not make it in her rush down to the farm. Tossing the bucket aside, she pelted across the meadow again. The goat and sheep, and the clutch of lambs, watched her curiously as she ran past them, jumping over fallen boulders and trees. The storm made leaping rivulets over the fallen branches, and her feet squelched in the wet socks in her heavy boots. She chased the water down the hill, fat, heavy drops of rain plashing on her arms and forehead, dropping off the leaves and branches of the trees high above.

A sudden fierce joy blazed in Oleanna, a sense of freedom she hadn't felt for months, even years. She leapt like a fox over the tumbling rocks graceful and strong, running branches and leaves through her fingers like the wool on her loom. She leaned her head back and let the water run over her eyes, across her temples and into her hair. And, tasting the rain on her tongue, she laughed, joy bubbling up from a place she thought she'd locked away again.

And then suddenly, she stumbled to a stop at the edge of the wood. Mama, she thought. She steadied herself against the bole of a tree, shivering. Why didn't I ask her what she saw in the forest? Why didn't I ask her what she left behind when she came to the lake? "Poor mama," she whispered. Oleanna took a deep breath, and straightening her skirt and tucking away stray wisps of hair, walked slowly into the farmyard, the rain drenching her to her skin.

Elisabeth was nowhere to be seen, but Torjus was playing at the lakeside, staying far out of the way of his mother and aunt's perpetual bad moods. Fishing pole abandoned on the rocks, he laughed and spun in circles, catching raindrops on his tongue, following the irregular gusts as they made patterns in the grass. He spun close, closer to the water's edge, the lakeshore shrinking under the deluge.

Oleanna froze, standing halfway between the forest's edge and the water. "Torjus," she croaked, her voice no more than a whisper. He continued to spin his circles, laughing as he tottered nearer the water's edge, losing his balance. "No," Oleanna moaned.

The door to the farmhouse banged open at that moment and Elisabeth stalked out, the storm in her face matching the gray fury of the skies above. "Torjus," she yelled, stamping over the ground, oblivious to Oleanna on the hillside. "Have you taken leave of your senses?"

Torjus righted himself at the sound of his mother's voice and Oleanna remembered to breathe.

"What are you doing? Come inside this instant," Elisabeth hollered, picking up his fishing pole and grabbing his upper arm with her other hand.

He gave the lovely storm and playful water a mournful look and was dragged by his mother away from the water's edge. Oleanna smiled in relief, and at the look Torjus gave Elisabeth behind her back.

Elisabeth looked up and saw Oleanna standing on the hillside. "What are you doing?" Elisabeth called, pushing Torjus through the door of the farmhouse. "Get inside!"

Oleanna stumbled down the last few meters to the farmhouse door. She closed it behind her and gasped at the steamy heat inside. A fire roared in the hearth, and the small window on the lake was closed tight.

"What on earth were you doing?" Elisabeth asked over her shoulder as she struggled to remove Torjus' sodden pants and shirt.

"I milked the goat," Oleanna said, struggling behind her back with the wet tie on her apron.

"Lea," Elisabeth said, stilling Torjus with a look. "Why were you just standing in the rain?"

Oleanna left off with the apron and brushed a strand of wet hair off of her warm forehead. "What?" she asked slowly.

"Oh dear lord," Elisabeth muttered from a long way away.

Oleanna awoke late that evening, sprawled in the bed she shared with Elisabeth. Even before she opened her eyes, she knew the window on the lake was open, as was the door. The evening breeze was deliciously cool on her skin. She pulled off the covers that were twined with her legs and opened her eyes. It was well after the sun dipped below the mountaintops; the room was dim and quiet. Elisabeth slept sitting up in the straight-backed chair, pulled close to Oleanna's bedside, her mouth open and curling dark hair all askew.

Oleanna shifted, attempting to rearrange the sweat-soaked pillows. Her arms felt heavy and she grunted in frustration.

Elisabeth awoke immediately. "Lea," she whispered, standing up and pushing hair out of her eyes. "Go back to sleep."

"You look like mama," Oleanna whispered.

"Hush," Elisabeth said, pushing Oleanna back down on the pillows. "Go back to sleep."

Oleanna grabbed Elisabeth's delicate wrist and pulled her down onto the bed. "You look like mama," she whispered again, searching her face.

Elisabeth recoiled, pulling her wrist from Oleanna's surprisingly strong grip. "You've got a fever," she said quietly. She stepped over to the small table against the far wall. It held the finest thing they owned, a delicate porcelain ewer, a gift from their uncle in Bergen. She poured a cup of water and handed it to Oleanna. "Drink this and go back to sleep, for pity's sake."

"Where's Torjus?" Oleanna said suddenly, sitting straight up, nearly knocking the cup out of Elisabeth's hand.

Across the room, Torjus murmured, awakened from a hard-won sleep. "He's fine," Elisabeth whispered, frowning at Oleanna as she crossed the room. She mollified her son and tucked him back under the covers. "Go back to sleep, both of you."

Oleanna shivered, and groaned as a fresh wave of aches began to wrack her legs.

Elisabeth returned and stood over the bed, forcing another cup of water into Oleanna's hands. "You're the one like mama," she said, so quietly Oleanna thought perhaps it was the last vestiges of an old dream, or the start of a new. "Running in the forest, standing in the rain, tsk," she whispered, shaking her head. She settled back into her chair. "Go back to sleep," she said, closing her own eyes. "You need to rest."

Oleanna woke again in the short dark hours around midnight, the birch branches of the elves' wood reaching out, wrapping her in their spindly arms. Her mother and Anna, and her eldest sister Severina, were singing, singing in the distance, the waves of the lake whipped by the cold autumn wind, pounding the shore in a marching funeral dirge. Lifting her head, she could see them, standing in the small boat, arms lifted, palms out: a warning, and a farewell. "Don't stand in the boat," Oleanna whispered. And then they were floating, white-faced and ghostly, just under the surface of the chill water, and she floated with them.

The boat rocked, and there was a confused noise just beyond her understanding, the keening voice of a man. "John," she groaned, curling around her sweat-soaked pillow. But the anguished voice was not John's. "Mathilde," he whispered, from a place far beyond Oleanna's understanding.

Then a crash, and with it a tumult of voices, pounding in Oleanna's head. She groaned and instantly the noise stopped, then began again seconds later as the soughing whisper of wind in the trees.

"How long has she been ill?" a man's deep voice sounded from the distance.

"Almost two days. Since Thursday," a woman's voice replied, high and floating like birdsong.

Oleanna slipped back under the water's surface, sliding quietly under the waves, when the man's voice pulled her back. "What happened?"

"I don't know. She's been working too hard. And then she was caught in the rainstorm."

"That's what delayed me. If I had just pressed on, I could have been here…"

Oleanna stirred and the voices stilled. Who were these forest people, talking like trees and flying birds?

The man's voice resumed, quieter now. "Should we try to take her to Skei? There's a doctor there."

"No, I don't trust them."

"What do you have here?"

The woman sighed, wind gathering on the mountainsides. "I'm out of valerian, and we've run out of whiskey. Could you go into Skei and get some more, and some aspirin?"

"Yes. Yes, of course."

"Thank God you've come back. I felt so hopeless. No wagon, no way to call for help. How I hate it here," she spat.

"I'll go water Terna now; I can leave in just a few minutes."

"Thank you. She and Torjus…she's all I have…"

After a moment, the man's voice replied, "And me."

Oleanna could hear the door open; she flung out her hand and opened her eyes.

Anders stood at the door, hand on the handle, eyes wide with surprise.

"You," she croaked, pointing at him. "And now you are dead too?"

"Oleanna," he whispered, kneeling at her bedside, resting his hand next to hers on the coverlet. Elisabeth hovered behind him, chewing her thumbnail.

"On the boat, and under the water," Oleanna whispered, nodding. "So you're dead too. Always leaving, only returning in the boats." She closed her eyes. "Always leaving, never returning." She felt a warm hand covering her own and opened her eyes.

"I'm here, Oleanna Tollefsdatter. I came back," Anders said, squeezing her hand.

She opened her eyes and looked up at him, then reached her free hand up and ran her fingers along the side of his rocky face. "They never return," she said. "I'm dreaming you, back from the depths. I can dream the dead back to life." Her eyes grew unfocused and she closed them again, her hand dropping back down onto the coverlet.

"But I have returned," he whispered.

Oleanna slipped back into the cool depths of the water and heard no more of the forest's song.

Later, when the midsummer twilight clung to the treetops, Oleanna awoke, clear-eyed and clear-headed. The farmhouse was quiet but for the snuffling snores of her sister and Torjus, curled together on John's bed across the room. The memory of Anders standing by her bedside returned to her, but she shook her head. I dreamed him, she thought. She crept out of bed quietly.

She pulled a wide-toothed comb through her snarled and damp hair, wincing as she went. The effort cost her, and she sat back down on the edge of the bed, panting. The restlessness of the lately recovered overcame her exhaustion, and she stood back up, pulling a coverlet off the bed. She stepped as quietly as her unsteady bare feet would allow, stopping briefly to fill a cup with the water from the porcelain ewer, and walked out the open front door.

Oleanna took a deep breath, the cool of the night filling her lungs, clearing her head. She wandered toward the long table set outside for their summer dining and sat on the bench, the small woven coverlet pulled tight around her shoulders. She faced not the dark forest, but the lake, and sipped her cool water.

The water, the water. How long ago had her father's people carved out this little corner of land, claimed it from the lake's rocky edges and the forest's dark fence? They had wandered the pilgrim's road to Trondheim, but came back, caught by the high mountains and deep fjords of Sogn. But why here? Why this barren lakeside?

She sighed. Another question, another mystery she didn't think of unraveling during the long, cold nights sitting together, her family huddled for warmth before the fire. Those long, dark days of winter, before Anton left for America, when Anna was still a baby and the boys still slept on the floor. She and her mother would sit in the corner, the shuttle passing back and forth as they worked quietly at the same loom.

In the spring it was all activity, carding the wool, spinning the yarn, dyeing it with the herbs they had collected when the snow began to melt. But in the winter, when the snow was deep and light hung low under the eaves of the wood, it was time to weave.

Oleanna liked the repetition, the same series of movements, the same patterns: the eight-petaled rose of Sogn, geometric, a rose only with a healthy imagination, rendered in orange-red, ochre-yellow, black and white. It was a common language she shared with her mother, the place they could reside together without speech. Her mother had taught Oleanna's eldest sister Severina the arts of weaving, and as a little girl Oleanna watched from the corner by the fire, fascinated, but not yet allowed to do more than hand her mother a new skein of wool. But then Severina had died and her mother left aside the weaving.

Elisabeth wasn't interested in her mother's weavings; she was more interested in reading by the fire, arguing with Anton and John. And so, when she was 12, Oleanna was allowed to touch the loom openly, previously only a furtive joy she had stolen when her mother was occupied elsewhere.

She pulled the coverlet closer and sighed. Were they that alike, she and her mother? And yet she still didn't understand her at all.

After long minutes watching the water, she set the cup down on the table behind her and sighed again. How she wished Anders really had been there. Maybe he'll arise, ghost-like from the shallow bank of the lake. Perhaps she could ask him why he was there, what drew him to his mean little cottage on the rocky lakeside...

Oleanna's eyelids fluttered and her head jerked slightly, and she realized with a smile that she was falling asleep. She gathered the coverlet and stood creakily, a fresh fever evidenced by her rapidly warming forehead. She turned to walk to the farmhouse and crawl back into bed, but stopped after just a few steps. Anders, or his ghost, stood at the edge of the forest, near the barn. He wore a white nightshirt over his work trousers, but no shoes.

"Oleanna," he said, running down the hill, remembering himself and slowing to a walk, and then evidently ignoring propriety and resuming his run.

She swayed slightly and reached out, resting her hand against the farmhouse to steady herself. He's not there, she thought, shaking her head. He is a ghost.

Anders skidded to a halt at her side and reached out his hand tentatively toward her face, then settled for resting his hand on her shoulder. "What are you doing out of bed?" he asked quietly.

"You're...you're not here," she whispered, sliding down the side of the farmhouse to sit, cross-legged, on the grass.

Anders knelt down next to her and felt her forehead. "I'm here, and you're feverish again. What were you thinking? You have to go back to bed—"

"You came back," she said, looking at him, her head cocked.

He smiled. "Of course I came back. I told you I would."

"They don't come back," Oleanna said, shaking her head.

"Come with me. You need to get back into bed," he said, standing and offering his hand.

Oleanna allowed herself to be pulled to her feet and stepped back,
resting against the sturdy comfort of the pine farmhouse. "How long have I been ill?" she whispered.

"Three days now."

"Oh lord," she said, looking wildly around the farmyard. "The chores..."

"She managed."

"What are you doing here?" she asked, looking at him suddenly.

"Looking in on you."

"You came back," she whispered, reaching for his hand. "Will you—"

He smiled. "I will tell you all about it, just as I promised," he said, squeezing her hand. "But you have to sleep now."

She nodded and allowed herself to be led by the hand inside, the coverlet trailing behind in her other hand. He turned his back as she crawled into the bed, pouring her another cup of water. When she had pulled the linen sheet up to her neck, she whispered, "Thank you."

Anders turned back and offered her two aspirin and the cup, which she drank in one long draught. She handed him the cup and folded her hands across her stomach on top of the sheet. "Will you stay?"

He grinned, lopsided, and shook his head. "Oleanna Tollefsdatter, you are a wild thing."

She smiled and chuckled. "You know what I mean."

"I'll stay until you sleep," he whispered.

"Are you real?" she asked, flipping onto her side and looking up at him.

"Of course."

"Good," she mumbled, burrowing deeper into her pillow. Anders' gentle laugh faded away as Oleanna dropped back into a fevered sleep.

# CHAPTER NINE

Lake Jølster, Sunnfjord, Norway
June 1905

"TORJUS, FOR HEAVEN'S SAKE, go back to sleep," Elisabeth muttered. "Please, on Sunday of all days."

"I'm. Not. Sleepy," he trilled.

Oleanna opened her eyes. Torjus was rolling back and forth, carrying the covers with him as he wriggled and writhed across the bed. "You've got to be quiet," Elisabeth begged.

"I'm awake," Oleanna said, yawning and pushing herself up.

"I tried to keep him quiet."

"I was awake anyway," Oleanna lied. She yawned massively, and Elisabeth followed suit.

"How are you feeling?"

"Thirsty."

"Here—" Elisabeth started, sitting up.

"No, no, lie back down," Oleanna said, waving her away. She yawned again and stretched, standing up on the tips of her toes, arms high above her head.

"Did you sleep at all?" Elisabeth asked, attempting to grab Torjus, who had jumped out of bed and was spinning in circles in the middle of the room.

Oleanna nodded, pouring herself a cup of water. "Thank you for taking care of me."

Elisabeth shrugged. "What else would I do? Besides, I need your help with the chores."

Groaning, Oleanna set the cup down on the table. "How far behind—"

"It doesn't matter. It's Sunday. Today we can rest – if this little jumping fish will let us," she said, reaching over and heaving Torjus back into the bed, tickling him as she did. He squealed and tried to squirm away, but she had him tight and blew kisses on the back of his neck.

"Lea!" he gasped between giggles, reaching out to her, "Help!"

"You're on your own, little one," Oleanna said, crawling back into bed. She watched the horseplay, smiling, until she drifted again into sleep.

A heavy knock at the front door rattled all three of them into wakefulness. Through the chink in the curtains, Oleanna could see the color of the mountainside across the lake, and discerned that the early morning was long since departed, midday rapidly approaching.

The banging on the door recommenced, this time accompanied by a male's deep voice. "Oleanna? Elisabeth? Are you in there?"

Oleanna sat up and smiled.

"Anders Samuelsson," Elisabeth mumbled. "God damned poxed son of a whore. Doesn't he know what time it is?"

Oleanna froze in place, gaping at her half-sleeping sister.

"What's going on in there?" he demanded, knocking again on the door. "Are you both ill now?"

"We're fine," Oleanna said, searching around for something to wear over her chemise. After a few moments of searching, she shrugged and pulled the coverlet off the bed again and, wrapping herself in it, opened the door. She squinted against the morning—or mid-day—sunlight and pulled the door closed behind her.

"Is everything alright?" he asked.

She leaned against the door and smiled, the sun warming her face. "It is now."

"I told you I would come back."

"So you did."

"How are you feeling?"

"Much better."

"Good."

Oleanna cocked her head. "What are you doing here?"

"Checking on you."

She smiled. "I wasn't that sick."

Anders shrugged and smiled back. "Do you plan on being lazy all day? Or could you be convinced to take a walk? Unless, of course," he said, a wry grin spreading across his lips, "you don't want to be in the company of a God damned poxed son of a whore?"

She whooped with laughter and immediately covered her mouth with her hand, glancing guiltily at the door behind her.

Anders' smile grew wider. "I'll wait for you out here, shall I?"

Pushing the handle, she leaned against the door and disappeared inside, watching him and grinning all the way in. She shut the door on his equally laughing face and spun around, searching for a clean shirt.

"Bottom drawer," Elisabeth muttered.

"Thank you."

Oleanna pulled on her clothes and shoved her feet into her battered boots.

"He's a good man," Elisabeth said, sitting up on her elbow.

Oleanna stayed her hand on the door. "What?"

"White as a ghost when he came in and saw you were ill. Went up to Skei to get some whiskey and aspirin for you."

"He did?"

Elisabeth grinned. "Enjoy your walk," she said, curling around her sleeping son.

Oleanna cocked her head and looked at her sister. A fluttering feeling snuck into her chest. "It doesn't do to hope," a voice whispered in the back of her mind. "Just for one day," she murmured, absently pulling her hair back into a plait.

"What?" Elisabeth said.

"Go back to sleep," Oleanna said, pushing the door open. Anders was not near the threshold, nor in the small farmyard, or near the store house. She hugged her arms to her chest and stood, irresolute.

"I'm right here," he said quietly, coming around the corner from the lakeside. His hands were shoved deep in his pockets and he smiled. "Are you ready?"

She dropped her arms. "Where are you taking me?"

"Where haven't you gone on the mountain?"

Oleanna laughed. "There's no place I haven't gone on the mountain."

He raised an eyebrow. "Nowhere?"

"I know every inch."

"We'll see," he grinned and walked off to the north.

Oleanna laughed and, picking up her skirts, ran to catch up with him. "What's so important that you have to wake me at first light?" she teased. She fell into step, struggling a bit to match his long stride, but keeping pace.

He looked down at her and grinned. "You wanted stories of the world. I hope you have time."

"All the time in the world."

"What do you want to know first?" he asked, holding back a birch branch that blocked their path.

She hesitated. "How was John?"

"He missed you from the moment you were out of sight."

Oleanna sighed. "Where do you think he is now?"

"Liverpool, I expect. Or maybe already on the crossing."

"Liverpool," she said, rolling the letters around on her tongue.

"There was a family he seemed to know, at the dock in Vadheim."

She looked up at him. "Do you remember the name?"

"Nelson, I believe."

"Good. I didn't want him to be alone."

Anders slowed, looking at her more directly. "Isn't that why he left?"

"He left because Anton asked him to." She stuttered to a stop.

He looked at her, but said nothing.

"He left because he couldn't stay," she whispered, looking out across the lake to the houses and mountains, picked out in sharp relief by the midday sun.

"Come with me," he said finally, turning and continuing along the path to the north. They walked quietly together, concentrating on the path that had narrowed along the lakeshore.

Oleanna watched Anders' tall, narrow form ahead of her, picking his way as easily and gracefully as an elk among the branches and tumbled boulders. He kept his long hands deep in his pockets, and hummed under his breath. She watched his head sway, back and forth to the half-heard melody, unconsciously graceful. He said something, and she started; Elisabeth's words rattled around her brain, something about the first apple of summer…

"Oleanna?" He had stopped in the middle of the trail and turned to her.

"I'm sorry," she said, blushing. "What did you say?"

He raised his eyebrows. "Are you feverish again?" he asked, reaching out to feel her forehead with the back of his hand.

"I—maybe," she said, feeling only a little guilty as she leaned into his touch.

"We should go back—"

"No!" she said, then smiled ruefully. "No, I'm fine. Where are you taking me?"

Anders dropped his hand and a smile tugged the corner of his mouth. "You'll see."

"You're so full of secrets."

The ghost of his smile faded. "Yes," he said after a moment, and turned back to the trail.

She followed after him and as they rounded another turn in the path, her heart began to race. She slowed to a stop, watching Anders disappear around the bend. Cold sweat beaded on her forehead and the bright sun of midday dimmed, covered by smoke and clouds.

"Oleanna," Anders said, dashing back along the trail, grabbing hold of her arms before she tumbled over. "What happened? You are sick, aren't you? I shouldn't have asked you to—"

"No," she whispered. "I'm fine."

"Oleanna. Look at me."

He swam in and out of her vision, ghostly, wavering.

"Oleanna," he said, shaking her slightly.

She gripped his arms. "I can't."

"What?"

"Around the bend," she said, shivering. "The stand of birches—"

"With the graves."

Oleanna nodded.

"What about it?"

"It's the elves' wood. My—my mother called it that. The trees there always blossom before the others, and keep their leaves after all the others' have gone."

Anders stilled.

She took a deep breath. "Mother and Anna are buried there. John and I..." she trailed off.

"Ah," he said quietly, taking her hand.

"They died just before you came." She turned away from the water.

He caressed the backs of her hand with his thumb. "I'm sorry."

She looked at him, and with a shock that took her breath away, recognized the depthless well of loss in his eyes.

"How are you feeling?" he asked, smoothing hair away from her sticky forehead.

"Fine," she said, brushing the question and his hand away. "Who did you lose?"

"This wasn't supposed to be a day to talk about loss," he said, shoving his hands in his pockets again. "Where would you like to go?"

"Answer my question. Who did you lose?"

His eyes narrowed. "Do you want to tell me about your mother?"

Her heart jumped. Mama. What could she say? That it was her fault that she died? That she didn't understand her, from the first day to the last? That burying her was the worst day of her life? "No," she whispered finally.

He nodded. "Where shall we go then?"

Oleanna sighed, unable to let her sudden grief ebb away because Anders Samuelsson wished it. "It doesn't matter to me," she said, looking back out across the lake.

"I'm sorry," he whispered.

She looked at him and felt the storm of grief speeding in, low dark clouds from the sea to the west. "They've all gone," she whispered, voice tight.

He nodded.

"But you came back."

Anders reached for her hand. "Let me take you back—"

"I'm not ready to go home," she said. "But I can't stay down here by the lake."

"I'll follow you, then."

They did not move from the narrow rocky trail next to the sparkling lake, but instead held hands and looked at each other. Finally, reluctantly, she squeezed his hand and dropped it. "Come with me," she said, turning and leading him not along the lakeshore, but away from it, into the forest and up the mountainside. They walked in silence, Oleanna picking out the easiest trail, Anders following close behind.

They crested the final hill and reached the wide sæter meadow, the goat and scattered sheep keeping the tall grass shorn close. She turned to look at Anders, grinning with pleasure and pride. "What do you think?"

He looked around, the brilliant afternoon sun illuminating valleys and lakes and fjords for miles. "Amazing," he breathed.

"That's Årdal, and that little smudge of brown is our farm. I can't see your cabin from here. If you squint, you can see Førde, and over there of course is Govabreen. And on the other side of the cabin," she said, "is the view toward Sognefjord." Anders followed, but at a slower pace, and Oleanna stopped, panting. "Don't you want to see—"

"I've seen Sogn, many times," he said. "Show me your cabin."

Oleanna shrugged and walked past him to the cabin's door. "John would bring me and Lisbet here, in the days before Midsummer—just like now—and tell us stories," she said, pushing open the door. She stepped back and allowed Anders to walk in ahead of her.

"Very comfortable," he said, nodding. "Who made the coverlet?"

"I did," she said, walking over and running her hand along the weaving. "I got tired of the rose, always the rose and the rutvev. So I sketched a new design. I was working on it when mama died."

"It's beautiful," he said, moving to sit on the bed, and then apparently thinking the better of it. He retreated to the hearth and picked up a book on the mantelpiece. "I didn't know you were an artist," he said, looking at the spines of the books.

"I'm not," Oleanna said.

Anders looked at her sideways and smiled. "You sell yourself short."

Oleanna shrugged.

"Are these your books?"

"No, Lisbet's novels. John always reads serious things, political tracts and farming techniques. Lisbet is forever losing herself in a fantasy."

"Don't you think that stories can tell you truths as well?"

"I don't know. I haven't read her novels. But the stories John would tell us, those felt real: the lost girl, the snowbird on Joutenheimen, and the trolls in the far mountains, and the world tree..." she trailed off and looked out the front door to the spreading meadow and tall mountains beyond. If she squinted, the tall, spreading branches of Yggdrasil could be seen, just beyond the furthest mountain peak, beautiful and terrible. A design for a weaving drew itself in the sky above the sæter, spidery branches and the heavy burden of fate.

"Oleanna?" Anders whispered after long moments of silence.

"Hmmm?" she muttered, turning dreamy eyes on him. "I'm sorry," she said, shaking her head slightly. "I was just remembering those stories." She turned her back on the door and sat in the hand-bent birch chair near the hearth. "John was—is—an excellent storyteller."

"I know," Anders said, leaning against the mantelpiece. "He told me stories about you and Elisabeth."

"Oh no," Oleanna groaned. "Telling secrets, was he? Well, I'll tell you," she said, pointing at him, "there was a girl, in Skei, that John—"

"No, nothing like that," Anders laughed. "He told me how he worried about you, and about the day your father died."

"He did?"

Anders nodded. "He also told me about how you and Elisabeth would pull each other's hair, and throw rocks in the lake—"

Oleanna looked up and laughed. "Do I have any secrets from you now?"

Anders smiled. "We all have our secrets."

She nodded, and he turned back to the mantelpiece. "An atlas," he said, picking it up and opening it immediately. "Who does this belong to?"

"Me," she said quietly. "Anton brought it for me, when he came home after a trip to Bergen."

Flipping through the dog-eared pages, a slow smile grew on Anders' face. "Did you turn down the corners?"

She blushed slightly. "Yes. I know I shouldn't, but I didn't want to lose—"

Anders laughed. "I don't care if you turn down corners."

Oleanna smiled.

"Scotland?" he asked, flipping to a particularly ratty page.

"Pardon me?"

"Why Scotland?"

"Why not Scotland?"

"Well," he said, flipping through the pages, "why not Egypt or India? Or Australia?"

She shrugged.

"What about America?" he asked, flipping to the map. "Wouldn't you like to see America, see John and Anton?"

Sighing, Oleanna stood. "This atlas is as close as I'll ever get to America. Or Scotland, for that matter," she said, taking the book from him and running her fingers along the outline of the American east coast.

"You never know," he whispered.

"I can't leave here."

"Why? There's so much—"

"What about you?"

He looked at her intently, and she flushed under his gaze. "This is my home," he whispered finally.

"Good," she said finally.

He stood not next to her, but just behind her, leaning down to speak into her ear. "Come with me."

Brushing past her out onto the porch, he turned back and held out his hand. She took it with a small smile, and they walked around to the far side of the cabin, facing south, facing the glacier.

"Beyond Govabreen, down there, beyond where that valley grows dark—over there," he said, placing hands on her shoulders and pointing her southwest. "That's Vadheim."

She nodded.

"And there, yes, right there," he said as she squinted, "that's Balestrand. There's a grand hotel there. The Kaiser of Germany stayed there."

"How far is that?"

"Three days' travel on these roads."

"Have you stayed there? At that hotel?" she asked, turning to look up at him.

He laughed, a full throated rumbling, like boulders tumbling down a mountainside. As he continued on, she folded her arms. "I suppose that means no?"

"No," he said, still chuckling. "Oleanna, do you think I would be a cotter on your land if I could afford to stay at Hotel Kvikne?"

"What do I know about you?" she asked. "Perhaps you were a rich man, living grand down on the fjord, having tea with the Kaiser."

"I have traveled up and down Sognefjord, down to Bergen and back, but I can promise you, I have never had tea with the Kaiser of Germany."

She softened. "Tell me more."

Anders offered her a seat on the grass, and she sat, black skirt billowing out around her. He stretched out next to her, resting on an elbow. "What would you like to know?"

"Everything."

He laughed. "That may take a while."

"I have all the time in the world, remember?"

"Well then. When I was a young man—"

"—a very long time ago, then," Oleanna interrupted, grinning.

Anders laughed. "Yes, a very long time ago. I'm surprised John didn't tell you stories of my youth among his tales."

"Oh, that was you? I thought I recognized a bit of the troll around the edges."

He pushed himself up, laughing. "Is that so?"

"It's the ears."

He gasped in mock shock. "Where are your manners?"

"It's your fault," she smiled. "You make me wild."

"No," he said, leaning toward her. "You're wild all on your own."

She leaned in toward him. "Is that so?" she whispered.

Anders reached up and cupped her face in his hand; she leaned into the touch and sighed. Leaning forward, he placed a chaste kiss on her lips, and withdrew. Oleanna moved forward, attempting to capture his lips with hers, but he backed away. "What would Elisabeth say?" he whispered, teasing.

She looked at him sideways. "I don't really care," she said, standing up. She offered him her hand and, with some effort, pulled him to his feet. "Come to the other side," she said. "Looking at the glacier gives me such a chill." She led him, hand in hand, back to the north side of the cabin, looking down on the lake and the familiar mountains beyond. They settled again on the cropped grass next to the cabin, sitting close and holding hands.

"Where were you taking me?" Oleanna said at last, quietly. "At first, this morning?"

"The Viking burial mound."

"Near the Sanddal farm? The one behind their store house?"

He smiled. "Yes. I saw it on the way back from Vadheim."

"I told you," she smiled, "I know every inch of this mountain, and the lakeshore. I can name every tree and every bird and every flower."

"Will you teach me?"

"If you'd like."

"I would."

After long quiet moments, she sighed. "I do love it here."

"I thought you loved it under the trees."

"Oh, I do," she said, scooting back to rest her back against the cabin. "But I love it here best." She sighed again. "Come on, grandfather," she said. He raised his eyebrows and she laughed. "Tell me your stories."

He leaned his head close and whispered stories to her of the winding, rocky road to Vadheim, of John's fears and sadness, of the shocking, severe gray cliffs of the Aurlandsfjord and the sturdy houses, painted red and yellow, right at the great Sognefjord's edge. He told her about the bustling marketplace at Bergen's harbor, the women, working and fashionable in Bergen's ancient streets, and the long lonely ferry ride east from Bergen on the Sognefjord.

They watched the light changing on the lake, fat clouds drifting by. "Where did you go?" she asked finally.

"Hmm?"

"After you left John in Vadheim. You were gone longer than I—than I thought you would be."

Anders leaned away, looking up at the sky. "I'll tell you. Someday."

"Why not now?"

He looked back at her. "Do you want to know all of my secrets?"

"Of course," she laughed.

"Do you want to tell me all of yours?"

She shrugged.

"Why don't you tell me about Søren."

"What do you want to know? I thought you already got all of the good gossip."

"Why did you break it off?"

She picked at the grass near her hand. Finally, she said, "He didn't approve of mama. And I suppose she didn't approve of him, either."

"But he's a pastor."

"He courted Elisabeth before me. And Jakob's sister Johanne."

"Ah."

"I didn't mind, at first. I'm an old maid, after all. And anyway, I'd followed him around like a dog when we were children."

"Surely you've had other interest."

"I suppose so," she said, waving the suggestion away. "But nothing serious."

"I don't believe that."

"Oh, I've had interest," she grinned, looking over at him.

He smiled, and in a split second, Oleanna leaned over and kissed him, eliciting a grunt of surprise. He shifted away but she followed him, wrapping her hands in the front of his shirt and kissing him soundly.

She had intended mostly to divert his attention, change the topic, an old trick she'd used when she was younger, when she tired of the sweet but slow boys who lived up and down the lake. But the low sound he made in his throat when she opened her mouth shifted something in her mind and she growled in response.

Anders chuckled and wove his hand into the hair at the nape of her neck, sending shivers down her arms. The tighter he held her hair, the more she wanted to devour him and so she did, until Elisabeth's teasing words came back to her, and she laughed low in her throat. They finally broke apart, panting.

Her giggling subsided immediately. Anders looked, to her, like a wild, desperate thing, his face both open and wary.

"What is so amusing?" he asked, his eyes hooded, reaching out to trail tentative fingertips along her collarbone.

Oleanna's eyes fluttered shut. "Elisabeth's been teasing me," she whispered. "About you."

"Mmm?"

"She says I look at you like you're the first apple of summer and I can't wait to take a bite." She flushed, despite herself.

He chuckled and she opened her eyes. He had shifted, leaning closer, and wove his hand back into her hair. "I thought that was how I looked at you," he whispered, leaning in and kissing her along her jaw line. She shifted and stretched her neck, which he obligingly kissed as well.

She shivered, from her toes to the top of her head. "Where did you learn how to do that?" she muttered.

"I am an old man, Oleanna," he mumbled into her neck.

"Lea."

"Oleanna."

"Why—"

"I like the way it rolls off of my tongue," he said, licking around the shell of her ear.

She moaned in reply.

Anders leaned her back onto the grass, kissing her as he did. He ran his fingertips along her collarbone again, ghosting them lightly along her breasts. After a few moments, her head spinning, she growled and, using surprise as leverage, rolled him over, pinned his arms down, and knelt over him.

He laughed, full-throated and merry. "Oleanna—" he began, but she had found a spot near his temple that made his eyes flutter shut.

"I like your laugh. You should laugh more often," she said, kissing her way down to his lips.

He reached up and cupped her breast, opening his mouth to her. Oleanna's head swam; the silly boys of Jølster bored her, tried to control her; even Søren. Especially Søren

This was something new. She explored him, slowly, eliciting sighs and grunts of approval that emboldened her. She covered his hand on her breast and squeezed, encouraging him. Anders rose up to kiss her, fiercely.

This felt like running through the forest. This felt like hope. A wild joy swelled in her. She was blinded by it and it drove her, reaching her hand up under his shirt, spreading her rough hand against his narrow chest. She tried to move his hand under her shirtwaist, and he broke the kiss, rolling her over onto her side next to him. She looked at him, surprised.

He nuzzled her neck. "You're going to get the both of us into trouble," he panted into her hair.

Oleanna laughed, running her fingers through his short hair. "With who? My parents? My brothers? I'm my own person."

"Good," he panted, laying her on her back. He began to unbutton her shirtwaist. "You seem to have recovered well from your illness," he said, kissing her exposed collarbones, the swell of her breasts under her shirt.

"Strong as a fjord pony," she gasped.

He laughed, the sound buzzing along her chest.

After a few minutes, by which time Anders had shed his shirt and Oleanna was down to her shift, she stood and held her hand out to him. She shook slightly, from nerves and excitement and need.

He looked up at her, his face closed and guarded again. "Are you sure?" he whispered.

Oleanna smiled. "I'm standing here in my shift, holding my hand out to you. Yes, I'm sure."

He leapt to his feet, crushing her against the side of the cabin, and kissed her fiercely. He pulled away, cradling her face with his hands. "I will never desert you. Do you understand?" he whispered, breathless.

"Anders—"

"Do you understand?"

Oleanna nodded.

He kissed her again, hard and possessive, and she broke away smiling. "Come with me," she said. She took his hand and led him into the cabin.

The sun had long passed its height, though it was hard to be sure so close to Midsummer. Oleanna stood at the small window looking south toward the Sognefjord, arms wrapped around her middle, her shift still sweat-damp

"Why?" she asked suddenly.

"Why what?" Anders asked, quiet on the bed.

"Why did you come back? Look at that wide world."

After long silent moments, he asked, "You don't know? Even now?"

She could feel him looking at her. "You weren't meant to be rooted," she whispered, still looking at the great fjord.

"Nor you."

Oleanna shrugged.

"We should go back," Anders said.

"No. We should stay here and never go back," she whispered.

She heard the bed creaking and sheets rustling behind her and she smiled, a thrill of energy tickling her arms and neck. A few moments later he was standing behind her; he wrapped his arms around her waist and she leaned into him.

"Elisabeth will be worried," he said, nuzzling her neck.

"I've waited up more nights for her than I care to think. She can wait." He chuckled and his breath on her neck made her head swim. "I am never leaving this cabin," she whispered.

"We don't have to."

Oleanna laughed. "Wouldn't that be nice?"

"Stay here with me. Stay tonight."

"You're scandalous," she whispered.

"Maybe I am," he whispered into her ear. "Stay."

She closed her eyes, the temptation coursing through her, warm and sweet like honey. After a few moments, Oleanna extricated herself and walked over to the window, looking out at the tall ridges of mountaintops marching down to the deep fjord in the distance. "We should go back," she whispered finally, brushing past him. She picked up her shirtwaist and held it tightly to her chest.

"Oleanna."

She shook her head, then slipped the shirtwaist on. "I have responsibilities. I have to—"

"Oleanna," he said quietly.

"Anders, leave it. Please. I need to go back."

The beautiful blue-sky openness of his face clouded and closed and he nodded once, curtly. "I'll wait for you outside," he said, picking up his trousers and shirt from the cold pine floor.

"Anders," she groaned, shaking her head. "I—" The door closed on her explanation.

She sighed and pulled on her skirt, fastening it with rough and jagged movements, tamping down the sob in her throat. I'm a fool, she thought. She found a comb on the mantle, next to the jumble of books and earthen mugs filled with wilting wildflowers, and yanked it through her snarled hair. After pulling her hair into a tight queue, she needlessly smoothed her blouse and, with a deep breath, pulled open the cabin door.

Anders, now fully dressed, waited for her on the step, hands in his pockets. She pulled the door closed behind her.

After a few moments, he finally spoke. "I told you I would never let you down and I would never desert you. Did you not believe me?" He leaned in slightly, one foot on the top step.

Oleanna looked past him to the wide grassy hilltop of the sæter. "Everyone leaves me," she shrugged. "You'll find a reason."

"No."

"We'll see."

"Yes we will."

She finally looked at him and shook her head sadly. "I—"

"Oleanna, hush," he said, stepping up and grabbing her upper arms. "I will show you." Anders leaned in to crush her lips, but at the last moment changed his mind, and kissed her gently on the forehead. "Trust me. Please," he whispered, releasing her arms and backing away.

She took a deep, shuddering breath, and looked past him to the lake valley below. "I trust you," she whispered.

His smile was slow and wide. "Good," he said. He leaned in and kissed her.

As he pulled away, she followed and kissed his cheek, his neck. She smiled shakily. "We really should go back."

"For now," he agreed, taking one of her hands. They wandered toward the line of trees that marked the boundary of the sæter. The ground was uneven, carpeted in old leaves, fallen trees, years upon years of growth, decay, renewal. They picked their way together down the hill, Oleanna leading, looking over her shoulder now and again to make sure Anders had not fallen behind; he smiled reassuringly each time.

When the turf-roofed store house appeared through the thinning trees, Oleanna slowed to a stop. Anders wrapped his arms around her from behind.

"You're welcome to stay to supper."

He nuzzled her neck. "I'll see you tomorrow," he whispered. "I promise." Anders dropped his arms and leaned in for a quick kiss behind her ear.

Oleanna sighed. "I'd better see what trouble they're getting into."

"They can take care of themselves."

A cry, accompanied by Elisabeth's muffled, angry voice made Oleanna turn and look up at Anders. "I'll see you tomorrow," she said with a half-smile.

He smiled, then leaned down and kissed her swiftly. He turned and walked down the path toward his own cottage. She watched him into the distance, and just before he reached the last bend where he would disappear, he turned and raised his hand. Oleanna grinned, waving back; moments later, he was gone.

She walked down to the farmhouse, smiling and humming to herself. As she approached, Elisabeth followed a filthy and crying Torjus out of the house, a paddle in her hand. "Wait right there," Elisabeth said. "Don't you dare come back into this house with those dirty hands. I'll wash you up in that cold lake if you're not careful."

"Yay!" Torjus cried, tears forgotten.

"Well then. A hot bath it is. Don't move," Elisabeth said, pointing at him. She noticed Oleanna and raised her eyebrows. "Have a nice walk?"

"Yes."

"You've been gone all day."

"Yes."

"Is he coming for supper tonight?"

"No."

Elisabeth walked back into the house, and Oleanna followed her.

"Will we see him again?"

Oleanna narrowed her eyes. "Why?"

Elisabeth shrugged, then began to gather clean clothes for Torjus from the dresser. "You're always telling me that they leave and never come back."

"Don't use my words against me."

"Are you sure you're ready?"

"What do you mean?"

"It's only been eight months since Søren."

"Why does everyone want to throw that in my face?"

"They don't," Elisabeth sighed. After a few moments, she said, "Don't let him hurt you."

"That's not in my hands," Oleanna said with a shrug.

Elisabeth stood in the doorway, a small smile tugging at her mouth. "There's still some fish, and an end of bread. You must be starving," she said with an arch look.

Oleanna colored. "I'm fine—"

"You should rest," Elisabeth interrupted. "You've been very sick, and then you've been exerting yourself—"

"Lisbet," Oleanna pleaded, though she smiled. "I need to get started on the wash."

Elisabeth grinned. "Leave the clothes. We can do them tomorrow."

Oleanna nodded. She was more exhausted than she cared to admit. "I'll just put these in the tub so I have a head start in the morning."

"Suit yourself." Elisabeth pushed open the door and Torjus was there, playing quietly. "Come with me, you demon. Help me draw some water from the lake," Elisabeth said, helping Torjus to his feet, pulling his filthy shirt off in the process and adding it to the pile in Oleanna's arms.

Oleanna watched them to the water's edge, then trudged up the hill to the store house. She pulled open the door, awkwardly with the bundle in her arms, and stumbled into the dark room, the door closing behind her. She stood still, her breathing loud in the echoing, empty building. The smell of drying herbs and old wool hit her all at once, overpowering but not unwelcome. She paused; the sense of being watched, the feeling that she held the weight of generations on her shoulders dissipated, floating away, momentarily, like morning mist on the lake.

She dumped the clothes onto the workbench and wandered back out into the evening. The sun had finally dipped beyond the edge of her world, at the far end of the lake, out toward Sanddal farm. The ring of jagged mountains glowed pink, briefly, before fading to a gentle lilac, the color of the fragrant bushes edging farmsteads out in Skei. In the stable, she could hear Terna's soft whinnying, and from the lakeside, Torjus' giggle. A gentle breeze lifted her collar, and brought with it the scent of cut grass and the cool evergreen heights of the sæter.

Oleanna sighed. She thought of Anders, around the bend in his own cottage, looking out at that same view, and smiled. Even the lake looks beautiful tonight, she thought. Almost.

# CHAPTER TEN

Lake Jølster, Sunnfjord, Norway
June 1905

THE NEXT MORNING, Oleanna slept in again, until the sky was pink with the coming sunrise. With a shock of panic, she threw off the covers and sat up, the last vestiges of a dream about plowing their field with a teaspoon lingering around her head.

Oleanna stumbled out of bed and the farmhouse, dressed haphazardly in an untucked shirtwaist and skirt, shod in her heavy work boots, just as the ever-present summer sun crested the mountains that ringed the lake, and trudged up the dew-covered hill to the store house.

She pushed open the door and propped it open with a bucket, allowing the sun to stream in, illuminating the piles of laundry, mending, and dyeing strewn about the room. Elisabeth had not been as successful with the chores during Oleanna's illness as she might have led Oleanna to believe. "What has she been doing?" Oleanna muttered. She dragged the washing tub out from under the worktable and pulled it toward the door where there was more light. She grabbed another bucket and walked down the hill to the lake, whistling tunelessly under her breath.

Oleanna knelt at the edge of the water, the lake glassy and still; she looked down at her reflection. Her hair was wild and her cheeks rosy. I look like a proper forest wife, she thought. She stood and stepped away from the lake. "What's gotten into me?" she whispered. With a slow grin, she left the bucket on the bank of the lake and walked along the water's edge, as if on a tightrope, toward Anders' cottage.

She climbed over the low rock-and-log fence separating their farm from Anders' plot and wandered into a stand of pines that grew all the way to the water's edge. Just beyond the treeline stood Anders' cottage. She heard singing.

Oleanna stepped carefully from tree to tree, until she could see Anders. He sat on the boulder next to his cottage, whetting his razor and singing quietly. "I mine kåte ungdomsdagar, eg minnest dei so vel. Eg va' så fri fe' plagur, og ha' sa glad ei sjel…"*

"Good morning," she called from the dark under the trees.

He looked up and smiled. "Good morning."

She emerged from the forest, smiling, and he stood to greet her. "That was beautiful," she said. "What is it?"

"A little song I learned a long time go," he said, reaching out for her hand and pulling her close. "Good morning," he smiled, smoothing hair away from her face.

"Good morning," she said. She reached up, running her fingertips along his whiskery jaw line. He closed his eyes, leaning into her touch, and her heart fluttered.

"Don't you have chores to see to this morning?" he whispered.

"They'll keep."

With a small smile, he opened his eyes and leaned down to kiss her. She opened her eyes and pulled back. "Good morning," she sighed.

He released her and stepped back. "Have you eaten?"

"No," she said, shaking her head. "I just woke up."

He raised his eyebrows. "You've grown lazy, Oleanna," he said. "I've been awake for hours."

"You're a terrible liar," she laughed.

"What?"

"You just woke up."

"How can you tell?"

*"In my reckless, youthful days, I recall them well, I was free of worries and was such a happy soul."

"You're warm. You smell like bed and sleep."

He grinned, his face warm and open like the summer's meadow at the sæter. "I haven't eaten, either. Stay, and we'll eat together. Unless you need to go back?"

Oleanna glanced behind her, toward her own farmhouse. She looked back and found him watching her expectantly, nearly on his toes. "They won't miss me, for a while at least." She broke into a wicked grin. "I'm not terribly hungry, though."

His lips twitched. "I'm sure we can find a way to pass the time," he whispered, carding his fingers into her hair. He looked at her, his eyes dark and lake-stormy. "Come with me," he whispered, and, taking her hand, led her into his small cottage.

Anders released her hand and stood in the middle of the room. The cottage was even smaller than her one-room farmhouse, with only enough room for one box bed next to the wall, a small table, and an even smaller stove. The wall opposite the door was taken up by a large, uncovered window looking out on the lake.

Oleanna had not been inside the cotter's house on their land since she was a very small child, the building dark and inhabited by a troll, or so her father used to tell her. She did not remember the window frame, or the ceiling, being covered in rosemal. She walked past him to the window and ran her fingers along the swirling acanthus and vines. "You did this," she said.

"Yes."

"It's beautiful."

"It makes me happy."

"And do you always just do things to make yourself happy?"

"Of course," he laughed. "Well, not always. Don't you?"

"No. Not really."

"What about your weaving?"

"Something to do with my hands during the winter."

"It's more than that."

After a few moments, she looked back at him. "Have you always painted?"

He shook his head. "No, I learned a few years back."

"You're very talented."

"I needed some beauty in my life."

Oleanna cocked her head. "Why are you here? On this farm?"

"What do you mean?"

"Why aren't you a fisherman anymore? Why are you here in this little cabin, hiding away your beautiful painting?"

"I'm not hiding it. I'm sharing it with you. And why does it matter? I'm content here."

She chewed her lip, swallowing down questions and protestations. She reached out to him. "Good," she said.

"Good," he whispered, leaning down and kissing her. He took her hands and wrapped her arms around his back and they held each other silently.

Finally, she said with a wicked smile, "I'm famished."

Anders grinned and, without warning, picked her up and set her on his narrow bed.

Later, when the sun had risen high above the encircling mountains, she rested her head on his chest. "Why here, though?" she asked.

"Why here what?" He swept his hand up and down the length of her spine, raising gooseflesh along her bare back.

"Why Jølster?"

His hand stilled.

"A friend of a—friend knew there might be opportunities for someone to start over here. So I came. I met John on one of his trips to Skei."

"You were fast friends."

"He's a good man."

Oleanna nodded. "Do you miss him?"

"Of course."

"Why did you need to start over?"

"Don't you wish you could?"

Oleanna looked up at him and smiled. "Don't answer my questions with a question."

He smiled. "It's a long story."

"I have time."

Anders looked away, up into the painted rafters of his tiny cabin and Oleanna laid her head back on his chest. After a long minute, he sighed. "I couldn't live on the fjord anymore. It was too painful."

She kissed his chest, and he resumed the fluttering along her spine. "It's like when I look at the lake," she whispered.

"Mmmm?"

"Sometimes all I can see is mama and Anna." Oleanna took a shuddering breath. "It feels wrong to look at it as anything other than a grave sometimes," she whispered.

He kissed the top of her head.

"She was so strange."

"How so?"

"It's hard to explain. It was as though you could feel her yearning for something; like waves of longing."

"What did she long for?"

"Another kind of life, I suppose."

"And what about you?"

Oleanna sighed. "I don't know. Elisabeth always talks about leaving the farm. She wants to live in the city."

"Has she ever left the farm?"

"No. Well, she's been to Skei of course, but that's all. Same as me."

"Cities do have an appeal."

She looked up at him again; he still gazed at the ceiling. "So why didn't you get lost in a city, rather than coming here to this lonely farm?"

"I hadn't planned on staying."

"Oh."

"I was going to start over here but it was always supposed to be temporary. Get my hands dirty, get my feet back under me, so to speak. I'd spent too long drifting."

"So what happened?"

Anders looked at her. "You."

Her heart jumped.

"I'm content here," he said.

Oleanna sat up, taking the thin sheet with her. Finally, she said, "You never told me who you lost."

He turned his head and looked at her, his face clouding by the moment. "It's a long story."

She nodded.

"Not now," he said, sitting up next to her. "Not here."

He kissed her on the shoulder; she turned and kissed the top of his head, and sighed. "I need to go back. They'll be wondering where I am."

He nodded, twisting her hair around his finger.

"Come to supper tonight," she said. "At seven."

"Like a proper suitor?" he grinned.

"I don't think you will ever be proper," she said.

"Nor you," he smiled. He rolled her over on her back again and kissed her thoroughly.

Oleanna began to drop into warm lassitude again, but with a sigh gently pushed him off and onto his side. "There's washing and mending to be done," she whispered.

"You're worth more than that," he said, tracing vines and flowers on her neck and chest.

She smiled.

Anders leaned over and kissed her forehead. She closed her eyes and sighed. "How am I supposed to leave?"

"You're not," he whispered.

"You are not making this easy," she sighed.

"I wasn't trying to."

Oleanna opened her eyes. "Come to supper tonight."

"You should go, before I can't let you," he said, swinging his legs off of the bed.

She smiled and reached for her shirtwaist.

Oleanna was whistling when she rounded the final bend along the lakeshore, carding fingers through her hair to drag out the snarls. She slowed when the sound of Torjus' laughter floated toward her and she peered between the last stand of trees between the farmhouse and Anders' cottage. Elisabeth was chasing Torjus around the table, face red with exertion and anger. Finally, Elisabeth caught him and, sitting down on the bench, put him over her knee and spanked him soundly, and his giggles turned to wails. "What did he do now?" Oleanna said, emerging from the cover of the trees.

Elisabeth looked up, hand poised above Torjus' backside.

"Where have you been?" Elisabeth demanded, releasing the sobbing Torjus and standing up. Torjus ran, as best he could, into the farmhouse. "Did you feed Terna?"

"Oh, no, I forgot," Oleanna said, eyes wide.

"What have you been doing all morning?" Elisabeth said, tying her hair back.

"I've been up at the sæter..."

"I was at the sæter."

"Oh."

Elisabeth glared. "Don't leave me with all of the chores."

Oleanna stepped back, but Elisabeth followed. "I-"

"And don't you leave me," Elisabeth hissed.

Oleanna pushed past Elisabeth, knocking into her with her shoulder, and headed for the farmhouse.

"You rude cow!" Elisabeth shouted, running to catch up with her.

Oleanna stopped and spun around; Elisabeth skidded to a stop. "Were you with Anders?" Elisabeth asked.

Oleanna folded her arms.

"Don't you dare let him take you away from here," Elisabeth said. She reached out and grabbed Oleanna by the wrist.

Oleanna wrenched her hand away and stepped back. "First it's 'don't let him hurt you' and now it's 'don't let him take you away.' You don't get to choose, Lisbet."

"Fine," Elisabeth said, "but don't come crying to me when he decides to leave."

"What are you saying?"

"They all leave. You said so yourself."

Oleanna scowled. "I—he came back. He came back, Lisbet. My God, can't you just let me be happy? For a little while?"

"It's on your own head."

The stared at each other.

"He's coming for supper," Oleanna blurted.

"Well, we'd better get started on the washing and the cleaning, then," Elisabeth said, walking away.

The afternoon passed in a dim blur of laundry and dyeing, mending and baking. By the time Oleanna had finished her share of the chores, the sun was just about to disappear behind the mountaintops, and it was well past time to begin cooking supper. Oleanna stepped out of the dark store house and shaded her eyes against the summer sunlight still reflecting merrily on the lake. She sat down and leaned against the building, feet out in front of her.

"Lea!"

Torjus emerged from the farmhouse and ran toward her. She opened her arms and he tumbled into her lap. "What is it?" He wriggled around until he could look up into her face, and she smiled.

"Mama said you smell bad and should come take a bath." He reached out and pulled at a strand of hair that had worked its way out of her braid.

Oleanna smiled, tipping Torjus out of her lap and standing up. "Is that so? She can smell me all the way from the farmhouse?"

He nodded earnestly. "I had to take a bath, too. It's alright, Lea, it doesn't hurt."

She laughed and took his hand. "You're very brave."

Torjus pulled his hand free and ran away, down the hill. "Mama, mama, she's coming," he hollered.

Oleanna stretched her arms up over her head, grinning, and then wandered down the hill after him. She pushed the door open and was greeted with the sweet, musky smell of angelica. Elisabeth was bent over the fire, picking up a boiling pot of water to pour into the small tin tub.

"You'd better hurry," Elisabeth said. "It takes ages for your hair to dry."

"Lisbet, you didn't have to go to the trouble—"

Elisabeth straightened and put her hand up. "Hush. Hurry up. You're starting to smell like Terna." She picked up a pile of linens from the bed and bustled out, shutting the door firmly behind her.

Just outside the door, Oleanna could hear Elisabeth shushing Torjus and his whining complaint as they walked up the hill to the store house.

Oleanna, with aching arms and hands, pulled off her skirt and shirtwaist, and kicked off her work boots. She piled them in the corner and stepped gingerly into the steaming water, wincing as her feet and ankles reddened. Gritting her teeth, she sat down all at once, a sweat breaking out on her forehead. The water worked its magic, unknitting the knots in her feet and the backs of her legs. She threw her head forward, her long hair soaking in the herb-scented water.

Before the water had cooled, she stood and stepped out of the tub and dressed. She sat on one of the hard, high-backed chairs before the fire and pulled the comb through her tangled hair, wincing and gritting her teeth with each snarl. The small calendar on the wall above the fireplace caught her eye: June 12. "Already?" she whispered. John, gone for less than two weeks. It felt like a lifetime.

She opened the farmhouse door and stepped out to find Elisabeth coming down the hill. "You're not done yet?" she called.

"I'm done. What's left to do?" Oleanna asked, tying on her apron.

"Boil the potatoes and chop the dill. We'll cook the fish right before he gets here. Which is—"

"Seven. I hope."

Elisabeth looked up at the angle of the sun. "Another hour, I expect. Here, help me dump out the tub," she said.

Oleanna followed her and together they hefted the tin tub the few feet out the door and dumped the water in the patchy grass near the threshold.

"Take this up to the store house, and ask my son to stop doing whatever it is he's doing." Elisabeth turned away, wiping her forehead. "I'll get started chopping the potatoes."

Oleanna nodded and headed toward the store house, but stopped suddenly. "You're getting better at this," she called. "I think this life could suit you."

Elisabeth turned around. "Don't say that," she said. "Ever again." She stalked into the farmhouse and slammed the door.

Oleanna shrugged. "Well, it does," she muttered, dragging the tub up the hill.

After Oleanna and Torjus had spun circles in the grass, named the birds in the trees, and generally kept out of Elisabeth's way, Oleanna deposited a sleeping Torjus on John's bed.

Elisabeth shut the door and they deposited the meal on the table. "How did you get him to sleep?" Elisabeth whispered.

"Running around," Oleanna shrugged. "Playing. Where did you get the akevitt?"

"John had it hidden in the stable," she grinned, opening the bottle and pouring them both generous portions.

Oleanna raised her glass. "Cheers," she said, tipping the burning liquor down her throat.

"Cheers."

Oleanna set her glass on the table and looked out toward the lake. "Oh, John," she whispered. "It feels like he's just left."

Elisabeth shrugged. "I've felt every hour. I haven't been quite as occupied as you have."

"I'm sorry," Oleanna said, looking into her glass. "I've been selfish."

Elisabeth sighed. "Don't listen to me. It's good to see you cheerful again."

"Not at your expense."

"I—"

"Hallo?"

Oleanna hastily set her glass down and stood, sucking the spilled akevitt off of her hand. Anders stood under the trees next to the stables, both awkward and smart in a stiff black suit.

"Hallo," Oleanna called, stepping around the table and walking up the hill.

He smiled, and walked out to meet her. "You've put your hair up," he said quietly, reaching a hand up to touch it, then quickly dropping it, looking past Oleanna toward her sister. He leaned in closer. "Does this mean you're taken?" he whispered.

Oleanna's heart thrummed. "Many times," she grinned wickedly.

Anders eyes widened and he threw his head back, laughing.

"Are you two going to come eat, or are you going to giggle like children up there all night?" Elisabeth called.

"Yes, yes," Oleanna called, not looking back. "Thank you for coming," she said quietly.

"I suppose it's time to court you properly," he grinned, though it stretched to a leer at the corners.

Despite her best efforts, Oleanna blushed. "Come on," she said. She turned and walked down the hill; he followed close behind. Oleanna slid onto the bench nearest the farmhouse and chewed her lip.

Anders approached slowly and, from behind his back, produced a ragged bunch of wood lilies, which he handed to Elisabeth.

"Anders Samuelsson," Elisabeth said, nodding.

Anders looked at Oleanna, who shrugged. "Elisabeth Tollefsdatter," he said, bowing slightly. "Thank you for—"

"Oh, hush," Elisabeth said. "Sit and eat." She grinned and Anders laughed, sitting down next to Oleanna.

Oleanna poured a round of akevitt as Elisabeth served the meal. Finally, Elisabeth settled across from them, and raised her glass. "Cheers," she said.

"Cheers," Oleanna and Anders answered.

They set to eating, Oleanna glancing between them.

"Aren't you going to ask about our crops?" Elisabeth asked.

"I hadn't planned on it," Anders smiled.

"Good. It's entirely too boring," Elisabeth said. "Tell us about the news from the wide world."

"You get the newspaper," he said. "I got it for you in Skei."

Oleanna's eyebrows shot up. "So you're the one!" she said, half-laughing. "Has it been you all along?"

"I brought the newspaper to John anytime I went into Skei," he said, looking between them.

Oleanna grinned. "You have your ways, do you?" she asked Elisabeth.

"Yes, of course," Elisabeth said. "I always stole John's paper before he was done."

"So who brought you your books? Anders?"

"No, I have other charming young men for that," Elisabeth said with a sly smile.

Oleanna laughed. "Elisabeth's the big tease of Jølster, don't you know? She can get whatever she wants."

"I thought that was you," Anders muttered, taking a bite of trout.

Oleanna gasped and laughed.

"You're a wild thing like mama," Elisabeth interrupted, "and don't pretend you're not."

"No. You're the one who is like mama," she whispered. "Not me."

"You're both wild," Anders said, reaching under the table and taking Oleanna's hand; he squeezed it gently.

Elisabeth looked at Oleanna and smiled. Oleanna's heart pounded again: the first true smile she'd seen from her sister in days and days, and it was dazzling. It was no wonder she usually got what she wanted.

Elisabeth leaned forward and pointed at Anders. "Tell us."

He blinked. "I beg your pardon?"

"Tell us about—all of it."

"I don't—"

"Have you been to Bergen?" Elisabeth asked.

"Yes, many times," Anders said.

"Kristiania?"

"No."

"Trondheim?"

"Yes."

"Bodø?"

"Lisbet—" Oleanna said.

"No," he laughed.

"Stop pestering him," Oleanna said.

"Tell us about it," Elisabeth said.

"What do you want to know?" Anders said.

"Everything."

He laughed. "You and Oleanna are very much alike."

Elisabeth laughed. "Don't change the subject," she said.

"I want to know about you," he said. "What do you do, besides tease all the men in Sunnfjord?"

Elisabeth blinked, then lifted her chin. "Do you think that's all I can do?"

"No."

"No," she said, tossing back a tumbler of akevitt.

"Oleanna weaves, and beautifully," he said, squeezing her hand again. "What about you?"

"I raise my son. I do the mending."

"Lisbet, he's just being polite," Oleanna said.

Elisabeth looked at them, then took a bite of fish. Her face colored and she shook her head.

"What?" Oleanna asked, laughing.

Elisabeth finished chewing, then said defiantly, "I write."

Oleanna lowered her fork. "You what?"

Elisabeth shrugged. "When mama died, it just started. I couldn't stop."

"Is that what you've been doing up at the cabin?" Oleanna asked.

Elisabeth looked away, out at the lake.

"Can I see—"

"No," Elisabeth said.

"But—"

"No."

"I started painting when someone close to me died," Anders said.

"That's when you started?" Oleanna said, turning to him.

"It's the only way I can face this farm every day," Elisabeth said. Anders nodded.

"It is?" Oleanna said.

"I don't know how you do it, Lea," Elisabeth said. "I don't know how you don't go crazy."

Oleanna looked between them, her head spinning. After a few moments, she shook her head. "I don't know that I'm not."

Elisabeth sighed, then laughed suddenly. "This is no way to have supper with your new beau," she said, pouring another round of akevitt. "Let's be merry, for once."

Anders leaned over and kissed Oleanna on the cheek, and she laughed. "Yes, let's be merry."

They finished supper, Anders providing what county gossip he knew, Elisabeth making them laugh with her stories, and Oleanna smiling quietly to herself.

Finally, Oleanna cleared the plates to the end of the table and Elisabeth poured yet another round. She had her glass halfway to her mouth when she stopped, gesturing toward Anders. "You're not going to run away, like John and Anton, are you?"

Anders stilled. "They didn't run away," he said. "They made a decision to start a new life. You can't fault them for that."

"Can't I?"

"No, they—"

"They ran away," Elisabeth insisted.

Anders grew still and silent.

Elisabeth downed her akevitt and glared at him. "You won't leave us here by ourselves."

Finally, he shook his head and downed his own glassful. "I have no plans to leave, no."

"Lisbet, leave it—"

Anders set his glass down on the table and folded his hands. "I'll never hurt her," he said evenly.

"No, you won't. Because you will answer to me."

Oleanna blinked.

"I will never hurt her."

"Mama!" Torjus cried from within the farmhouse, the final A extending into a drawn-out wail.

"You keep your word, Anders Samuelsson," Elisabeth said, standing up and pointing at him as she walked past.

He nodded. They sat very still next to each other, Oleanna hardly breathing.

Soon, the sounds of Elisabeth soothing Torjus faded into the background. "I'm sorry she was talking to you like that," Oleanna said.

"I don't mind."

She took his hand and squeezed, leaning into his shoulder. He turned his head and kissed the top of her head. "I should go," he murmured.

"No, don't," she whispered.

"Like a proper suitor," he laughed.

She sighed. "Meet me at the sæter tomorrow morning."

"Neither one of us is going to get any work done at this rate."

"If you'd rather work—" she said, scooting away with a laugh.

He grabbed her around the waist and pulled her back, kissing her on the back of the neck. "I'll see you tomorrow."

Oleanna closed her eyes. "I'll get away as quickly as I can."

"Good," he whispered into her skin, then with a quick bite that made her yelp, he stood. At that moment, Elisabeth emerged from the farmhouse, closing the door quietly behind her. She folded her arms and grinned. "I can go back in—" she said, pointing over her shoulder.

"I'm just leaving," Anders said, retrieving his jacket. "Thank you very much for a lovely evening." He walked over and offered Elisabeth his hand.

With a laugh, she shook it. "Good night."

Anders shrugged on his jacket, then leaned down and kissed Oleanna on the cheek.

"I can walk with you—" she said, starting to get up.

"I can find my way. Good night." He grinned and walked away, into the darkness of the forest, hands in his pockets.

Elisabeth set to clearing up their dishes, but Oleanna watched Anders until he was well under the eaves of the wood. Then, shaking herself, she helped Elisabeth gather the remains of their feast.

The next day began early, as ever, and Elisabeth and Oleanna set to their chores: the hops and the potatoes, the mucking and the milking, the washing and the mending and the dyeing. They worked quietly, separately and together, though Oleanna found Elisabeth looking at her strangely now and again. When Oleanna questioned her, Elisabeth shook her head and moved on.

By mid-day, they were not quite half done with the work. Elisabeth disappeared into the store house, and Oleanna took a moment to lean against its walls and rest under the sod-covered eave.

"We need milk," Elisabeth called.

"Oh no oh no oh no," Oleanna groaned, squinting up at the sky. "How could I forget?" She pushed away from the wall and stuck her head in the door. "I'm going up to the sæter. I'll milk the goat."

"Bring down any mending from the cabin."

"I'll be back." Despite the fact that her legs were cramping and her back aching, she picked up her skirts and dashed into the forest.

Anders stood on the crest of the hill next to the cabin, looking south toward the Sognefjord. His hands were clasped and still behind his back, and he was swaying slightly, like a great birch tree caught in a breeze. Oleanna stopped and watched him. "I'm sorry I'm late," she called finally.

He turned around, smiling, his hands still behind his back. "I've kept myself busy."

"Good," she said, stepping up to him and smiling. "Thank you for coming to supper."

He wrapped his arms around her, and she leaned into him. "Does Elisabeth approve?"

"Does it matter?" she asked, pulling back and looking up at his face.

"Of course," he laughed.

"I think she does," Oleanna smiled. "Though I think she would have preferred to have you for herself."

Anders grinned.

"So. How have you kept yourself occupied?"

"I have something to show you," he said, taking her hand and leading her to the cabin door.

She raised an eyebrow.

"Later," he laughed. "I have something else to show you."

Oleanna laughed.

"Close your eyes."

She did as he asked. She could hear the door opening and he maneuvered her to stand on the threshold.

"Open your eyes," he whispered in her ear.

Oleanna gasped. The mantle above the fireplace was emptied of books, and decorated with a twisting acanthus and rose design. "When did you paint this?" she asked, walking as if in a dream into the room.

"This morning."

She turned to find him smiling. "It's beautiful," she breathed. "Beautiful." She took his hand.

"You need a beautiful place to keep your dreams."

Oleanna stilled, looking up into his face. After a few moments, she whispered, "Thank you." She turned back to look at the artwork, exquisite in black and aqua and red. She sat in the chair before the fireplace and he sat next to her on the floor, holding her hand. They sat quietly, Oleanna sighing now and again, looking between the mantle, and the wide world outside the window, and Anders.

"Your hands must be cramped," she said finally.

"No," he laughed.

"That's a lot of work."

"I'm not afraid of a little hard work for a good cause," he smiled.

"I like that about you."

He smiled, broad and sunny.

She cocked her head. "Was it hard work, before you came here? When you were a fisherman?"

"Yes."

She leaned over and kissed him quickly. "Tell me about it."

He took a deep breath. "What do you want to know?"

"Everything," she said, sitting back in the chair.

"Of course," he laughed. "I shouldn't expect anything else from the girls of Myklebost."

"Tell me."

He paused. "It was hard work. I was always cold, and the freezing water and the ropes shredded my hands."

"It's what your father did?"

"Yes."

"Is he disappointed that you're not a fisherman anymore?"

"I think that would be hard to know. He died many years ago."

"Oh, no. I'm sorry."

"Don't be sorry. I didn't tell you."

"What was he like?"

Anders shrugged. "Stern, and kind. Like most fathers I suppose."

"Not all fathers."

"When did your father die?"

"Years ago," she shrugged.

"Were you close to him?"

"No one was close to him," she said. "He was stern, and hard. We learned how to work."

"He had a lot of mouths to feed."

"Yes," she said. "And bottles of akevitt to drink."

"Oh."

"We were never quite sure…" She sighed.

"Go on."

"He would be quiet, quiet, quiet, working and sweating, and then…he would change. He would explode, like a cannon. He beat Anton so badly once that mama's medicines and poultices couldn't help him. The doctor from Skei had to come to look at him. He couldn't work for a week."

"Is that why Anton left?"

"Wouldn't you?"

Anders nodded.

"I don't know where he got the money to go," Oleanna said quietly. "I think mama had some, or maybe she gave him jewelry to sell. It broke her heart." She sighed, and he rubbed the top her hand with his thumb. "Do you have any brothers or sisters?"

He shook his head.

"Has your family lived in Sogn a long time?"

"No," he said, looking up at the mantel. "My parents met there. He was from Hyllestad and she was from Hardanger."

"Adventurous."

"Yes," he smiled. "And what about you?"

"Me?" she laughed.

"I've seen your atlas."

Oleanna sobered. After a long pause, she said, "My father's family have lived here for generations out of mind."

"So there is nothing keeping you here except history."

"And Elisabeth. And my responsibilities. And you."

He squeezed her hand.

"Let's talk about something cheerful," she said, leaning down and kissing his cheek. "I'm tired of talking about history."

"How about politics?"

"Oh, no. No thank you," she laughed. "I said 'something cheerful.'" After a few moments, an image of Anders on Constitution Day came to her. "Wait. Was your friend at the Seventeenth of May party the one who suggested you come to Jølster?"

"My friend?"

"The one who spoke."

"Oh. No. I just happened to meet him in Skei the day before. He has a bright future in government, if he can get to Bergen."

"So you follow politics closely, then?"

"Don't you?"

Oleanna shrugged. "Father was passionate about it. He spoke quite often up in Skei for farmers' rights. But after a while, it bored me."

"Why?" Anders laughed, surprised. "How could it be boring?"

"Can I vote?"

"What?"

"Can I vote? As a woman—an unmarried woman?"

"Well. No."

"It's theory with no practical application for me."

"And you prefer practical applications."

She smiled. "Yes. I prefer to work with my hands."

Anders chuckled. He rubbed the top of her hand with his thumb and she allowed her eyelids to flutter closed with a sigh of contentment.

After a few minutes, she opened her eyes and stood, then leaned against the windowsill; he followed, still holding her hand. She looked out at the broad expanse of the Sognefjord, many miles and valleys away. "You had to start over because you lost someone."

He sighed. "I thought we weren't going to talk about history anymore."

"Just answer the question."

"Yes."

She traced patterns on the inside of his wrist with her fingertips. Finally, she whispered, "Who did you lose?"

"Someone close to me."

"Who—"

"Tell me more about your mother."

"What?" she asked, dropping his hand.

"Tell me about your mother."

She looked up at him, his features strange and shadowy profiled against the bright midday sun outside the window. He looked down at her, his eyes still and quiet, waiting.

"Why—" she whispered, her throat tight.

"Just tell me," he said.

She took a deep breath, then abruptly let it out in a short laugh. "I don't know what else to say about her," she said.

He nodded but did not speak.

"She—she looked like Elisabeth," Oleanna said, looking away from Anders and out the window at the hillside and far valleys beyond. "Her hair was dark and curling, and she was so graceful. Well, graceful when she wasn't bent over the washbasin or beating out the rugs or gutting a fish," she said.

"Was she a good mother?"

Oleanna shrugged. "What does that mean?" she said, looking back at him. "She beat us when she was angry and smothered us with love when she was happy. Toward the end—though, I suppose we didn't know it was the end—she grew pale. She looked like a ghost. It's almost like she knew what was coming," Oleanna shuddered.

"Go on."

"Why don't you tell me about—"

"Go on, Oleanna."

She sighed. "I remember, when I was very young, she would walk into the forest in the morning and come back late at night. To gather herbs for dyeing, she said. She stopped going a few months before she died."

"What do you think she was doing out there?"

"I don't know. But sometimes think I would do the same, if I could."

Suddenly, Anders leaned in and turned her face to his, kissing her greedily. She clung to him, pouring all of her sadness and pain and loneliness into him; he pulled back, eyes strange and wild. Oleanna lifted her chin, defiant, heart throbbing, tears on her cheeks. He leaned in again and kissed her soundly, rubbing circles into her back.

Later, Oleanna finally yawned and stretched, kissing Anders on the neck and sitting up.

He rolled over and captured her hand. "Stay. Stay with me, here. Tonight."

Oleanna sighed. "I can't. I have chores."

He wrapped his arms around her from behind and kissed her neck.

"I have responsibilities, which I have been neglecting, thanks to you," she said, closing her eyes, and leaning into his kiss.

He chuckled and drew her closer. "Let's escape."

"What?"

"Let's go—somewhere. We can spend all day in bed. I can paint, and you can weave, and—"

"And where is this magical place where we don't have to work?"

"We could go anywhere."

"No matter where you go, you will still have to work. Don't be silly," Oleanna said, shrugging him off and standing up. She pulled on her shirtwaist and buttoned it.

"Don't go. Please."

She pulled on her skirt and boots silently, avoiding his gaze. Oleanna smoothed her hair and walked toward the door. When she reached it, she turned around, to find Anders still sitting on the small bed, the linen sheet barely covering him. "I'll come to you tomorrow," she said.

"I'll be working," he spat.

"Don't be childish."

"Don't leave me." He stood up and walked over to her, the sheet dropping away. He leaned down and carded his hands into her hair, looking at her but not kissing her. "You're a free thing, Oleanna. You are free."

She stilled. "Am I free to go now?" she whispered.

He dropped his hands and stepped back.

"I'll see you tomorrow."

He sighed. "I'm sorry."

Oleanna reached up and kissed him on the mouth. "Goodbye." She opened the door and stepped out onto the porch, peering out at the sunny, breezy hilltop. "Damn," she muttered.

The final onion pulled, Oleanna stood and put her hands on the small of her back, stretching and groaning with relief at each pop. Though Elisabeth complained that she had been late, they made up as they always did and spent the evening sitting together at the table outside, doing the mending while Torjus chattered himself into sleep in the short grass near the farmhouse.

As ever, the next morning had come too quickly, and Oleanna, bemused and ashamed by her behavior, was determined to make up for her absence. By the time Elisabeth and Torjus had woken, the stable was mucked, Terna watered, and the rugs beaten. As they ate their breakfast in bewilderment, Oleanna pulled a basket full of onions from the dirt and hummed under her breath.

She had not gone to Anders that morning, nor had he come to her, though she hardly noticed deep in the recesses of the store house, organizing the winter clothing and taking inventory of their linens. She finally emerged, blinking, into the mid-day sunlight.

Elisabeth was in the middle of their small patch of hops, showing Torjus how to train the bines so they caught the best summer sun. Oleanna wiped her hands on her apron and wandered down the hill. "We're nearly out of flour," she said, kneeling down next to Elisabeth. "One of us is going to have to go into Skei to sell some of those ratty onions. We need to sit down and look at John's book tonight. We're going to be out of supplies and money before we can blink if we're not careful."

"How much flour do we have?" Elisabeth asked, turning her head and holding her hands out as Torjus began flinging dirt in every direction. "Stop that," she begged, trying to grab his hands without looking at him.

"Enough for a few more days. We also need turpentine."

Elisabeth finally succeeded in grabbing Torjus' hands, slapping them. "Stop. Go wash your hands, now."

With a pout, Torjus stood and kicked some more dirt, then ran off laughing toward the lake.

"Inside!" Oleanna called, and he made a radical turn and headed instead for the farmhouse. She stood up, creakily, and Elisabeth held her hand out to be pulled up. They stood together, looking out at the lake, and sighed at the same time. They looked at each other and laughed. "We're out of eggs, and I don't think any are going to appear this afternoon. I'll go over to Anders' to see if he has any. Maybe he'll have some flour too."

Elisabeth raised an eyebrow. "Don't take three hours this time."

Oleanna blushed. "I'll be back soon. I promise."

"We'll see," Elisabeth said, shaking her head.

Oleanna headed to the lakeside and the path to Anders' cottage. Across the lake, two boats bobbed on the sparkling water, and high above, a gyrfalcon cried, circling its prey and diving suddenly, lost in the dark forest that crept nearly to the water's edge. She ran her hands along the slender birch branches that barred her way, humming as fleeting images of her brothers and sisters, playing in the lake and under the trees flashed through her mind. She slowed as she reached Anders' land, and watched him from between the branches.

"So ro, godt barn, mor spinner blått garn, by, by liten ting. Snart kommer papp'n din, han kjører plogen…"*

The lake shushed quietly on the shoreline, the only sound other than his song. He was digging in a rocky dirt patch, fussing with the handful of onion sets John had given him when he had taken the cabin in February, a meager welcome gift.

With a smile, Oleanna stepped through the fence of branches. "You're industrious," she said, leaning against the smooth bole of a young birch.

Anders looked over his shoulder and grinned. "I've been chastened," he said, brushing off his hands and standing up.

"A forest wife has been keeping me from my work."

Oleanna pushed off the tree and grinned. "Funny. A strange grandfatherly troll has been keeping me from mine."

Anders laughed and leapt over the row of onions, standing inches from Oleanna but not touching her. She itched to take his hands, to lean into him, but she stood still, chewing her lip. He leaned down and kissed her chastely, then stepped away and leapt back over the row. "What can I do for you, Oleanna Tollefsdatter?"

She smiled and stepped around the patch of dirt, pushed him against the wall of his cabin, and kissed him ferociously. He smiled into her kiss and pulled her close. After a few minutes, he broke away. "I thought you had work to do today," he said.

Oleanna sighed. "I do," she said, stepping back and smoothing down the front of her shirt. "I came to see if you had any eggs."

"I don't," he said, "but I'm going into Skei shortly. I'll bring you some."

"No," she said, brows furrowed. "You can't afford—"

"Don't," he said, holding his hands up. "What else do you need?"

* *"Rest now, sweet child, mother's spinning blue thread, bye, bye my little one. Your daddy will be coming soon, he's out ploughing in the field…"*

"What else do you need?"

"Nothing, we're—"

"Flour. And turpentine."

He turned and disappeared into his cabin, reappearing moments later with his coat. "I'll be back by this evening. Is there anything else—"

"Anders, please, you don't need to—we don't need you to save us."

"Is there anything else you need?" he said, folding his arms.

"No. I'll pay you by Sunday. I swear "

"I'll see you this evening," he said, kissing her gently. He turned and headed for the path east.

"Thank you," she called, and he waved his hand without looking back.

The afternoon passed more slowly than the morning, Oleanna searching for Anders along the lakeside or under the forest's eaves every few minutes. She finally gave up and retreated to the farmhouse, where she and Elisabeth finally took out John's instruction book and delved into the secrets of planting and harvesting while Torjus napped.

After an hour or two, Oleanna's head was spinning with planting schedules and yearly yields. She rubbed her eyes and sat back. "I can't read anymore today," she said.

Elisabeth rubbed her temples. "My head hurts."

Oleanna stood, stretching. "I'm going to take the wash up."

Elisabeth nodded and waved her off. "I'll get supper started."

She trudged up the hill with the basket of washing. As she pushed open the door of the store house, she heard Anders' voice just beyond the treeline. "Oleanna," he called.

Her heart jumped. She paused just on the threshold and smiled. He emerged from the trees, carrying a basket and waving. He jogged over the short distance and, without warning, grabbed her around the waist, bent her back, and kissed her thoroughly. He stood her back up, laughing, and showed her the basket's contents with a flourish. "Eggs, flour, and turpentine. And some pork."

"Pork? Anders, you shouldn't—"

"Hush."

"Thank you," she said, holding the basket of wash against her hip with one arm.

"It was my pleasure."

She smiled and pushed the door open, walking into the store house and pausing to let her eyes adjust. He followed behind.

"You're cheerful," she said, her heart skipping a beat at his wide grin. "Oh, please prop the door open." She walked to the middle of the room and dropped the pile of clothes next to the great round wooden washtub.

Anders sauntered to Oleanna's side. She turned to him suddenly and grabbed the front of his jacket, pulling him close and kissing him. "Welcome back," she murmured.

He laughed and kissed the palm of her hand, then stepped back. "I have news," he said, his blue-gray eyes wild, like the lake during a spring storm.

"Yes?"

"You won't believe this."

"Don't tell me you took all that time in Skei for the county gossip," she laughed.

He took her hands, and paused, looking suddenly serious. "The union has been dissolved," he said.

"What?"

"The Storthing dissolved the union. King Oscar has been deposed."

"When?"

"Last week."

"How do you know?"

"It's all over the papers."

"The union is dissolved."

He laughed then, his joy ringing around the ancient rafters.

She scowled at him. "Don't laugh at me."

"I'm not." He sobered and took her hands. "It's freedom, don't you see? It's what we've been hoping for!"

"We?"

"We are running our own country. Six hundred years! They even raised the Norwegian flag, the proper one, in Kristiania!" He leaned in and kissed her.

"But surely the Rigsdag hasn't approved. Sweden won't stand for this."

"Doesn't matter," he shrugged impatiently. "We're free again."

"Right now? As of this moment?"

"No. No, they've demanded a referendum."

"The Rigsdag?"

"Yes. They want to be sure that the people are in agreement with this decision. Oh, we'll show them!" he laughed.

Oleanna grinned, catching his mood. "When is the referendum?"

"Sometime in August. At least that's what I've heard."

"Who told you?"

"Jens."

"And Jens is—"

"The man who spoke at Constitution Day. He's heading down to Bergen tomorrow."

She leaned against the washtub, folding her arms. After a few moments, she looked up at him. "But it won't make any difference, will it?"

"What? What do you mean?"

"It doesn't matter who's in charge," she shrugged. "Not really. We still have to darn socks. We still have to wash clothes. It's all well and good for you to talk about freedom. You're a man! It doesn't really make any difference to me who the king is, or what country we have allegiance to."

"I don't believe you think that."

"I still have to make breakfast every morning. I still have to work this farm."

"But it's bigger than that."

"Really, though. What difference will it make, except to some men down in Kristiania?"

"It makes all the difference in the world."

She shook her head and started to turn away. He grabbed her hand and turned her back to face him. "It's a chance to start over."

The world around her grew very quiet, shockingly still, until all she could hear was the thudding of her heart and his words echoing in her mind. "Say that again," she whispered.

"Oleanna."

She pulled her hand free and stepped away. "You're leaving," she said, her voice flat.

"You don't have to stay here," he whispered, his voice tight.

"I thought you liked it here," she said, picking laundry out of the basket and throwing it into the washing tub. "I thought you liked our world here."

Anders reached out and grasped her arm again. "That's not the point—"

"It is the point!" she thundered, shaking his hand off and stepping away.

Anders stilled. "Why are you doing this?"

"Doing what?"

"Why do you insist that you have to stay here?"

"Because I do."

"There's more to it."

"No. Why do I have to keep—"

"Is Torjus yours?" he interrupted.

She turned around and laughed, startled out of her increasingly dark mood. "No, I think I'd remember that," she said.

Anders smiled, smoothing his hand down her arm to take her hand. "Then nothing should keep you here."

Oleanna shrugged.

"Oleanna..."

"It's my debt to the dead," Oleanna said in a rush.

He squeezed her hand. "You owe the dead nothing," he said. "The dead are gone."

She pulled her hand away.

"You'll have to let the dead go someday. Come with me."

"Anders—"

"Come with me. Escape. Please."

"I can't."

Anders sighed heavily. After a few moments, he smiled, a tight, sad thing that did not reach his eyes. "Goodnight, Oleanna Tollefsdatter." He kissed her forehead, then turned and walked out of the dim store house, into the lilac gloaming, hands buried deep in his pockets.

Oleanna swallowed a sob and then steadied herself with her hands on the worktable, scattering herbs. "They all leave," she whispered. "They all leave."

Some time later, Oleanna woke to find Torjus tapping her on the forehead, his small form barely visible in the darkness of the store house. "Lea, wake up, wake up, wake up," he said, punctuating each word with a tap.

She groaned and stilled his hand. "I'm awake."

"Mama says you should stop working and come eat supper."

Oleanna nodded and sat up, dislodging Torjus from her chest. He rolled over onto the packed earth floor of the store house, giggling.

"Run and tell her that I'm coming," she whispered, pulling herself up by the edge of the worktable. "I'll be right there."

Torjus bounced up like a jack-in-the-box and raced away, slamming the door back against the wall. Oleanna squeezed her eyes closed and edged slowly out of the store house, feeling her way toward the open door. She stood on the threshold, blinking; the gloaming had turned less lilac, more blue. She could see Elisabeth bustling around the table, a lantern set at the end, illuminating it and the grass down to the lakeside in a wavering circle.

Elisabeth looked up suddenly and waved her down. Oleanna made her way slowly down the hill, the world fuzzy and uneven.

"You've been working in there too long," Elisabeth said when she arrived. "Did Anders bring the flour?"

Oleanna nodded, rubbing the side of her head. "And pork. I—I forgot to bring it down."

"What's the matter?" Elisabeth asked sharply, setting the plates down on the table with a clatter.

"Nothing," Oleanna winced, realizing at that moment a sharp headache was slicing into the side of her head and behind her eyes.

"Don't lie to me."

Sighing, Oleanna sat gingerly on one of the benches. "I think I fainted."

"Not again," Elisabeth groaned, spooning potatoes onto Oleanna's plate. "Torjus, come sit down," she called.

Torjus appeared from the other side of the small farmhouse and bounced his way onto the bench next to his mother.

"What happened?"

Oleanna looked up at Elisabeth, her brain churning into gear. The conversation with Anders rushed back all at once. "Did you hear?" she asked quietly.

"Hear what?" Elisabeth said, admonishing Torjus to sit quietly and eat.

"About the dissolution?"

"The Storthing dissolved the union, yes, I heard."

Oleanna set her fork down. "How do you know?"

"Read it in the paper," Elisabeth shrugged.

"Why didn't you tell me?"

"I didn't think you'd care."

# CHAPTER ELEVEN

Lake Jølster, Sunnfjord, Norway
June 1905

OLEANNA STOOD ON THE FAR SIDE of the sæter cabin, hand shielding her eyes from the rising sun, looking out south and east toward the far, shining ribbon of the deep Sognefjord in the distance.

Her eyes felt gritty, dry and bleary from a sleepless night. The aspirin Elisabeth had given her served to ease the pains in her head, but not the sickness in her gut, the dull panic of impending loss.

"Oleanna?"

She stiffened, her heart pounding.

"Are you up here?"

"Yes," she called finally. She walked around to the front of the cabin where Anders stood. He leaned forward to kiss her, but she turned at the last moment and he gave her a glancing kiss to the temple.

"Oleanna," he said, voice tight with pleading.

She folded her arms.

He looked at her for long moments, then exhaled. "I want to be there, to be a part of it," he said. He began to pace, his hands flexing, expansive. "It's a time in our history that's unparalleled, don't you see? Not since Harald—"

"Yes, yes, yes. We haven't been free for hundreds of years. But we exchange one set of rulers for another."

"But Norway can take its place in the world again."

"And again: explain how that makes any difference to me. And explain why it's more important than me."

Anders sighed.

"John has been gone only a few weeks, and now you?"

"Come with me."

She turned away from him. "You are leaving."

"Yes," he said quietly.

"When? Where?" Oleanna held her hands in tight fists, her body stiffened against the blow.

"Bergen."

"Bergen?" she asked, spinning back to face him. "Are you going with Jens?"

"No. Karl Nilsson asked me to come."

"Who?"

"An old friend."

Oleanna stood very, very still.

Anders reached out to take her hand, then dropped his own and stepped back. "Karl took a place in the city government in Bergen last year. He sent a telegram, asking me to come. It's a paid position," he said.

"And that's all it takes?"

Anders raised his eyebrows.

"An old friend contacts you, and you're off?"

"Oleanna, if it weren't something this important—"

She snorted. "And what do you think you can do there?"

His eyes narrowed. "Do you think all I am is a farmer?"

"No, of course not. You're also a fisherman," she spat, cheeks burning.

"Well. If that's all you think of me, maybe it is time for me to go."

They stood a foot apart, glaring at each other. Finally, Anders took a step back. "They need willing hands, Oleanna. It's a chance to do something important."

"Farming isn't important now? Being with me isn't important now?"

He ignored her and pressed on. "I can help Norway start over. You have to understand—"

"Go," she interrupted, waving him away, "if it's that important to you." She winced at the pain in his face, then turned away, her cheeks flaming.

"Oleanna."

After a few moments, she sighed. "You said you would never desert me," she said quietly.

"I'm coming back," he protested.

"That's what they all say. They all lie."

"I am."

"When? When?" she cried, her voice tight and high. "Can you tell me that?"

"No."

"You're throwing away your art, and your little farm, and me. I hope whatever you find is worth it."

He reached out and turned her to face him. "You can't live on this farm forever. You can't live with those ghosts. They'll take you with them. I speak from experience." He held out his hand. "Come wi—"

She quelled him with a look.

"You're being childish," he said, dropping his hand.

"No more than you."

Anders stepped forward and grabbed Oleanna's shoulders, squeezing her until she winced. "You can't hide up here forever."

"I have no choice."

"That's a lie, and I'm tired of hearing it," he said, leaning down and kissing her fiercely.

After a few moments, she pushed him away. She looked up into his face, forbidding as the mountainside, and slapped it with all of her might. "Go," she said, stumbling back, her palm tingling.

He narrowed his eyes, and stepped forward.

Oleanna stood her ground. "If all of that," she said, waving her hand vaguely toward the Sognefjord and beyond, "is more important than me, go. I don't want you here."

"You're being childish," he whispered.

"Go. Now," she said, pointing beyond his shoulder toward the forest and the trail back down to the lakeside. "And don't bother to say goodbye."

Anders stepped away. "You're a foolish woman," he whispered, shaking his head. He turned and began to walk away.

"And you're a faithless man."

He hesitated, but continued down toward the forest.

Oleanna watched him until he disappeared into the trees. She sank down onto the crooked step leading into the cabin, shaking.

"He's what?" Elisabeth said.

Oleanna nodded, arms folded, leaning against the doorframe. Her walk back from the sæter had been numb; the usual thoughts spinning in her head had stilled, and the forest itself was silent of even a birdcall. "I can't believe it," Oleanna whispered. "He had the gall to ask me to go with him."

After a moment, Elisabeth whispered, "You're a fool."

Oleanna narrowed her eyes. "What?"

"Go with him. Go while you still can."

Oleanna shook her head. "I can't leave. I can't leave you and Torjus here. What are you saying?"

"You're an idiot. You have a ridiculous and misplaced sense of duty."

"But—you two can't—"

Elisabeth grabbed Oleanna's wrist and squeezed. "If you don't take this opportunity to leave, I will really hate you."

Oleanna froze, staring past Elisabeth to the mirrored lake. "I can't," she whispered finally.

Elisabeth flung Oleanna's wrist away. "Then you're a coward and a fool."

"There's too much work on this farm for just your hands," Oleanna said, rubbing her wrist.

"Do you think I wouldn't know how to manage?"

Oleanna shrugged.

"You think I can't do this?" Elisabeth said.

"I think it's a lot of work."

"You think I'm an idiot who can't handle this."

"I think you're too smart for this," Oleanna said, gesturing behind her toward the stables and store house. "You're made for better than this."

"That's ridiculous."

"It's the truth."

"And you're not?"

"I'm not what?"

"Made for more than this?"

Oleanna paused, then shook her head. "It doesn't matter. I can't leave."

Elisabeth folded her arms and cocked her head, examining Oleanna; after a few moments, Oleanna looked away.

"I could have saved them, too, you know," Elisabeth said quietly. "I could have kept mama from getting in the boat. We all knew there was a storm coming, and I still let her go."

"Why did you run away? After the viewing?"

After a moment, Elisabeth said, "I'm a coward."

"That's what John said."

"When?"

"When I asked him why he was leaving."

Elisabeth opened her eyes and looked long at Oleanna. "We're all cowards," Elisabeth whispered finally.

"Now you know why I can't leave."

Elisabeth turned away and looked out across the lake. She folded her arms and after a short huff that sounded to Oleanna like both a sigh and a laugh, said, "Jakob is coming to live with us."

"What?"

"He doesn't know it yet," Elisabeth said, looking at Oleanna over her shoulder and smiling. "I've decided I like it here," she said over Oleanna's chuckles. "Despite everything, God help me, I love it."

Oleanna sobered. "The world has gone mad," she said quietly.

"The world is moving on. It always does. You can stay here, and be underfoot with me and my husband—"

"What?"

"He doesn't know that yet, either," Elisabeth grinned.

Oleanna laughed, shaking her head.

Elisabeth sobered. "You'll end up a wraith in the forest like mama if you stay here."

"And you won't?"

"No. I talk a lot," Elisabeth said. "But I'll never leave. You have a chance to go. Take it."

When Oleanna woke, the sun had already risen, industrious so close to midsummer, and Oleanna hurried out the door, already feeling behind. She stuffed her feet into her work boots and sidled out the farmhouse door, shushing Torjus' sudden chatter with a finger on her lips.

After sticking her head into the barn to check on the pony, she laced her boots and set off toward the sæter.

By the time she reached the wide meadow, she was covered in a cold sweat and shivering. She stumbled to the cabin and dropped onto the step, wiping her forehead with a shaking hand. The goat and sheep wandered by, heedless of her confusion, her sadness, her distress.

The door behind her opened and she jumped up with a shout.

"Oleanna?"

Anders stood in the doorway, his clothes rumpled and misbuttoned. "What's wrong?"

"What are you doing here?"

He looked down at his clothes and attempted to smooth them. He shrugged. "I was hoping you'd come back."

"Were you here all night?"

He nodded.

"You look terrible."

"I wanted to apologize—"

"Don't," Oleanna said. "I'm sorry."

He sighed. "This would all be much easier if you would just come with me."

"Don't you think I want to? Don't you think I want to see the world? To see it with you?"

"Then come with me. Stop this foolishness."

The morning breeze swept up, and Oleanna brushed the hair out of her face. She hesitated. "When are you leaving?"

"Come inside," he said, pushing the door wide.

She paused, then shook her head.

He slumped against the doorframe. "Tomorrow."

"Tomorrow?"

"One of the Sanddal boys is going down to Vadheim to pick up a cousin at the ferry. He said he'd give me a ride. Come with me."

"I can't," she whispered. "I just can't."

"I'll be back. I promise. I will come back."

She turned her back on him and looked out across the meadow, down toward the lakeside and her farm. "I won't hold my breath."

After a few moments, he said, "I should go."

She nodded.

"Can I see you before I leave? Tomorrow?"

"It's on your way, isn't it?"

"Oleanna—"

"You should go."

Anders reached out to touch her arm, but thought better of it and dropped his hand. He walked past without touching her and made his way slowly across the wide meadow. She watched him, still and cold as the glacier. Finally, she moved, stepping across the threshold into the cabin. Anders' coat was hung over the back of the chair; she picked it up and dropped onto the bed, clutching the coat to her chest.

In the bright morning sun, Oleanna loitered close to the farmhouse, having dispatched her barn and store house chores before the dawn had fully given way to sunrise. After breakfast, Elisabeth had taken pity on Oleanna and sat her down at the table outside, setting out a pile of mending. Eventually, Elisabeth joined her, and they looked up every few minutes, watching the trail from Anders' cabin.

Finally, he appeared as he had the night of John's farewell feast, all at once from out of the forest. He wore a dark suit and carried his bowler in one hand, a small case in the other. Oleanna dropped the mending into her lap. He looked so strange, and so handsome.

He paused for just a moment, then headed down the hill, jogging slightly with the incline. "Ladies," he said, slowing and stopping a few yards from the table.

"Anders," Elisabeth said, standing up.

Oleanna remained seated.

"Good luck," Elisabeth said, extending her hand.

He shook her hand. "Thank you."

She leaned in closer to him. "Take her with you."

"What?"

"Take her with you."

Anders laughed, a short sound with little joy. "Do you think I haven't tried?"

"I'm right here, you know," Oleanna said.

"Is Anders leaving too?" Torjus asked, tugging on Oleanna's hand.

"Yes, he is."

Anders sighed. "Not for good. I'll be back."

Oleanna shrugged.

"Can I speak with you? Alone?"

"Do whatever you please."

Elisabeth lifted Torjus from the bench and carried him into the farmhouse.

"I'll be back. Maybe by the end of the summer."

"I'm sure you think so."

"Oleanna," he said sharply.

She looked up and glared at him. "Go."

"This is ridiculous."

"I agree."

Suddenly, he leaned down and kissed her, holding the back of her head. She struggled feebly at first, but returned his kiss with gusto.

"If you won't come with me, at least wait for me."

"We'll see," she shrugged.

"Oleanna—"

"Just go."

He leaned down and picked up his case, then set the hat on his head and walked away. After a few moments, she stood and watched him leave.

He headed toward the Sanddal farm, the same path that they all take: Anton, father, mama, Anna, John. And now Anders.

As he disappeared around the corner, Elisabeth emerged from the farmhouse and placed a steadying arm around Oleanna's shoulders. "Don't you dare faint this time," she said.

Oleanna straightened and smoothed down her shirtwaist. "Let's get back to work."

# CHAPTER TWELVE

Lake Jølster, Sunnfjord, Norway
June 1905

ELISABETH AND OLEANNA sat with their backs against the farmhouse, stretching their legs and resting their backs. The daytime chores were done, and they enjoyed their brief respite before supper had to be made by tossing pebbles in the water.

Oleanna looked out across the lake, the houses tiny splotches of color against the blue-green mountainsides. "Have you ever been over to Årdal?" she asked.

"No. Severina went over, when we were small. She had a sweetheart there."

"She did?"

"Nels somethingorother."

"Father allowed that?"

Elisabeth grinned. "Father didn't know."

"How do you know?"

"John told me."

"Don't say his name," Oleanna said.

"John, John, J—"

"Stop."

Elisabeth's impish smile faded and she sighed.

"I can't bear it," Oleanna whispered. "Not anymore."

"Yes you can, you idiot. You have, and you will."

"You're starting to sound like me."

"You've made your choice, Lea. You had your chance to leave, and you tossed it aside."

Oleanna nodded but said nothing.

After a few moments, Elisabeth softened. "Was he just a distraction? Or do you love him?"

Oleanna closed her eyes. She loved the smell of him, the feel of him. She loved his sudden smiles and gentle hands. She loved his art and his stories and even, if she was very honest with herself, his passion for Norway and the coming change. After a few short weeks, she had honestly and truly fallen in love with Anders Samuelsson. Had she told him? Did he know?

"Yes," she whispered finally.

"And you let him go."

Oleanna nodded. Then, out of nowhere, like a spring storm, she began to cry. The tears soon turned to wracking sobs, and Oleanna buried her face in her hands, and rocked back and forth.

Finally, Elisabeth whispered, "Shhh, shhh, don't wake Torjus."

Oleanna sniffled and wiped her face with her sleeve.

"It's your own fault for being a stubborn ass, you know," Elisabeth said, smoothing Oleanna's hair away from her face.

"I'm not stubborn."

Elisabeth raised an eyebrow.

"I'm not that stubborn."

They shared a smile. "Why didn't you go with him?" Elisabeth asked quietly.

"You know why."

Elisabeth shrugged. "Do you think he'll come back?"

"No," Oleanna said. "They never come back."

Elisabeth looked out at the lake. "Sometimes I feel like I could fall to pieces, right here. Little bits of me scattered along the lakeshore, carried by the wind."

"Yes," Oleanna whispered.

"I miss her so much. Looking at you every day reminds me of her."

Oleanna's heart constricted.

"So many losses, so many deaths. Do you realize that it's only been three years since father died, and Anton left?"

"It's worn me down, Lisbet. I feel old. You would think time would make it easier. But it only seems to get harder."

"It's only harder if you keep carrying all of the weight."

"What do you mean?"

"You have to let them go. All of them. They're crushing you."

"They're not—"

"With every loss, you've grown colder, Lea. Anders started to thaw you out—"

"Don't," Oleanna whispered.

"Let them go."

Oleanna sighed, then tossed a pebble into the water, watching the circles expand out deeper and deeper. Finally, she said, "I'm afraid to let them go."

"Why?" Elisabeth said, bemused. "They're crushing—"

"I don't want to forget them."

"You won't forget them. They're a part of you."

"Maybe I don't want that either."

Elisabeth laughed. "You are impossible," she said, but took Oleanna's hand. "Come with me."

They stood and she led Oleanna around the corner, back into the farmhouse. They tiptoed in, careful not to wake Torjus. Elisabeth pulled out her drawer in the dresser, and after digging around and scattering chemises and woolen winter stockings, pulled out a small leather-bound book. "This," she said quietly, "is where I keep them."

Oleanna smiled at the warring looks of excitement and shyness on Elisabeth's face. "Is this your writing?"

Elisabeth nodded, and handed her the book. Oleanna took it, handling it gingerly. "Can I?"

"Yes."

They stepped back outside. Oleanna opened the book and flipped to a page in the middle. Nearly the entire book was filled with Elisabeth's surprisingly tight and tidy handwriting.

"Where did you get this?"

"I asked John to order it. From Bergen."

Oleanna walked over to the table and sat on the bench, flipping through pages; Elisabeth sat across from her, perched nervously.

Pages of dialog and description alternated with paragraphs detailing hurt and pain, confusion and joy. And then, a long passage describing a woman Oleanna recognized as their mother behind a loom, weaving in the firelight during the darkest nights of winter.

Oleanna began to cry again. "It's beautiful. Absolutely beautiful," she whispered.

Elisabeth blushed.

"Does it help?"

"Yes," Elisabeth said, more serious and solemn than she'd ever seen her. "I might have gone mad."

Oleanna nodded, wiping her eyes.

"I keep them in there, so I can remember them," Elisabeth said. "But I lock them in the pages so I can face another day."

"Isn't it frightening to write about them?"

"Terrifying."

Oleanna ran her fingers across the pages. "I'm not like you, Lisbet. I can't write like this."

"Then weave them into a coverlet. Run naked through the trees. Scream. Leave this farm. Do something. You are becoming a ghost of yourself, Lea. You must do something. Anything."

At that moment, Torjus wandered out into the sunlight, rubbing his eyes. "Mama?" he said, pulling on Elisabeth's sleeve.

Elisabeth stood and picked Torjus up, kissing his warm, sleepy face. "What are you doing awake already?" she said. He shrugged and snuggled into her arms. She looked down at Oleanna. "The world is moving on, Lea. Don't turn into a ghost too."

Elisabeth carried Torjus back into the farmhouse. Oleanna looked up into the dark forest on the mountainside. "How?" she whispered. I feel as though I'm half ghost already.

Days later, Oleanna wandered through Anders' garden and found that the reedy saplings were already dying. She had contemplated keeping them alive, hoping perhaps that would, by some alchemy, lure him home. In the end, she decided she had enough work of her own to do, and let them die on their own.

Though she was tempted, she did not push open the door to his cabin; instead, wiping away tears, she continued on the path, toward the small church: the site of the Constitution Day party, only weeks before.

She waited under the trees, watching the parishioners filing out of the tiny church, disappearing away on their horses, in their wagons, on foot. When the last matron and recalcitrant child had gone, Oleanna took a deep breath and walked across the newly shorn grass and up the steps of the small wooden church.

"Søren," she said quietly, standing on the threshold.

He stilled, then set the Bible back on the altar very slowly. "Oleanna," he said, turning around.

"I'm sorry to bother you. I—"

He remembered himself, and quickly walked down the aisle, stepping just a pace shy of where she hesitated. He reached out and took her hands firmly in his. "How are you?" he asked, leaning forward slightly, bending down to look in her eyes.

"It's busy at the farm," she said, removing her hands from his grasp.

He hesitated for just a moment, then stepped back and folded his hands before him. "How are you?"

Oleanna shrugged. "There's a lot of work to be done."

"I expect so," he said, inclining his head gracefully. "And how is Elisabeth?"

"Well enough. That's why I'm here."

"Oh?" he said. "Come, sit down. Let's chat." He took her under the elbow and led her to the last row of pews, sitting on the outside and blocking her in. He let his hand rest on the pew behind her.

"You've been out of the neighborhood too long, Søren," she smiled. "Not getting the good gossip up in Skei?"

He smiled, his teeth perfect and his nose straight, his eyes crystal blue and his hair soft and brown. "I have the souls of my parish to attend to."

"Of course."

He smiled and dropped his hand. "What kind of trouble is your sister in now?"

Oleanna laughed. "She's finally ready to marry Jakob."

Søren's eyes widened. "Really?"

"That's what she says. We should perform the ceremony right away, before she changes her mind."

Could I make myself fall in love with him again? she wondered. A consolation prize for staying on the farm. Anders' rocky face appeared in her mind's eye, and she shook her head slightly.

"I have to go back to Skei on Wednesday, and I won't be back until next Saturday," he said.

"Oh no, that's too long to make her wait. She'll change her mind. When is the soonest—"

"This is highly unusual, Oleanna."

"I know," she said. "Please, can't you find an earlier time? Think of Torjus."

He sighed. "It is not my usual practice, but…I could perform the service Tuesday. Would that suit?"

"That would be perfect," she said, taking his hand and squeezing. "Thank you, Søren."

He tilted his head again. "How are you keeping, Oleanna?"

"I'm tired."

"And is Jakob coming to live with you, or are Elisabeth and Torjus going to live with him?"

"He's coming to live with us."

"Ah," he said, raising his eyebrows.

Oleanna shrugged. "It's about time."

"Won't it be awkward?"

"Oh. I suppose. But I can't leave."

"Don't be silly."

"What?"

"Don't be silly. Of course you can leave."

Oleanna sighed. "No. I really can't."

"Yes you can. You can marry me."

She stilled.

"Leave the farm to Jakob and Elisabeth. Come live with me in the parsonage."

"We've already been through this."

"I am willing to take you back."

Oleanna's eyebrows shot up.

"You weren't thinking straight," he continued, grasping her hands again. "It was a terrible time, after all. Terrible. I forgive you."

She pulled her hands away and folded them in her lap. She grew very still.

"Come live with me in the parsonage," he said again quietly. "You'd hardly have to lift a finger."

"I can't."

"Why? There's nothing holding you on the farm now."

"This is why…Oh, you wouldn't understand."

"Oleanna, please."

"I can't leave Elisabeth and Torjus."

"Is that why you broke off our engagement?" he asked quietly.

"I don't want to talk about this right now."

"I think you owe me an explanation."

Oleanna lifted her chin and glared at him until he blushed. After a few moments, she said, "It was a terrible time."

"Yes."

"I had hoped you…" Oleanna shrugged. "It doesn't matter now."

"I can give you a good life," he said, scooting closer to her. "You would be treated with respect and honor. By me and my congregation."

Oleanna smiled. "Even that old gossip Ingeborg?"

"Even Inge. I've known you since we were children. I know you. I can take good care of you."

Oleanna stilled. His indifference and his arrogance seemed a lifetime removed. He was so lovely in the dappled light, so earnest and insistent. Right there before her; he would not leave. Don't be faithless, she thought finally, shaking her head. "No."

"Why?" he asked, cheeks coloring. "There can be no good reason for you to refuse me again."

"I'm in love with someone else."

"Who?"

"It doesn't matter," she said quietly.

He stood and backed out of the pew, his crimsoned face giving off heat. "You—just like your mama, like a huldra," he muttered. "Beautiful but hollow on the inside." He turned and hurried down the aisle toward the door.

"Søren—" she said, standing.

"Tell them to be here Tuesday afternoon at 2:00," he said without looking back. "And don't be late. I'm a busy man." In a moment, he disappeared into the bright light of midday.

"Damn," she muttered. She sank back down and closed her eyes, rubbing her temples.

Oleanna remained in the pew for minutes, or hours, watching the shadows shift between the rows, watching the sun highlight the rough-hewn crucifix at the altar and the rutvev altar cloth she and her mother had woven many years before.

She stepped out into the afternoon sun and half-heartedly looked for Søren, knowing full well he had retreated to his parsonage. She stood, shielding her eyes, seeing not a limitless horizon, but the familiar, beloved trees and rocks and mountainsides of her home. Could I leave this? she wondered.

When she returned to the farm, she found Elisabeth kneeling in their vegetable patch, dirt-covered to the elbows. "He said Tuesday," Oleanna said, stopping and folding her arms. "What are you doing?"

"Looking for potatoes. Who said Tuesday?"

"Søren."

Elisabeth stopped digging and looked up at Oleanna. "Guess I should let Jakob know."

"You haven't told him?"

Elisabeth grinned. "Surprise!"

Oleanna shook her head, laughing. "You do love him, don't you?"

"Desperately."

"Why have you waited so long?"

"I thought I'd feel trapped," she shrugged. "What time did Søren say?"

"Two."

"We have some work to do then, don't we?" She flashed a brilliant smile, and Oleanna thought she had never looked so beautiful, covered in mud, her dark hair askew.

While Elisabeth went to break the happy news to her unsuspecting new husband-to-be, Oleanna threw herself into a frenzy of cleaning, mending, cooking, baking. With only a few days to prepare, she raced to provide her last, her only, sister with a proper wedding.

Later that day, Oleanna squinted in the dark of the store house. Standing straight and stretching her back, she wandered to the open door. Elisabeth appeared, walking slowly from the woods next to the barn down to the farmhouse. She looked, for once, contemplative. Oleanna folded her arms and watched her sister disappear into the house. He had to have said yes, she thought, wiping her hands on her apron and hurrying down the hill.

Oleanna pushed open the door. Elisabeth knelt next to the chest of drawers, rifling through their underthings. "So?" Oleanna said.

"So?"

"What did he say?"

"Yes, of course," Elisabeth said, glancing up and grinning.

Oleanna smiled. "Good. Are his brother and sister coming to the wedding too?"

"No."

"What?"

Elisabeth stood, dropping the shift back into the drawer. "His mother doesn't approve, and has forbidden anyone else from being there. She doesn't like me to start, and then complained that there were no proper negotiations—"

"Who was supposed to negotiate on your behalf? Torjus?"

"John had offered before he left, but…" Elisabeth shrugged. "They're all close-minded farmers, anyway."

"And what are we?" Oleanna laughed.

"Just farmers." Elisabeth turned away and began to tidy the room.

"I'm sorry."

Elisabeth shrugged again and continued her cleaning. "He'll meet us at the church, with his cart and horse, and his tools. He has some ideas about how we can improve the farm."

"Good." Oleanna stepped forward and put a hand on Elisabeth's shoulder.

Elisabeth turned around and hugged her. "I wish mama were here," she whispered.

"She would have loved the excitement, and seeing you so happy. Was he surprised?"

Elisabeth laughed, wiping her nose with the back of her hand. "No."

"Really?"

"He said he knew I would see reason eventually."

Oleanna smiled. Just outside, they heard Torjus' voice echoing from the edges of the forest. "Lea! Lea!" he cried. Heart jumping, she turned and raced out the door, to find that he was not in danger, but running down the hill, waving a chubby handful of tiny wildflowers. "I got it! I got it!"

She put her hand over her racing heart and half-laughed. "You frightened me, little man!"

"I did?" he said, skittering to a stop.

"I—never mind. Your mama is back. She has something to tell you," she said, ushering him into the farmhouse.

Elisabeth sat on the bed and invited Torjus to crawl into her lap; he obliged with delight. "Would you like Jakob to live with us?"

Torjus looked from Elisabeth to Oleanna and back, eyes wide. "Yes," he said quietly.

"Jakob and mama are getting married in a few days, and then he's going to come live with us. How does that sound?"

Torjus started to bounce in Elisabeth's lap. "Yay yay yay!" He wriggled out of her grasp and spun a few circles.

"I think he likes the idea," Oleanna smiled.

"Can he come today?" Torjus stopped, weaving slightly.

"No, on Tuesday," Elisabeth said.

"When is Tuesday?"

Elisabeth and Oleanna smiled at each other over his head. "What is today, little man?" Oleanna said.

He shrugged. "I don't know."

"It's a good thing Jakob went to school," Elisabeth said with a sigh. "It's Sunday. So what is tomorrow?"

"Monday."

"Yes, and then after that?"

"Tuesday!"

Oleanna laughed and took his small hand, spinning him around again. "We have a lot of work to do for our feast."

"Lea, you don't need—"

Oleanna raised her eyebrows. "This is a proper wedding, no matter how many people will be here."

Elisabeth grinned. "We'll show them."

They finally crawled into bed, somewhere around the fleeting hours of darkness near midnight. Torjus took up the entire bed he shared with Elisabeth, so the sisters got into their old bed together. "What else do we have to do?" Elisabeth muttered into her pillow.

"Nothing," Oleanna said, flexing her aching feet and hands. "Go to sleep."

Elisabeth snuffled and suddenly, she was still, breathing shallowly and snoring a little.

Oleanna put her arms behind her head and sighed, wondering yet again where Anders was on his journey. Already in Bergen, most likely, working and already forgetting about her. She pushed the thoughts away and turned over, falling asleep within moments.

By Monday evening, most of the preparations had been completed: the fiskeboller prepared, the lefse made and wrapped carefully, the small kransekake wedding cake on a protected side table in the farmhouse. Just the flower garlands left, Oleanna thought, surveying the room with her hands on her hips. Suddenly, her heart skipped. "Oh no!" she said, eyes wide.

Elisabeth sat on the far box bed, combing out her wavy dark hair. "What?" she asked.

"The crown. How could I forget?"

Elisabeth shrugged. "I'm sure Søren has one I can borrow."

"I've never seen one at the church."

"How about at the parsonage?"

"No, not there either."

"I'll be fine. It's not—"

"Hallo?" A man's voice outside stilled them both. Oleanna pushed open the door to see Jakob walking down the hill, his younger sister Johanna in tow, white-blond and lovely like her brother. Oleanna had spent many hours toiling over sums with Johanna, years and years ago when she was allowed to go to school, before the work on the farm claimed her time.

"Jakob," Oleanna said, stepping out to greet them. She wiped her hands on her apron and pushed the hair out of her face. "We weren't expecting—"

"Lea!" Johanna said, stepping in front of her brother and offering her hands to Oleanna.

"Hanna," Oleanna smiled. "I didn't see you at the party."

"Mother was punishing me for—oh, something," Johanna said, grinning.

"I'm not surprised. You were always the first to be sent out of church for making a racket."

"Not the first," Elisabeth said, emerging from the farmhouse. "Second. After me."

Johanna laughed. "We've brought you something."

From behind his back, Jakob produced a delicate silver crown. With a small bow, he handed it to Elisabeth. "It was my grandmother's," he said quietly.

Elisabeth looked, wide-eyed, from the crown to Jakob and back. "Does your mother know—"

"I told her I was taking it for you to borrow," Johanna said.

Oleanna leaned in, squinting at the fine detail on the tips of each flowering leaf of the crown. "It's beautiful."

"Thank you," Elisabeth whispered. She reached out to caress Jakob's cheek, but he smiled and stepped away. He bowed and said, "We'll collect you at 1:30 tomorrow."

"I thought we were meeting at the church," Elisabeth said.

"You need a proper procession," he smiled.

Oleanna glanced at Elisabeth who, to her amusement, was blushing. "I'm sorry there's no party tonight," Oleanna said. "I didn't think anyone would come."

"Don't mind that," Johanna said. "It just makes tomorrow better. Come on, Jakob. You have a busy day and night tomorrow."

Oleanna laughed. "See you in the morning," she said over her shoulder, pushing the door open with her foot. She set the crown gently on the table next to the cake.

A few moments later, Elisabeth pushed open the door. "Well, I didn't expect that," she said, fingering the delicate silverwork.

"He's got a good heart."

Elisabeth nodded but didn't turn around. "Where did Torjus get to?"

"Up at the sæter I think."

"I'll go get him," Elisabeth said.

"I can go."

"No, I'd like the walk."

"I'll tidy up."

Elisabeth turned around. "Thank you," she said, opening the door and stepping back out into the evening air. Oleanna closed the door behind her and in the darkened room, fingered the delicate wrought leaves of the silver crown.

The next morning, Torjus bounded out of bed when the first hint of light touched the mountains across the lake. "It's time, it's time!" he hollered, launching himself out of bed, racing across to the door.

"What time is it?" Elisabeth mumbled.

Oleanna sat up on her elbows and squinted at the clock above the fireplace. "Three-thirty."

"Torjus," Elisabeth groaned. "Get back into bed."

He allowed them another hour's sleep, but the excitement and the sunlight were too much for him, and they were soon sitting side by side before the fire, sipping coffee and willing themselves awake.

Oleanna tried to keep Elisabeth occupied throughout the long morning: checking and double checking the food, dressing Torjus, then sending Torjus out of the farmhouse so Elisabeth could have a soak in the tub.

Finally, Elisabeth and Oleanna changed into their best dresses, the embroidered skirts and vests they'd worn only a month before for the Constitution Day party. As Elisabeth buttoned her vest with a shaking hand, Oleanna tilted her head. "Something's missing," she muttered, tapping her lips with her finger.

Suddenly, she knelt down and pulled open the bottom drawer of the dresser; buried beneath her last weaving was her mother's sølje brooch. She stood and pinned it at the neck of Elisabeth's blouse. "That's better," she said stepping back. "Protection and memory."

"Thank you," Elisabeth said quietly.

Oleanna picked up the crown and placed it on Elisabeth's head. She tied the two red ribbons under Elisabeth's chin, then stepped back to admire her work. Wide-eyed and pale, Elisabeth looked like a child playing at dress-up. "There," Oleanna said. "How do you feel?"

Elisabeth took a deep breath and set her jaw.

"You look beautiful."

Suddenly, Elisabeth's face broke into a wide grin. "I'm ready," she said, walking past Oleanna and out into the sunshine, where the crown sparkled and shone.

Oleanna paused on the threshold, watching Elisabeth, slim and fair, looking like an elven queen. And now she's leaving me too, Oleanna thought with a sigh, following her out the door.

Moments later, the droning sound of a fiddle reached them from just beyond the treeline. They looked at each other and laughed. "Who is that?" Oleanna asked, shielding her eyes to peer into the forest.

Torjus stopped his circuits around the table and ran, crookedly, towards the sound. A few moments later, a fiddler emerged, tow-headed and grinning. "Bjarne!" Elisabeth said, laughing. Jakob's younger brother led the way out of the dark of the trees, Torjus dancing alongside, Jakob and Johanna walking behind and grinning. Oleanna and Elisabeth walked out to meet them, laughing.

"You can't have a procession to the church without music," Bjarne said, leaning in and kissing a laughing Elisabeth on the cheek. He leaned in to kiss Oleanna and she smacked him gently on the cheek. "Keep dreaming."

He grinned and played a little melody on the fiddle. "Can't blame me for trying."

Johanna stepped in front of her younger brother and hooked arms with Oleanna. "He insisted on coming. Mother was furious!" she laughed. "Jakob wanted to bring the wagon, but I told him it would be much more fun to walk!"

"But how—" Oleanna started.

"We'll trundle home in it after the ceremony," Johanna said, spinning Oleanna.

Jakob held his hand out to Elisabeth. "Are you ready?"

Bjarne's fiddle quietened, and Johanna's giddy laughter faded away. After a few moments, Elisabeth nodded.

He offered her his arm, and she took it, glancing back at Oleanna with a grin.

Bjarne whooped and put the fiddle back under his chin, half-dancing toward the trail through the forest. Jakob and Elisabeth fell into step behind him, Oleanna and Johanna bringing up the rear, holding tight to Torjus' hands.

Though Søren was stiff and businesslike throughout the ceremony, which both embarrassed Oleanna and made her cross, the following hours passed in a merry blur. The wedding party returned to the farm by the lakeside in Jakob's wagon, his pony festooned with flowers.

The newly married couple was offered the ale bowl, and there was feasting on cheese and bread, pickles and salmon, potatoes and fiskeboller. The wedding cake was passed around, along with the akevitt, and then a giddy attempt to dance off the crown and pass it to Johanna, the next girl to be married, ended with Johanna red-faced and breathless.

Bjarne pulled Oleanna into a dance while the others laughed and clapped, and she let herself be spun around, dizzy with exhaustion and akevitt, while Torjus spun in his own circles around them. After a few minutes, Bjarne tripped to a stop and Oleanna tumbled to the grass, panting and laughing.

She watched Bjarne and Torjus caper together in the tall grass. The sky was painted pink, casting the ragged tops of the mountains in alpenglow. The fingers of white glacier and lingering spring snow snaked down the sides of the mountains toward the water, and in the distance, she could see a twirling writhe of bonfire smoke from a distant valley.

The sound of another fiddle tuning and starting a merry tune floated to them from across the lake, and the scent of lilac and pine suffused the night air. She leaned back and cradled her head in her hands. Perhaps this is what heaven is like, she thought, closing her eyes with a happy sigh.

After a few moments, she heard Bjarne and Torjus' trampling and laughing growing closer. Suddenly, someone nudged her side with his boot. "Come on, sleepyhead," Bjarne said with a laugh. "Get up."

She opened her eyes and grinned up at him. "You are a troublemaker, Bjarne Evenson."

He laughed. "Get up."

"You're worse than Torjus."

"You don't know the half of it."

Oleanna laughed and sat up.

"I forgot, this came for you up in Skei," Bjarne said, pulling an envelope from his vest. He dropped it from a height, watching it flutter toward her. "I told the fellow at the post office I'd bring it to you."

She grabbed it before the coming night breeze from the lake could flutter it away. "Who is it—"

Before she could glance at the envelope, Bjarne grabbed her hand, pulling her up and spinning her again. Stumbling, she shoved the envelope into her apron pocket before it flew out of her hand.

Torjus joined in, and then Johanna again, and their dance turned into a particularly exuberant game of snap the whip, both Johanna and Bjarne ending up tumbling in the grass, laughing. Elisabeth called for another round of akevitt. The envelope remained, forgotten, in Oleanna's pocket.

Late in the evening, when the last hints of light disappeared from the sky, Bjarne and Johanna finally stood from the table. Elisabeth and Jakob sat side by side, holding hands, while Oleanna kept an eye on an animated Torjus, who had no intention of growing sleepy or slowing down.

"We had better be going," Johanna said, walking a little unsteadily.

"Mother will be wondering what terrible accident has happened."

"She'll be furious," Bjarne said, grinning broadly.

"I'll talk with her," Jakob said. "I'll—"

"Oh, I think you have more important things to worry about at the moment," Bjarne said.

Jakob laughed, shaking his head.

"I'm so glad we're really sisters now," Johanna said, leaning in and kissing Elisabeth on the cheek.

Elisabeth blushed and looked more shy than Oleanna had ever seen. "And me," Elisabeth said.

Oleanna smiled, though her eyes prickled with tears.

Bjarne picked up his fiddle and played a slow, languorous tune, half lullaby and half fairy tale. "Come on, Hanna," he said, wandering away. Johanna kissed Jakob on the top of the head, and with a last look, turned around and followed Bjarne.

Torjus ran to meet them, weaving around their feet as they wandered up the hill. Johanna stopped first, turning back and waving at Oleanna. "Torjus, go back to your other auntie now. Go on. We'll see you soon, Lea."

"Goodbye!" Oleanna called, as Torjus tore past her, toward the farmhouse.

Bjarne blew her a kiss and she shook her head. "Go!" she called, laughing.

And finally, Bjarne and Johanna turned away and took leave of the tiny Myklebost farm, disappearing back into the dark forest from which they came.

Oleanna watched them leave, smiling and waving, trying hard to keep her feet and keep her head from spinning. When she could hear no more of Bjarne's fiddle, she turned and set her shoulders. "Torjus," she called. He was helping himself to another piece of wedding cake. "Come help me, please." He hesitated and she put her hands on her hips. "Now."

He grabbed the piece of cake and, smooshing it in his hand, wandered up the hill.

"We need to clear the dishes. Help me, quick as you can."

Shoving the rest of the cake in his mouth, he nodded and, without a word, raced back down the hill. She followed him and together they hauled the remains of their feast to the store house, to be dealt with in the morning.

Elisabeth and Jakob were wandering along the lakeshore by the time Oleanna and Torjus had finished their work. "We're going up to the sæter," Oleanna called from beside the farmhouse. Elisabeth nodded and they steered their path back toward them.

"Why?" Torjus whined, tugging on Oleanna's hand.

"Your mama and papa need to be alone."

"Why?"

"They just do."

"I don't want to go," Torjus said, starting to cry.

Jakob picked him up. "It's just for tonight."

"No," Torjus cried. "Don't make me go away."

"We'll come back tomorrow," Oleanna said.

"I'll see you tomorrow," Jakob said, setting him down on the ground. "I promise."

Elisabeth knelt down and kissed Torjus on the top of the head.

"We'll see you late tomorrow morning," Oleanna said, pulling Elisabeth into a hug.

"Thank you," Elisabeth said.

"Yes, thank you," Jakob echoed.

Oleanna released Elisabeth, then reached up and kissed Jakob on the cheek. "Have a nice evening," she grinned, then turned to Torjus. "Come with me, little man. Let's go up to the sæter and light our midsummer's eve fire."

"Our what?" he asked, his eyes wide.

"St. John's bonfire," she said, taking him by the hand and leading him away. "We send away the evil spirits tonight."

"How?"

"We build a great fire and let the flames and the wind take the bad spirits away."

"Ohhh."

She held tight to his hand and walked into the forest, striking the trail to the sæter, marked out by the tall stand of pink foxgloves. He turned to look behind him and she squeezed his hand. "Can you name all the birds in the forest?" she asked.

He looked up at her. "All of them?"

She nodded. "I'll bet you can. Here, I'll start. Goldcrest."

"Lark."

"Good," she said. He pulled his hand from hers and ran ahead into the forest, calling out names of birds, and animals not remotely resembling birds.

Mental and physical exhaustion caught up with her, and she fell behind, Torjus' voice fading and distant, a breeze caught in the treetops. It was dark under the trees, and the desire to sink down at the base of a swaying fir pulled at every limb. But she pressed on, gathering kindling as she went, naming the flowers and the plants, the trees and the birds. Naming everything but the melancholy, the bitter and the sweet wreathing her heart.

She suddenly remembered, with a start, the envelope in her apron pocket. She pulled it out, squinting at the faint writing in the dark under the trees. Though it was close to her eyes, she couldn't read much more than her name. With a frustrated grunt, she put the envelope back in her pocket and pressed on up the hill.

Near the edge of the forest, at the top of the hill, she could hear Torjus calling for her. "Lea, Lea, come on!" he cried. "What are you waiting for?"

An hour later, after chasing each other around the open meadow, gathering more kindling, clearing high grass, and searching the cabin for the tinderbox, the bonfire crackled in the purpling night. They sat together, watching the flames dance, their backs to the Sognefjord.

"Where do the wraiths go?" Torjus asked after a few minutes.

"Hmmm?"

"Are the wraiths here right now?" he asked, scooting closer to her.

She put an arm around him. "No, not now that we have the fire going."

"Where do they go?"

"Hm?"

"Where do the wraiths go?"

"Oh. Well, where do you think they go?"

"Søren says they go to hell."

Oleanna scowled. "Søren," she huffed. "Well, what do you think?"

"I think they go into the lake."

Oleanna shuddered, then pulled him close.

He pondered for a moment. "Was bestemor?"

"Was she what?"

"A wraith?" he asked in an impossibly small voice.

"Oh, little man," she said, kissing him on the head. "She was a lot of things, but she is definitely not a bad spirit."

"Good," he yawned.

She kissed him again and said quietly, "Do you still have your violets?"

He nodded and pulled a crumpled wad out of his vest pocket. Oleanna picked up her own carefully gathered wood violet and held it up. "Think of the things that make you sad," she said quietly.

Torjus screwed up his face, a pout creeping in.

"When you throw your violets on the fire, it will burn up those sad thoughts and carry them away on the wind."

He stood and with great ceremony threw his flowers into the flames, where they crackled and were quickly gone.

"Well done," she said.

"Now you," he said, reaching down and tugging on her hand to stand up. "You have a lot of sad thoughts."

She half-laughed, then quickly sobered. "You're right," she said, standing. After a moment, she tossed the wood violet onto the fire and watched the tiny slip of silver smoke twist up and then out across the meadow, and disappear.

Oleanna looked down at Torjus, who was watching her intently. "Thank you, little man," she said. "Now it's time for you to go to bed. Come on." She took his small hand and they walked up to the cabin.

"Who made the flowers?" he asked with a yawn, crawling, still clothed, under the covers.

"No, no, you must take your good clothes off first," Oleanna said, pulling back the coverlet. He did as he was told, and she folded the embroidered short pants and vest neatly on the chair.

"Who made the flowers?" he asked again.

"Anders," she said quietly, looking around at the rosemaling on the mantelpiece.

"I like him."

Oleanna smiled. "Me too."

Torjus crawled over to the far side of the bed, and curled into a ball. "G'night," he mumbled, and in less than a moment, was fast asleep.

She grabbed the spare coverlet and walked back outside, shutting the cabin door quietly behind her. The fire still crackled and the sky was shot with gold around the edges. She walked down the slight hill and stood before the fire, the coverlet warm around her shoulders.

The smoke drifted with the shifting of the night wind, now to the south and the west, toward the long fjord and the wide sea that she'd never seen. She sunk to the ground, sitting cross-legged and huddled under the coverlet, and wondered yet again where Anders was. She stared into the fire, her eyes growing unfocused.

What a long few days it had been. The image of Elisabeth, blushing and quiet in the church made her laugh, and the joy on their faces as Bjarne led them back to the farm made her heart skip. It's so easy for Elisabeth, she thought, pulling the coverlet closer about her shoulders. Say the word, and the world drops what it's doing to help her, to fall at her feet.

Oleanna sighed. That's unfair, she thought, plucking a handful of grass and braiding it together. She watched the last streaks of color and light leave the sky, and in their wake, broad pathways of mottled stars. She fingered the grass braid, listening to the dying crackling of the fire. The circular arguments commenced: Could I leave? I can't leave. Why did he leave? Why can't I? Elisabeth needs me. Or does she?

Nearly an hour later, exhausted and cold, she sat up and sighed. The last flicker of firelight disappeared, and she stood, stretching her back and shivering. She kicked the fire out, realizing too late she was not in her work boots, but her best pair of buckled shoes and hose. She jumped back and cursed under her breath.

Oleanna bent down and pulled off her shoes, then walked back up to the cabin, where Torjus snuffled quietly in his sleep. She took off her vest and her hose and laid them on the chair. After a moment's hesitation, she reached out and trailed her fingertips along the rosemal acanthus leaves on the mantelpiece. As the moon rose, the room grew more bright, and she could study Anders' work closely for the first time. Though the brushwork was delicate and precise, the colors were bold. She tilted her head and smiled, tracing the same leaf over and over along the edge. I will never hurt you, he said. She closed her eyes, leaning her head against her hand.

Oleanna wiped the tears from her cheeks and glanced over at Torjus. After the whirlwind of the last few days, the reality of the change in her life finally hit her. Jakob had moved in; his things were in the wagon, his horse stabled with old Terna.

It was at that moment she remembered again the envelope in her pocket. Lighting a lantern, she peered at the handwriting and unfamiliar stamp. She opened the envelope and shook out the first piece of paper; a handful of ten kroner notes fluttered to the floor. She picked them up and her eyes widened.

Dearest Lea,

I'm sorry it's taken so long to write. I'm sure you've forgotten about me already! The voyage has been long, but I'm finally in New York. I'm going to post this before I get on the train. I've been here for a few days. It's loud and dirty, nothing like home. I think I might like it. You could lose yourself and your worries in these crowds.

I hope you're well, and Lisbet and Torjus. How are the crops coming along? I think by the time you get this it will be time to start pulling some of those onions.

I'm taking a long time to write this, as I hesitate to write the next line. Lea, I think you should come to America. Elisabeth can handle the farm. If she can't, well, she can sell the farm and maybe come to America too. Anton has plenty of room for all of us, and I know you at least aren't afraid of hard work.

I'm enclosing enough money for your ferry fare to Bergen. There is a steamer leaving for Liverpool from Bergen on June 28, and there should be enough here for you to make the trip to Liverpool if you're very frugal, though I think you should sell mama's brooch and some other things to afford the passage to New York, and the train. I'm enclosing another sheet with the information you need on the steamers, and how to take the train to Anton's farm in North Dakota.

If you don't come, keep the money and use it for the farm. Whatever it is you decide, please write me back (care of Anton's farm) and let me know. All I ask is that you don't ask me how I got the money.

I miss you and Lisbet and Torjus terribly. It will be good to see Anton, though. Did you know he has a son already?

Please write soonest and let me know your decision.

Your brother,

John

"Oh John," Oleanna breathed. "What have you done?"

# CHAPTER THIRTEEN

Lake Jølster, Sunnfjord, Norway
June 1905

SHE WAS PALE AND SHAKING with lack of sleep and overwrought nerves by the time Torjus finally woke the next morning. Oleanna sat on the step of the cabin, watching the goat and sheep scampering in the early morning sunshine. Her decision was made during the long hours of pre-dawn and dawn, while Torjus snuffled in his sleep.

"Lea?" he said, pulling the door wide and yawning.

"Good morning," she smiled, and he climbed into her lap. "Did you sleep well?"

"Mmmhmmm," he said, burying his face in her arm.

"Good. We should go back to the farm soon. Are you hungry?"

"No."

"Well, we should go back anyway. We need to milk the goat first, though. Can you help me?"

He nodded sleepily and stood up, rubbing his eyes with his little fists.

They chased the goat around the meadow, laughing and exasperated, and finally succeeded in getting a bucket's worth. "Can you carry this?" she asked handing him the splintery bucket.

He tried, but staggered a bit under its weight. "Here," she said, taking it from him and settling it on the step of the cabin. She pushed open the door and gathered their discarded fine shoes and, at the last moment, the dog-eared atlas. She pulled the door shut behind her and handed Torjus his vest and jacket. "I need you to carry something very important," she said, pulling her own vest on.

He looked up at her, eyes wide, small hands outstretched.

Oleanna smiled and placed the atlas in his arms. "Do you know what that is?"

"A book!" he crowed.

"Yes. Be very careful with it while we go through the forest. When we get home, I want you to put it in my dresser drawer, quick as you can. Can you do that?"

He nodded and clasped it to his small chest. Oleanna picked up the sloshing bucket of goat's milk. "Are you ready to go see your mama and papa?" she smiled, though her heart constricted.

"Yes, yes, yes!" he said, spinning a couple of circles and then bolting away toward the forest. Oleanna laughed, then took a deep breath. The sæter was so beautiful this morning, the meadow soft and the sky blue and the glacier forgotten. She set her jaw and, without a backward glance, headed straight for the forest herself.

"Mama!" She could hear Torjus hollering, his tiny voice echoing. Oleanna winced and continued on, emerging from the forest only having lost a few inches of milk from the bucket, and luckily not onto her best skirt, though she had half-slept in it.

"What are you doing up?" she spluttered, seeing Elisabeth and Jakob already at work, clearing the last of the dishes from the feast, Elisabeth with an armful of linens.

Elisabeth looked up and grinned. "Good morning!"

Jakob nodded and smiled on his way to the store house.

"It's nearly eight," Elisabeth said, meeting Oleanna and walking with her to the store house as well. "We've been up for hours. Well, all night, really," she grinned.

Oleanna laughed.

"Did Torjus behave?"

"Fell asleep before the fire burned out."

Elisabeth stopped before they reached the store house and Oleanna stuttered to a stop, nearly spilling more milk. "Thank you for last night, and for yesterday."

"Don't be silly," Oleanna said, shrugging. "You would do the same for me."

"Maybe," Elisabeth said, then walked the last few steps to the store house.

They spent the rest of the morning setting the farm back to rights after the small feast, along with their daily chores. Oleanna tried to convince them to take the day off and rest, to enjoy the warm lilac-scented breeze and blue skies, but Jakob insisted on delving into the accounts and the planting schedule.

"What's wrong with you?" Elisabeth said at mid-day, narrowing her eyes.

"What?" Oleanna said, looking away.

"You've been skittish all morning."

"Have I?"

"What's going on?"

"Nothing," Oleanna shrugged. "Just tired. Didn't sleep last night."

Elisabeth looked at her askance. "Something's going on."

At that moment, Jakob emerged from the store house, rubbing his eyes and stretching. Torjus clung to his leg, and Jakob looked down with a grin and took a few strides, dragging Torjus along with him. "We're going fishing," he said, nodding down at his son. "We'll be back shortly."

Elisabeth untied her apron. "I'm coming, too."

Oleanna looked at them, her heart pounding. "That's too many people in the boat," she said, the words sticking in her throat. "It's too dangerous."

"I'll protect them," Jakob said. "I promise."

"Take a nap, Lea," Elisabeth said, taking Jakob's hand. "You need some rest, I think."

Oleanna nodded and watched them away, around the corner to where they tied their small boat, out of her sight. She looked around the farm: the sunlight bright on the lilac, and the pine forest, and the swaying birches, and the little vegetable patch, and old Terna, eating grass up near the stables. Her heart skipped, but she set her jaw, and stepped into the dark farmhouse.

The atlas was in her drawer in the dresser, and she pulled it out, sitting on the bed and flipping to the pages showing the tall mountains and the long fjord between their little lake and Bergen. She glanced around the room; already, Jakob's hat and shaving cup sat on the mantelpiece, just as John's had, just as her father's had. Oleanna, heart pounding, stood and began pulling clothes from the dresser.

She didn't have any fancy dresses like the women in the big cities wore; her plain woolen skirt and linen shirtwaists would have to do. Eschewing John's boots for her best buckled shoes, she gathered her things and carried them to the store house. She kicked the door open and set her things on the long worktable.

Along the far wall, where they kept the linens and winter clothes, was an embroidered canvas bag, brought to their mother by their uncle from Bergen many years before. "It will have to do," Oleanna muttered. She opened it, and found in the depths a yellowed sheet of paper: her uncle's last address in Bergen. Maybe she was thinking of leaving, too, she thought, an idea which both heartened and saddened her.

After a few minutes, her packing was done and she leaned against the long worktable. The herbs had dried and were ready for the dyeing vat. She picked up a handful and smelled, the scent woody and warm. She smiled, and put some into the bag with the rest of her things.

She put the bag under the worktable and walked out, wandering over to the barn where Terna chewed the grass. "Hello, my love," she whispered, running the tips of her fingers along his short mane. The fjord pony nuzzled into her arm, making soft whinnying noises. "I know. I'll miss you, too," she whispered.

Oleanna walked back to the store house and retrieved her bag from under the worktable. She reached up and re-braided her hair, patting the errant wisps back into place, then set her shoulders and after the slightest pause, pushed the door open.

"Oof," she said, colliding with Jakob.

"I'm sorry," he said, holding her shoulders to steady her.

"What are you doing here?" she asked, holding the bag behind her back.

"I forgot the net." He narrowed his eyes. "Why do you have a bag?"

Oleanna colored. "It's—"

He stepped back and folded his arms. "You don't have to leave because I'm here, you know," he said quietly.

Her eyes widened. "It's not—"

"There's plenty of room for all of us."

"It's not that."

"This farm belongs to you, too."

"I—I'm going to Bergen," she said in a rush.

"What?"

"John sent me money. To go to America."

Jakob's eyes widened. "He did?"

She nodded.

"And you're going?"

"Please don't tell Lisbet."

He laughed. "Of course I have to tell her. She'll notice you're missing."

"Tell her," Oleanna said, shaking her head, "I don't know. Tell her I went to find Anders."

"Are you?"

"Am I what?"

"Going to find Samuelsson?"

"No. He left me. He made his choice. I'm going to America. I'll get to Bergen, and then...oh, I don't know. Jakob, you have to understand. I have to go now, or I will never go." She reached out and grabbed his arm. "If I don't go now, right this moment while I have my courage up, I will never leave this farm. Ever." She dropped her shaking hand; her heart thudded wildly.

"I'll drive you to Vadheim."

"No!" Oleanna said, stepping back.

Jakob's eyebrows shot up.

"It's not—that's kind of you—I just—"

"How are you going to get there?"

"I'll walk."

"Let me drive you in the wagon. It will take less than a day."

"No," she said, shaking her head vigorously. "No. I won't take you away from Lisbet, even for a day. You've waited too long."

"It's just a day," he laughed.

"No. I'm not going to argue about it anymore."

Jakob smiled. "You and Lisbet are very much alike."

She smiled. "Don't tell them for a while, please. Please."

"I won't. They'll miss you, you know. So will I," he said. "I was looking forward to many merry evenings with you, and Bjarne and Johanna."

Oleanna nodded, and then, to her surprise, and Jakob's, began to cry. Jakob reached a tentative hand and patted her awkwardly on the shoulder. Eventually, she wiped her eyes with her sleeve. "Take care of them, and the farm. Don't ever leave them."

"I won't leave them, ever. I promise."

"Thank you," she said, offering her hand.

He shook it smartly, then leaned in and kissed her on the cheek. "Good luck," he said.

She looked down and checked the fastenings on her bag. Taking a deep breath, she began to cry again. "Don't tell Torjus for a while," she whispered through shaky sobs. "Tell him I'm at the sæter." She looked up at him. "Please."

Jakob nodded. "Are you sure about this?"

She laughed and cried at the same time. "No."

"You must promise to write when you get to Bergen. And all along your journey. Promise me. Lisbet will be heartbroken if you don't."

She sniffled and nodded. "I promise. I have to go now, or your talk will make me change my mind again."

After a moment, he said, "Do you know how to get to Vadheim?"

"Past the Sanddal farm, follow the road south."

"Be careful."

"I know how to take care of myself."

"You're a woman alone," he shrugged. "You must be very careful."

"I know how to take care of myself."

He tilted his head. "Don't be too proud to ask for help along the way."

She nodded.

"Good luck, Oleanna."

"Goodbye," she said, squaring her shoulders again. With a deep breath, she walked past Jakob and down the hill, toward the south, along the road upon which nearly everyone she loved had vanished.

As she rounded the corner, the urge to look back seized her, and she stuttered to a stop. She stood, hesitating, fingers gripping the bag until they were white. "Go now, go now, go now," she whispered. Is this how John felt, and Anders? she thought. Did they pause here, looking out at the lake, with the scent of lilac on the air, and the sounds of the farm behind them? Did they have this urge to drop their bag, to run back, to never think of leaving again? "Damn you, John," she muttered.

Go now.

Oleanna stumbled forward, and had reached the stand of birch at the edge of the lake where she and Anders had talked after her illness, only weeks ago. "Keep going," she whispered.

She kept walking, though her heart pounded her hands shook. "Keep going, keep going, keep going," she whispered. And then, all at once, she came upon the elves' wood, the graves of her mother and sister. "I'm sorry," she said.

Oleanna ran full out, the bag bouncing against her leg, until she had nearly reached the Sanddal farm. She stopped and bent over, her lungs burning, and chanced a look behind her: no spirits, no one chasing after her, dragging her back.

She trudged along the path that turned into the road past Førde, on the way to Vadheim. She carried the bag in both arms, hugging it to her chest; dust from the road where she'd dragged it clung to her shirt and trickles of sweat dampened her collar. The road wasn't heavily traveled, and the first wagon that trundled by caused her to scurry off the road and hide in the cover of the trees.

Oleanna scolded herself for silliness, but the feeling that she did not want to speak with anyone, at least not just yet, was strong. She needed to focus on moving forward, one step after another. If she looked side to side, if the spell was broken by an unfamiliar voice, she would lose her nerve and give in to the strong impulse to run all the way back to the farm.

The tiny road cutting through the thick forest was dark, impenetrable, the sky high above bright, but only guessed at under the branches. She stumbled along the deep ruts, weary, forcing one step at a time, eyes on her feet. She rounded a bend and suddenly the forest was lit with a strange illumination, as if the ground itself was glowing.

After a few steps, she looked up and was saw a city in the distance, gleaming yellow with what she assumed was electric light. She dropped her bag and sagged against a tree; the reality of what she'd done was suddenly very clear. The adrenaline ebbed away and left hunger, thirst, and mental and physical exhaustion. She slid down the tree and sat at its base, face in her hands.

She woke when the first streaks of light appeared above the trees. The trees were the same, and the sky, but she realized with a jolt where she was and shuddered. "Sleeping next to the road, what was I thinking?" she muttered, standing and brushing the dirt and leaves from her skirt and her hair. Her stomach gave an almighty growl and she closed her eyes with a sigh. No food, no water, no map, little money. She walked a few paces into the road, heading back toward the farm.

Oleanna stopped and closed her eyes. "I can't go back now," she whispered. "I can't. There's nothing left for me there." After a deep breath, she opened her eyes, turned around, and after another moment's hesitation, started the long walk down the road she hoped would take her to Vadheim.

# CHAPTER FOURTEEN

The Sognefjord, Norway
June 1905

THE LITTLE PORT TOWN OF VADHEIM, a collection of twenty white, red, and sky blue houses, was perched over the deep Sognefjord, clinging to the steep mountainside that tumbled toward the water. The fjord was darker and broader than Oleanna had imagined in her dreams at the sæter those many miles away. The water was so blue it was nearly black, the depths only guessed at, though she thought perhaps the fjord was as deep as the mountain behind her was tall.

She sat on a boulder at the side of the road, watching the town and its few inhabitants walk between the tiny homes and smaller farmsteads, tiptoeing along the narrow line of meadow grass along the water's edge. The mountains were taller here; the sun struggled to break free of the jagged ring of rock, though she knew it had risen hours before, illuminating her way past Førde and then south, to this spot.

Her stomach growled again, and Oleanna grimaced, but she did not move from her perch. Perhaps there was a place to buy some food in that small town, like the small general store away in Skei, but she was reluctant to move from her spot, despite the gnawing in her stomach. Where would the ferry dock? And when? From her place on the hillside, she could keep an eye on the town and the port.

She pulled her feet up onto the rock and hugged her knees. "What am I doing here?" she whispered. "What have I done?" At that moment, the bell on the tiny white church, tucked gently in a fold of the rocky mountainside, began to toll. The remaining residents of Vadheim emerged from their homes and wandered toward the church, and Oleanna looked again up at the sun. "Services? Today?"

The thought intrigued her. She watched the crowd grow at the door of the church, wondering at their dress, and the fact that none of the women wore the pointed caps so common in Jølster. The view, at once so familiar and so strange, made her heart constrict.

She imagined Jakob getting ready for church, because certainly he would insist that they go. She smiled, imagining Elisabeth's reaction and Torjus' wriggling energy confined to a back pew. And then she imagined Jakob telling Elisabeth and Torjus, perhaps right at that moment, what she'd done. "They'll be fine," she whispered, over and over.

Despite her misgivings, she scrambled off the boulder, dragging the bag with her, and struck the road again, moving forward, moving forward.

When she reached the water's edge, she found she was not the only one waiting for the ferry. An older woman in an elaborate feathered hat and a dove gray washed silk dress stood in front of what appeared to be a café, shuttered and dark. She glanced up at Oleanna and raised an eyebrow, then returned to her perusal of the closed restaurant.

Oleanna looked down at herself: mud on the hem of her skirt, her brother's work boots, undoubtedly leaves in her hair and dark circles under her eyes. She laughed, and the woman looked up sharply. "When does this café open?" the woman demanded.

"Oh," Oleanna said, shrugging. "I have no idea. I've never been here." She cocked her head, wondering where the woman was from with that outlandish accent.

"It is ridiculous that there is nothing open, when there is a ferry that will be docking soon. Is everyone in this part of Sogn so irresponsible?"

"I expect they're all at church," Oleanna shrugged.

"Well, I'm starving." The woman looked at her, hands on her hips.

Oleanna suppressed a laugh. "Me too," she said.

The woman gaped, then laughed, a deep-bellied guffaw that echoed around the hills. She walked over to Oleanna, shaking her head. "I'm sorry, I'm just nervous and hungry, and evidently, that makes me rude." She offered her hand. "I'm Gjertrud Moe. From Ålesund."

"Oleanna Tollefsdatter Myklebost. From Jølster."

Gjertrud cocked her head, hands on her hips again. "Do you know Nikolai Astrup?" she asked.

"Who?"

Gjertrud smiled, though Oleanna could tell she suspected her slow. "The painter. He grew up along your lake, in Ålhus."

Oleanna waved her hand. "Oh, Ålhus. That's across the lake."

"One of his paintings was just accepted into the collection at the National Gallery."

Oleanna nodded sagely, though she had no idea who Astrup was. Elisabeth would know, she thought. After a moment, she said, "Do you know when the ferry is supposed to arrive?"

Gjertrud pulled out a gleaming pocket watch. "In less than half an hour, if my watch is correct, and it always is."

Oleanna's heart fluttered; she turned and looked back at the road, the path back home. No wraiths pursued her down to the water's edge, but she shivered nonetheless. What am I doing? she wondered for the hundredth time.

"You look green. Come sit down," Gjertrud said, taking Oleanna firmly under the arm, and leading her to a bench near the café. "There, that's better," she said, eyeing Oleanna. "Where are you going?"

"Bergen. For now."

"Yes," the woman smiled indulgently. "But where in Bergen?"

"Oh." How big could it be? "I—I don't know." Oleanna reached into her bag and pulled out the crumpled piece of paper with her uncle's address. "Fjellgaten, I suppose."

"Are you going to take a position as a maid?"

Oleanna dropped her hand and looked at Gjertrud. "Why would you think that?"

"That is often why women your age leave the country."

"Women my age," Oleanna whispered, then shrugged. Anders' face, never far from her mind's eye, returned, and her heart clenched. What if he comes back and I've gone? No, but he's left me. He's not coming back.

"You are looking unwell again," Gjertrud said, taking Oleanna's hand. "Flushed."

"I'm fine, really."

The half-hour wait for the ferry was filled with Gjertrud's monologue about the sorry state of education in Sunnfjord, and the split from Sweden, and her kind but stupid husband, whom she'd left to tend the general store they owned. Oleanna nodded and smiled at the right times, but let the words flow over her, wondering if she could find Anders in a city as big as Bergen, and wondering if she should even try.

She saw and smelled the belching black smoke before she saw the ferry itself. Oleanna reflexively covered her mouth and nose. "Is that the ferry?" she mumbled from behind her hand.

"Yes, and right on time," Gjertrud said, standing up brushing off her dress. "Are you feeling better now?"

Oleanna nodded though the stench of the smoke made her gag.

The sounding of the ferry's horn signaled the end of services at the little church. As the boat came into view from the east, the town's inhabitants appeared, in pairs and in groups, until the tiny strip of land was filled with people, talking and laughing, all straining for a look at the boat.

Oleanna hung back and was soon separated from Gjertrud, who chatted happily with anyone who would listen. Oleanna clutched her bag to her chest, watching the crowd and the ferry's noisy approach with apprehension. The ship's crew tossed long ropes to men standing on the quay, then let down a narrow, rickety plank. A man with a large canvas mailbag sauntered down the gangway, followed by a mother with three children, who were welcomed by a large family. Gjertrud called up to one of the crewmen, who came down and helped her with her large trunk. Halfway up the gangway, she looked back over the heads of the crowd. When she spotted Oleanna she waved her hand.

Oleanna closed her eyes, frozen to the spot. "John, what have you done to me?" she whispered, her heart pounding, breath coming in short gasps. She clutched her bag tightly, then with a deep breath, opened her eyes. "It's now or never," she muttered, and took a shaky step forward.

She broke into an ungainly run, forcing herself forward without thinking. She reached the deck of the ferry, breathless, before she realized where she was: on a boat, in deep water. The world grew fuzzy around the edges, until she felt a strong hand close around her wrist. "Come along." Oleanna forced herself to focus, and followed Gjertrud into the passenger's seating area. "You'd best make yourself comfortable, my dear. It's a long ride."

Much to her surprise, it took Oleanna only a few minutes to get her sea legs, and soon she realized the grinding in her stomach was not nausea but hunger. Leaving her bag with Gjertrud, who was regaling a small man in wire-rimmed spectacles with her well-worn tale about her husband, Oleanna took her first tentative steps toward the small café counter.

She stepped up to the counter and hesitated, chewing her lip.

The young man turned to look at her and smiled. "What can I get for you, madam?"

"I'm starving," she said, flushing as soon as the words left her mouth.

"One of everything, then?" he smiled.

Oleanna smiled in return, and released the grip she'd had on the counter. "What do you think is good?"

"I'm partial to the brown bread and cheese, myself."

"Oh, yes, I'll have that," she said, relieved to find something so familiar. "And a cup of strong coffee, if you have it." She leaned against the counter.

"Of course. If you'd like to pay now," he said, smiling kindly, "I can bring you a tray in a moment."

"Oh," she said, pulling out a bill. "Thank you."

He set her change on the counter and nodded toward the windows behind her. "The table there has the best view."

"Thank you," she said, flushing again and walking, still a bit unsteadily, toward the table. She sat down in the chair, her head spinning, and looked out the window at the passing mountains.

A few minutes later, the young man appeared with her tray. "Will there be anything else, madam?"

Oleanna shook her head. "No, thank you—oh!" she said.

He turned back.

"Do you have any paper?"

He nodded and returned a few moments later with a handful of sheets marked *MS Solundir*, and a pencil.

"Thank you," she said around a mouthful of bread.


Dearest Lisbet,

I don't know how to start this letter. I'm sure you're angry that I didn't say goodbye, but if I had, you know I wouldn't have left. I couldn't have. I suppose John knew you'd come to your senses about Jakob eventually. Maybe he knew Anders would leave. Maybe he was hoping I would choose America over Anders. I hope you're not sore that he asked me.

I'm writing to you now from the ferry to Bergen. I suppose I'm trying not to think much at all, either about you and Torjus and the farm, or Bergen, or Anders, or John and America. It is beautiful here, down on Sognefjord, though not so different from home as I thought it might be. We'll see if I lose courage when I arrive in Bergen.

You understand, don't you? Perhaps I will understand why I did this someday as well. If Anders happens to come back...well, I don't know. Tell him that he's not the only one who gets to leave, I suppose.

Oh! There's the sea... Lisbet, you would not believe how vast it is. It is so beautiful...

# CHAPTER FIFTEEN

Bergen, Norway
June 1905

THE FERRY DOCKED AT THE BRYGGEN late in the afternoon, the ever-present Bergen rain obscuring the mediaeval buildings that ringed the old wharf. As they stood on then gangway, Gjertrud pressed her address into Oleanna's hand and extracted the promise of a visit, then disappeared down into the noisy crowd milling on the docks. Her ears pounded with the sounds of ferries and fishwives, automobiles and tradesmen's wagons, people laughing, shouting, complaining.

Oleanna took a deep breath, then spluttered with the choking smoke that was an ever-present component of the rainy fog. After a moment's pause, she walked down the gangway, clutching her bag tightly to her chest.

The crowd on the dock represented more people she had seen in one place than she'd ever seen in her life, and the chaos momentarily stunned her. After a few moments, she regained her footing and hurried along the edges, unsure what direction to go, but sure she needed to get away from the throng. She reached a relatively empty sidewalk and pressed herself back against a building, trying to catch her breath. What is America going to be like? she thought, her heart sinking.

After a few minutes of trying to gain her bearings, and searching for Anders' face in every one that passed, she pushed herself away from the wall and approached what looked to be a policeman. "Pardon me," she said.

"Yes, madam?"

"I'm looking for Fjellgaten."

"Just up that way, shouldn't take you more than a half an hour if you're walking." He turned and pointed behind him, up a long street that wound into one of the many hills that ringed the harbor.

Oleanna nodded. "Thank you."

The street was steep and slick with rain, but her legs were accustomed to climbing hills and she welcomed the physical exertion. Every few minutes she turned around and looked down at the town spreading beneath her, strange and beautiful, peeking out from the fog.

After a half an hour, she reached Fjellgaten and, after minutes of searching, found what used to be her uncle's house. What am I doing here? she thought, taking a deep breath. It's been years and years. He'll never recognize me. Will I recognize him?

Oleanna stepped up to the door and knocked smartly. She stepped back and looked up and down the hilly street. Tradesmen hurried by, dodging carts pulled by huffing horses, and in the distance, the rumbling sound of an automobile. Her head began to throb.

Suddenly, the door swung open and a tiny woman in a black dress appeared. Her dark hair was styled as many women's were in Bergen, in fashionable poufs around her face, which served to set off the sharp angles of her cheekbones and the blue of her eyes, rather than the tracery of wrinkles.

The woman raised her eyebrows. "Yes?"

Oleanna cleared her throat. "Does Gunnar Johannson still live here?"

"Who's asking?"

Oleanna laughed in surprise. "You have pretty manners here in Bergen."

The woman raised an eyebrow. "And you smell like a farm."

Oleanna blinked. "And you smell like a whorehouse," she spluttered.

The woman's brows shot up; she chuckled and then grinned outright. "You must be one of Gunnar's relatives."

"Yes. How—"

"Come with me." She pulled the door open and stepped back, allowing Oleanna to pass inside. The long entryway was dark, but at the far end she could see tall windows, letting in the gray light. She stood back against the wall, gripping the handle on her bag.

The woman shut the door and laughed. "You're one of Brita's daughters," she said, brushing past Oleanna and walking down the hall.

Oleanna hesitated, then followed the woman. "Yes."

"Oleanna?"

"Yes," Oleanna said, narrowing her eyes. "Who are you?"

"Katrine," the woman said over her shoulder. "I look after your uncle."

Oleanna's eyes narrowed further. What does that mean?

Katrine led her into the bright room at the end of the hall. The tall windows looked out into a tiny back garden, dominated by a tall, spindly birch. Rather than a feeling of relief, of something green and lovely in the dirty town, it felt sad and sorry. She sighed, thinking of the sæter.

"Have a seat," Katrine said, taking the bag from Oleanna's grip. "You must be tired. Would you like a cup of coffee?"

"Oh, that would be wonderful," Oleanna said in a rush. "Just show me where the pot—"

"Don't be silly, I'll bring it to you. I'll search out your uncle; he usually reads in his room at this time of day." Katrine turned and disappeared down the hallway, her tiny form nearly overpowered by Oleanna's bag.

Oleanna sat on the edge of one of the chairs, folding and unfolding her hands in her lap. After a few moments, she stood and paced; if she slowed down now, if she sat for more than a moment, the enormity of what she'd done, and the exhaustion of the past days, would catch her. So she took a turn of the room, imagining herself one of the women in the Ibsen play Elisabeth had read to her one long, dark night in winter: proper, fashionable, miserable. She laughed softly to herself. I'll never be proper.

The chairs faced the broad windows and small garden, but on the other side of the sparsely decorated room, a mosaic of books covered a wall-sized bookcase. The leather spines were cracked and worn, a well-loved library of novels she'd never heard of in both Norwegian and English, treatises on geology, thick tomes on the modern building styles of Europe, the latest fashion magazines from Paris. And in a place of honor on a brass stand, a great spinning globe.

Oleanna ran her fingers along the cool, smooth surface, outlining Norway. She gave the globe a spin, then stopped it with a finger: Egypt. Another spin: Spain. Another spin: America. Where was John right now in the vastness of that country? Was he still in New York, or was he on a train heading toward his oceans of wheat? She shivered and rubbed her arms. Is that what I want? Oceans of wheat?

"He'll be down momentarily," Katrine called, and Oleanna jumped. "Do you take sugar in your coffee?"

"No." Why would you do that to coffee? Who could afford sugar to waste on coffee? She heard Katrine's skirts swishing away down another narrow hallway, presumably toward the kitchen. Oleanna turned back and gave the globe another spin, pushing the great world around and around, until the outlines of countries and oceans blurred; she stopped it with a squeak, her forefinger right in the middle of Norway.

"I always end up in Norway. What about you?"

She jumped and turned around. Her uncle, tall and dark-haired, leaned against the bookshelf, a small smile pulling the corners of his wide mouth.

"You're quiet as a cat, like mama," Oleanna said.

The ghost of a smile faded. "Have a seat," he said, indicating one of the chairs. He sat and leaned back, crossing his long legs.

She sat on the edge of the other chair. "We buried her at the elves' wood," Oleanna blurted.

He cocked his head. "With the birch trees?"

"Yes."

"Good," he said. He looked at her for a long moment. "It's been so long since I've seen you. How old are you now?"

"Nearly thirty."

"Thirty. It can't be that many years."

Oleanna shrugged.

"You're not married—"

"No."

He paused. "Is there something wrong on the farm?"

"No. John left for America."

"Did he?" Gunnar raised an eyebrow. "Is he going to live with Anton?"

"Yes. He's going to farm wheat in North Dakota."

"Ah," he said, nodding.

They sat quietly, Gunnar looking past Oleanna out the window, Oleanna studying her uncle's face. He had the same startling ice blue eyes and dark hair of her mother. She found it hard to believe that he was well over 50; older than her ancient Anders. She smiled.

"What's so amusing?"

"It's nothing," she said, blushing again.

He cocked his head again. "I am glad to see you here. Why did you come to Bergen?"

What could she say? My lover left me? I'm sailing across the sea? I'm staying here? I had to escape the ghosts? I had to leave before I became a wraith myself? Finally, she settled on, "John asked me to join him. In America."

"When do you leave?"

Oleanna paused. "I—haven't decided yet."

He uncrossed his long legs and sat forward. "Do you still have the atlas?"

Surprised, she laughed. "Yes, of course. I looked at it every day for years."

"Good," he nodded, then looked down, tracing the intricate designs of the Turkey carpet. Finally, he said, "Brita was not made for life on a farm. Perhaps you're not either."

"Perhaps," she shrugged. "How did you come to leave?"

"I'm a man," he shrugged. "You know, every farmer in Norway wants their son enter the ministry or a trade. So I went to school, and Brita was married off to your father." He looked up at her, a kind of pleading in his eyes. "I hated leaving her, but I couldn't go back. She didn't begrudge me my freedom. Well, at least I think she didn't."

She hesitated, then said, "She didn't."

"You can't know that. I know how close and silent she could be."

Oleanna sat back, cheeks blazing. "I'm sorry."

"No, don't apologize. I appreciate your kindness," he said, a faraway look on his face.

Katrine arrived at that moment with a tray of coffee and cookies. They watched her silently as she set it on the small table between them and poured their cups. "Black for both," she said, handing a cup and saucer to Oleanna. After handing Gunnar his coffee, she stepped back and folded her arms. "She looks more like Tollef, wouldn't you say?"

"Her eyes remind me of her mother's."

Oleanna narrowed her eyes at Katrine. "Did you know my parents?"

"I've seen them," Katrine said, smiling and sharing a look with Gunnar. "Dinner will be on the table at six o'clock sharp. You'll want to bathe before that, I'm sure," she said, looking Oleanna up and down.

"Oh, no, I don't want to intrude. I just need to get my bearings, and then—"

"Don't be silly," Gunnar said, blowing across his coffee. "You're welcome to stay as long as you'd like."

Oleanna sat back against the tall-backed chair. A wave of profound exhaustion washed over her. "Thank you," she whispered, closing her eyes.

"You might draw her a bath, Katrine, if you don't mind."

"Of course."

A few sips of strong coffee was not enough to counteract hot water and exhaustion, and after her bath, Oleanna barely made it, half-clothed, to the bed in the small bedroom set aside for guests.

She crawled under the coverlet, and as she drifted off, realized the design was the same that she had woven over the long, cold winter and gave to Elisabeth and Jakob.

A knock on the door woke her moments later. "Oleanna, it's nearly time for dinner," Katrine called. "Your uncle doesn't like to be kept waiting."

Oleanna sat up and looked around wildly. It couldn't be six, I've just closed my eyes, she thought, yawning and pushing the hair out of her face. She stood and looked out the small window, feeling woozy, still half-dreaming. The second storey window offered a view across the rooftops and down the hill toward Bergen's busy harbor.

She leaned her forehead on the glass and watched the intricate moving parts of the city: the boats and the carts, the automobiles and the people, the ladies with their fashionable flowered hats, the men scurrying by with umbrellas and a hurried sense of purpose.

She picked one person out, a woman with a startling purple hat, and followed her down Steinkjlellergaten, heading toward Øvregaten and the harbor. Where is she going? she wondered. Is she a housemaid? A governess? Is Gunnar wealthy, or is this how one lives in the city? How easy would it be to get work here? And where is Anders, down in all of that activity? Maybe he didn't come to Bergen after all. Maybe it was just an excuse to get away from the lake. From me.

With a sigh, she twisted a strand of hair around her finger and picked out another person, and another, following them all toward the harbor: always the water. Finally, she stepped back and stretched, then with a huff wiped the forehead smudge off the window with her sleeve.

A few minutes later, she was seated at a delicate table, shimmering with candles, though the summer sun had finally broken through Bergen's gloom and shone throughout the house. Her hair was properly, if painfully, combed and queued, and she had changed into her only other shirtwaist.

"Claret?" her uncle said, offering her a glass.

"Oh. Yes, thank you." She sniffed the wine and took a sip, for politeness' sake, though she would have much preferred to drink a tumbler of akevitt. Or two. She sat again at the edge of her chair, staring at the delicate candles that didn't smoke and smell, and the fine place settings, and the crystal shimmering in the light.

"Oleanna," Gunnar said, reaching out and covering one of her hands with his.

She looked up, surprised.

"You are with family. This is really no different than sitting at the table outside by the lake."

Her mouth twisted in to a wry smile. "You've lived in the city too long."

He laughed, rolling and smooth like water over rocks. "Perhaps you're right."

"He's always talking about the lake," Katrine said, serving them roast. "You would think he would spend more time outside here if he missed the lake so much."

Gunnar shot her a look that Oleanna could not interpret; she blushed and pushed her chair back. "Here, let me help you with that," she said, reaching out to take another serving plate from Katrine.

"Don't be silly," Katrine snapped, stepping back.

"Oleanna, sit down," Gunnar said quietly.

She did. "I'm sorry, I—"

"I am the help here," Katrine said, dishing out potatoes, her movements jagged. "You let me do my job, and I will leave you to yours." She set the plate back on the sideboard with a clatter and left the room in a swift rustle of skirts.

Oleanna fiddled with her fork; then, out of nowhere, a laugh bubbled out of her throat. She covered her mouth, but the laughter kept coming, a waterfall of mirth. She could hear Katrine smashing pots and pans in the kitchen, which made her laugh harder.

Gunnar said nothing, but raised his eyebrows.

"She—" Oleanna gasped.

"Yes?"

Oleanna took a deep, steadying breath. "She reminds me of Lisbet," she said, still chuckling. "With the—" She made complicated hand motions that were meant to express "outspoken" and "emotional" and "silly" and "wonderful". Instead, it looked like Oleanna was a bit mad.

Gunnar watched her, his hands still resting gracefully on the arms of his chair.

"I'm sorry," she said finally, wiping her eyes.

"It's a long journey, to leave the farm."

She paused. "Yes," she whispered finally.

"I don't spend much time outdoors here," he said, unfolding his napkin and settling it in his lap. "It is beautiful here, but it is nothing like the lake, and I do not like to be reminded."

"But," she said, still sniffling and wiping her eyes, "you can go back—"

He looked at her sidelong. "Please, let's not wait for Katrine, she will be a few moments. I would hate for your food to go cold. She makes a particularly delicious roast."

Oleanna held her uncle's gaze for a moment longer, then smoothed her crumpled napkin in her lap.

They ate together in silence until Katrine returned a few minutes later, settling herself in the chair across from Gunnar.

"This is the best roast I've ever had. Honestly," Oleanna added at Katrine's raised eyebrow.

"Good," Katrine said, applying herself to the meat.

They all ate again in silence, Oleanna casting around for topics of conversation and rejecting each in turn. Finally, she settled on, "What is your business, here in Bergen?"

"I'm a builder."

"He's an architect," Katrine said around a mouthful of potatoes.

"What kind of buildings do you design?"

"Homes. For families down south in Årstad."

"Wealthy families," Katrine said, still chewing. She stood and retrieved the bottle of wine, pouring a glass for herself.

Oleanna smiled. "What does that make you?" she asked her uncle. "Wealthy, too?"

"I suppose."

"No," Katrine interrupted, leaning forward. "So is that why you're here, out of the blue?"

Oleanna's face flushed. She set her fork carefully on her plate and leaned forward as well. "I don't give a fig if uncle is wealthy or poor," she said quietly. "I was simply looking for a friendly face in a big city. I'm not a child, and clearly neither are you. Stop playing games."

Katrine's eyes widened; she sat back in her chair and laughed.

Oleanna looked over at her uncle, who was sitting very still. He glanced over at her, and smiled. "Welcome to Bergen."

"Thank you," she said, taking another sip of wine.

"She looks like Tollef, but she's Brita through and through," Katrine said, shaking her head and reapplying herself to her plate.

"Not through and through," Oleanna muttered. "I'm at a disadvantage here," she said. "You seem to know everything about me, but I don't know anything about you."

"Not much to tell," Katrine shrugged.

"She's an officer in the local suffrage organization," Gunnar said, his cool, even voice warming for the first time since Oleanna had arrived.

"Are you really?" Oleanna asked. "Why?"

"We have the same right to have a say in our own lives as men."

Oleanna shrugged and looked past Katrine to a brightly colored painting of a wide blue lake hanging on the wall. After a few moments, she turned back to Katrine, as if coming out of a dream. "But this is how it has always been."

"Yes. And we are working to change it."

"How?" Oleanna said, half-laughing.

"We talk to government officials when we can, explain to women why they would want the vote."

"The way I see it, it doesn't matter if we get the vote, or if we have a new government. We still have to do the washing and the mending."

Gunnar sat forward. "Why don't you go with her to a meeting, and see for yourself?"

Oleanna shrugged noncommittally, suddenly quite tired. She looked past Katrine, the bright painting again drawing her eye. "Who painted that?"

"A fellow who lived across the lake from your farm, as a matter of fact," Gunnar said.

"Astrup?" Oleanna said.

"Yes, do you know him?"

"No, though a woman on the ferry kept talking and talking about him." She pushed her chair back and stepped around to look more closely at the painting. "She said the National Gallery had bought one of his paintings for the collection. This is probably the only chance I'll get to see his painting."

"That's Jølster," Katrine said, turning around in her seat.

Oleanna nodded. The young women in their shirtwaists and pointed caps, the green of the meadow and the snow on the dark mountain and the midnight blue of the lake made her shudder.

"What do you think of it?" Gunnar asked.

"I don't know," she whispered. "I feel...exposed." The exhaustion she had been battling suddenly weighed her down again, like a heavy dress in the water. She swayed on her feet. I am not going to faint here, she thought, balling her hands into fists, breathing through her nose.

"Oleanna?"

She could hear her uncle's chair being pushed back. She turned around, forcing herself to focus on his face. "I'm sorry," she said, walking back toward her chair. "It's been a long few days."

"Come with me," Katrine said, putting a gentle hand on Oleanna's
back. "There's no need to fuss with dinner. Say goodnight to your niece, Gunnar."

Gunnar smiled. "Goodnight, Oleanna."

"Goodnight," Oleanna said as Katrine guided her out of the dining room towards the stairs. "Thank you for–"

"Goodnight, Oleanna," he said again.

She nodded and allowed Katrine to maneuver her up the stairs to her guest room; each step up felt as though she was treading through heavy snow to reach the sæter. She sat on the edge of the small bed with a sigh. "Thank you."

"Get some sleep," Katrine said, shutting the door with a soft click.

Oleanna closed her eyes. "What am I doing here?" she whispered.

# CHAPTER SIXTEEN

Bergen, Norway
June 1905

OLEANNA LAY BACK ON THE BED, her feet still on the bare floor. She closed her eyes, but her head was spinning, from wine and exhaustion, and she opened them again. The white ceiling was like a field of fresh snow. It put her in mind of Torjus, tramping through the middle, laughing and spinning, darting after skittish wild things under the eaves of the forest, then returning to her side red-cheeked, putting his small hand into the mitten with hers.

"Have you broken the ice for the ponies?" Elisabeth asked sleepily, pulling all the covers off of Oleanna with surprising suddenness and speed.

"No, it's your turn," Oleanna muttered.

"I did it yesterday. Go." Elisabeth put her cold feet on the backs of Oleanna's legs; she yelped and rolled out of bed with an inarticulate grumble.

"Don't forget to pick the valerian while you're out."

Oleanna nodded as she stepped into her boots. "Where's Torjus?" she asked, looking around the dark farmhouse.

"Who?"

"Torjus."

"Who?"

"Your son?"

Elisabeth pulled a pillow over her head. "Ha ha. Go break the ice for the ponies."

Oleanna pulled on a heavy gray coat, big enough for a tall man, and pushed open the door. The meadow and field between the farmhouse and the barn and store house was covered with fresh snow, sparkling and icy in the moonlight. She pulled the coat closer and stepped forward, the snow grasping at her ankles as she walked toward the barn.

After a few steps, the wind was knocked out of her. Oleanna stumbled back, gasping for breath. She looked around, and found she could barely see the barn or the store house. The meadow was filled with people, shadowy and substantial at the same time. She backed away, heart beating itself out of her chest. As she did, she ran into another body, and another, and another. She turned to run, heading for the bend and the freedom of the Sanddal farm. Every step she took sent her back, toward the farmhouse, rather than forward.

And then, she heard her mother's voice, echoing across the distance. "Lea," she called. Oleanna turned, but as she did, she stumbled and landed face-first in the suffocating snow.

Oleanna awoke suddenly, her mouth filled with linen pillowcase, her face smashed into the down pillow on the narrow guest bed. She flipped herself over, with grunting effort, and sat up against the headboard. The summer sun was already streaming into the bedroom, glancing off the delicate porcelain washbasin and inlaid mahogany mantel clock. "Six?" she muttered, rubbing the sleep from her eyes with the heels of her hands. She dropped her hands to her lap and cocked an ear, listening for the sounds of Katrine in the kitchen or her uncle in the library.

Hearing nothing, she scooted down in the bed and laid back, hands behind her head. No chores, no Torjus, no one to make demands, and nothing she had to do.

The feeling of indulgent lassitude lasted all of five minutes, until she heard the first ship's horn in the harbor and the rattle of carts and automobiles in the streets below. An impatient buzz began in her gut and though she tried to give in to sleep again, the effort was wasted and she sat up.

She looked out the window toward the water; in the distance the Bergen gloom approached, but in the green hill town surrounding the busy harbor, the morning sun gilded the windows and the white and red and ochre buildings. Did mama like it here? she wondered. Mama, who couldn't decide if she would let her go after all.

Oleanna turned away from the view and pulled on her skirt and shirtwaist, rolling the sleeves to her elbows. She made the bed and patted her hair down into a kind of submission, then left the room, pulling the door closed silently behind her. She tiptoed down the stairs and toward the front door, when Katrine's voice stopped her in her tracks.

"Leaving already?"

Oleanna spun around to find Katrine standing in the hallway leading to the kitchen. "No. I wanted some fresh air."

"You won't get it in Bergen," Katrine laughed, turning on her heel and disappearing down the hallway.

Oleanna hesitated; the pull of the morning air was strong, but the pull of responsibility was stronger, and she followed Katrine into the kitchen.

Katrine stood over a simmering pot on the small gas stove and looked up, surprised, when Oleanna appeared in the doorway. "You're up bright and early."

"I'm usually up by four to feed the animals," Oleanna shrugged. "Can I help?"

Katrine stared at her. "Four? How awful."

"You grew up in Jølster, didn't you?" Oleanna laughed.

"My father was a school teacher in Førde."

"Oh."

"Did you go to school?"

"When I was young," Oleanna said. "But then we didn't have time. There was too much work to do. So, can I help?"

"I'm just making coffee. Would you like some?"

"Yes, please."

Oleanna watched Katrine move around the kitchen, graceful and assured. "How long have you lived here?"

"In Bergen? Or with your uncle?"

"Both."

Katrine looked over her shoulder and smiled. "Jølster women are always so inquisitive."

Oleanna raised her eyebrows. "All women from Jølster?" she laughed. "I don't think—"

"Maybe it's just the ones from the farms."

Oleanna shrugged. "How long have you lived here?"

"Ten years."

"And uncle?"

"He's lived here for almost 20."

"Did you come to Bergen to live with him?"

"No," Katrine laughed.

Oleanna waited, but got no further explanation.

Katrine bustled around the kitchen. "What are your plans?"

"I'm not sure," Oleanna admitted.

"You should wander around town. The rain looks like it's holding off, at least for now."

"Is it safe, to go by myself?"

"You got here by yourself, didn't you?"

"Well, yes."

"Then don't worry. Here," Katrine said, handing Oleanna a cup of coffee. "Go occupy yourself in the library. Breakfast will be ready in an hour."

"I can help. Please. Give me something to do."

"I have my ways and it will take longer to explain them to you than for me to just do it. And breakfast needs to be ready in an hour."

"There must be something."

"You can get out from underfoot," Katrine said, though Oleanna could see the hint of a smile. "Go, read some books or write a letter."

Oleanna nodded absently and wandered off toward the library, the coffee cup jittering noisily in its saucer. I should finish the letter to Elisabeth, she thought. She sank into one of the side chairs and set the cup and saucer on the delicate side table.

And what about Anders? The size of Bergen was unnerving, so much larger and louder than she had expected. Elisabeth wouldn't be rattled by the city, she thought. She would own the city by the end of her first week. Oleanna grinned, but only briefly. And what about America?

She stared at the wall of books in her uncle's library until her eyes were unfocused and it was no more than a smudge of brown. She reached for her cup of coffee and took a sip, wrinkling her nose: it was cold and bitter. She set the cup back in the saucer.

"Oleanna?" Her uncle's voice carried from the stairway.

She stood and stretched her back, then walked toward the hallway. "I'm in the library," she called.

He rattled down the stairs and landed on the polished wood of the foyer. "Excellent," he said. He took her by the shoulder and led her back into the library. "Katrine," he called over his shoulder.

She appeared after a few moments, wiping her hands on her apron. "Yes?"

"Let's eat outside this morning," Gunnar said.

Katrine folded her arms.

"In honor of Oleanna's visit."

Oleanna looked between them. "Oh no, uncle, it's not—"

He raised his eyebrows. "Come," he said, sweeping past Katrine and out toward the small garden just off the library. "And bring the coffee," he called again over his shoulder.

He pushed open the tall windowed door that led out to the small garden. A delicate table perched among the grasses and lilies of the valley; Gunnar pulled out a handkerchief and wiped off the seats, pulling the chair out for Oleanna. She paused, then sat with a muttered thank you.

"Did you sleep well?" he asked, settling into his own chair.

"Yes."

"You were up before dawn?"

"Yes," Oleanna laughed. "Mostly."

He sat back as Katrine spread a tablecloth and set coffee for them. "I did the same, when I went to university," he said, draping a napkin over his lap.

"Did you like university?"

"Yes. Very much."

"Did you miss the farm?"

"I missed Brita."

Oleanna sipped her coffee. "I don't recall you visiting very often, at our farm. But I was so young."

"I visited more when Anton and Severina were young, when I wasn't so busy. Before you and Elisabeth were born. I came to your christening, you know."

"Did you?" Oleanna laughed.

"You screamed and kicked the entire time," he said, grinning.

"I did not!"

"Oh, yes. Elisabeth, on the other hand, was an angel."

"Now I know you're joking."

He shrugged noncommittally. "How is Elisabeth?"

Oleanna took another sip. "She's well enough. I think she's happy. She's married now."

"Married?"

"Yes, finally."

"When was the wedding?"

"Tuesday."

Gunnar's eyebrows shot up. "Tuesday? This past Tuesday?"

Oleanna nodded.

"Who did she marry?"

"Jakob Evenson, from the Logard farm close to Skei."

"His father is Even Olafsson?"

"Yes, you know him?"

"Yes," Gunnar smiled. "We would meet at their sæter and get up to no good."

Oleanna waited for an explanation, but understanding one was not forthcoming, simply smiled.

"And what about you? Will you marry soon?"

"Oh," Oleanna said, her heart constricting. Finally, she said, "I don't think that I'm the marrying type."

At that moment, Katrine returned from the kitchen, a tray piled with brown bread, jewel-like lingonberry preserves, and a hunk of caramel-colored gjetost. She set it on the table and stepped back, hands on her hips. "It will have to do. We weren't expecting guests."

Katrine settled into the chair next to Oleanna and they applied themselves to their breakfast, the sounds of the waking city muffled by the tall trees lining the garden.

"Have you decided when you'll leave for America?" Gunnar asked eventually.

Oleanna's knife clattered on her plate; she picked it up and set it gently on the table. "No, not yet," she said.

"The steamer to Liverpool doesn't leave until Monday," he said. "The next after that isn't for another week."

She nodded.

"You should have a look around Bergen, while you can."

Her heart constricted. "Yes. Yes, I'll do that." Can I really say goodbye to Norway?

As she slipped into reverie, they ate again in silence, Gunnar and Katrine casting looks at each other over her head which they thought she did not see.

Finally, Gunnar said, "Do you hear much about the referendum out in the fjord country?"

"Oh," Oleanna said. "I suppose."

"We must make sure everyone participates," Gunnar said. "It is our duty as Norwegians."

"Oh, here we go," Katrine muttered. She stood up and began clearing away the dishes, though she smiled as she walked away.

Gunnar ignored her and began to sing quietly, his deep voice soft and solemn.

> Yes, we love this country
> as it rises forth,
> rugged, weathered, above the sea,
> with the thousands of homes.

Love, love it and think
of our father and mother
and the saga night that sends
dreams to our earth.
and the saga night that sends
dreams to our earth.

Oleanna hummed the next bars of the national anthem. "All this talk about freedom. You and Anders seem convinced that it's possible."

"Anders?"

"He is my—friend. He's here in Bergen. Somewhere."

"Please tell me you didn't leave the farm to follow a man," Gunnar said.

She sat very still and considered for a long time. Finally, she said quietly, "No. He left me behind." She sat forward and looked her uncle in the eye. "I didn't leave the farm to follow him. He was never going to come back."

He nodded and sipped his coffee. "Why America?" Gunnar asked eventually.

Oleanna shrugged. "John asked."

"John leaving was the right decision for him. Are you sure it is the right decision for you?"

She paused. "You know the ghosts. I had to go, when John gave me the chance, or I would never have left." She sighed and shook her head. "Though I wish I hadn't left Lisbet to them."

"Elisabeth has her new husband, and Torjus."

"Yes. There's nothing left for me at the farm."

"Oleanna," he said quietly. "I won't tell you not to go to America, nor will I tell you to go back home. But I will suggest that you think about what you're doing."

"It's not in my control," she said. "It's never been in my control."

"Of course it is."

"Life has always acted upon me. Mother and Anna died. Anders chose to leave. Elisabeth chose to get married. John chose to force my hand. And so, here I am."

"You could have stayed at the farm."

"Could I?"

He took her hand. "We all choose our lives."

She laughed, though it felt wrong and ungrateful, and she stopped abruptly. "Mother had no choice. You've said so yourself."

He squeezed her hand and sat back. "In her circumstances, no, but that was an age ago. It's a new century, Oleanna. You can choose your life."

Oleanna shrugged. After a few moments, she said, "Thank you for breakfast, and your hospitality," she stood and brushed off her skirt. "I'm sorry to impose on your kindness here."

"You are not imposing."

She smiled politely, then, as she was about to walk away, paused. "Was mother always so unhappy? As a girl?"

"No," he whispered. "She was as merry as a lark."

Oleanna watched her uncle, his sharp-featured face now pale against his dark hair. He slumped back, his delicate hands still gripping the arms of the chair.

"I understand," she said and walked back into the house, leaving the windowed door ajar. As she walked toward the stairway, Katrine came out of the kitchen. "Where is he?"

"Battling ghosts," Oleanna said, rushing past the staircase to the front door. She unlatched it and stepped out, heart pounding. Though a noxious smoke hung over the city from the noisy automobiles and ferries, the scent of the water and the pine trees was strong. What am I doing? she thought, head spinning. She took a steadying breath, and after a few moments, headed off down the lane, toward the water.

She wandered the streets, maids hurrying past, rushing down the steep alleyways to buy the first catch of the day at the fish market, children sent out of doors, men walking in pairs and threes, discussing the latest news, everyone heading down to the harbor. The novelty was a welcome distraction, and she gave herself over to it. She fell into step with a tiny young maid, a giant market basket nearly toppling her over. "How are you going to get that home after the market?" Oleanna smiled.

The young girl looked over at her, surprised. "I manage," she said, her voice high and clear. She walked away, the great basket bouncing against her side, knocking her into a zigzag pattern down the street.

"Oh Lisbet," she whispered, following the now-disappearing maid down the street. I think you would like it here.

She pressed on, forcing her gallery of ghosts deeper to the back of her mind, attempting to bury them all not under dirt and meadow grass, but under cobblestoned streets that rang with every step.

After only a few minutes, she lost sight of the girl and was finally alone in the street, though the cacophonous roar of the automobiles and crowds throughout the city carried easily on the sea air. A strange frisson passed through her, tingling her fingertips, making her heart race.

She picked up the pace, her shoes ringing and echoing around the narrow street. Her speed increased, and by the time she reached the bottom of the hill, she was nearly toppled over by her momentum. She skidded to a stop a few yards from a busy cross street and bent over, hands on her knees, catching her breath.

"Are you unwell, madam?" A young man in a stiff gray suit and impeccable bowler took her by the elbow and led her out of the way of the oncoming cart traffic.

She nodded and stood straight, wiping the sweat from her forehead with the back of her hand as she followed him to the side of the road. She laughed at his horrified look, but stifled it as he narrowed his eyes and stepped back. "I am well, thank you."

"Do you need any further assistance?"

She looked out across the street, the Bergen harbor alive with people, the sun sparkling on the waves, the fishermen's boats bobbing up and down as maids and matrons and young boys leaned over the quay to haggle for the best fresh salmon and shrimp. The summer sun lifted her spirits, and she turned to the man and smiled. "I do not, thank you very much. You have been very kind."

The man smiled uncertainly. "Are you sure you're well?"

"Yes. Very well." Without another word, she walked past him and dodged the traffic to reach the throng milling around the quay.

"What's your name?" the young man called.

Oleanna smiled and disappeared into the crowd.

She lingered at the fish market and around the quay, strangely soothed by the presence of water, and disappeared into the anonymity of the crowd. The ancient old Bryggen, the mediaeval wharf buildings, shone red and yellow in the morning sun and across the harbor to the north, the New Church dazzled white. Leaning against the wall of a building that was home to the ferry company, Oleanna watched the variety and multiplicity of life in the city swirl and surge.

And as she watched the crowds gather and disperse in waves, she watched for a dark head, a stern jaw: any glimpse of Anders. The sheer energy, the sheer noise of the city was wearing and her excitement soon dissipated, resolving itself into a throbbing headache. She turned her feet back toward her uncle's quiet neighborhood.

She crossed the main thoroughfare and wandered up one of the narrow, steep streets. Rather than taking her to her uncle's neighborhood, however, she found herself standing before a great forbidding stone building, its double towers dwarfing the narrow gabled building in between. She craned her neck to see the very top, and stumbled backward, into a solid body.

"You again." She heard a voice behind her and spun around. The young man with the bowler hat stood there, a stern look on his face that did not match his youth.

"I'm sorry," Oleanna said, stepping away.

"Are you new in town?"

"Is it that obvious?"

He smiled. "Would you care for a tour?"

"What is this place?"

"It's Mary's Church," he said.

"Mary's church?"

"It's the oldest building in Bergen. Building began in the twelfth century but it was quite destroyed in 1248 in the great town fire…"

"I'm afraid I can't pay you for a tour."

"Oh, payment is not necessary. I'm Tor," he said.

"Nice to meet you, Tor," she said, shaking his hand firmly. "And you are?"

"A visitor," she smiled, looking back at the church.

"How long are you in Bergen?"

"How old are you, Tor?"

"Twenty-one."

She smiled. "Are you a student here?"

"Yes."

"What else can you tell me about this church?"

"It is significantly more beautiful on the inside."

Oleanna smiled. "Then lead the way."

They walked in silence into the church. The moment she crossed the threshold, a hush spread through her body. The city noise was left behind and in its wake was the murmuring sounds of a church at mid-day. A row of candles spluttered in a side aisle, barely visible in the dazzling light shining through the tall glass windows. At the far end of the church, an enormous golden altar shone, Mary and her blue robes at its center.

Tor walked into the church, but Oleanna hesitated at the doors. Painted saints floated above pedestals at the top of the stone walls, and above them, tall, graceful arches pointed the way up to heaven. Though Tor was already chatting and explaining the intricacies of the church's history, she sank onto a chair at the back of the church, feeling strangely heavy and very lonely. When did her family settle the land on the lake? Were they wresting oat from the land and fish from the lake when these stones were being hewn?

The image of her tiny parish church, with its clean walls and bright windows and views of the green trees came in a rush, and her heart ached.

"As you can see, there is a..." Tor's voice echoed from somewhere near the altar and she opened her eyes. As he walked back toward her, she looked up at the intricate pattern of arches, whitewashed in the broad spaces between the joints. And along the gray lines of stone supports, a delicate, weaving vine and leaf pattern. Anders would love this, she thought.

Tor approached and stood a short distance away, holding his hat in both hands. "When did I lose you?" he asked.

She wiped her eyes and laughed. "As soon as we walked in."

"Oh," he said, fiddling with the brim.

"I'm sorry," she said, standing. "I was a bit overwhelmed."

He nodded.

"Where are you from, Tor?"

"Voss. And you?

"Jølster."

"I have been here for two years," he said.

"Are you lonely here, in the city?"

He shrugged. "Sometimes. And you?"

"It's strange," she said. "It is amazing, all of the people, and the automobiles. But I still feel quite alone."

"How long have you been in Bergen?"

"Oh," she laughed. "Only a day."

He smiled. "Let me show you the church. It always helps me feel less alone."

"Thank you. It's good to talk with someone from home."

He escorted her around the church, naming the martyrs and explaining its long history. Too soon, the bright sun of the morning gave way to Bergen's gray drizzle, dimming the church and shadowing the saints.

Oleanna smiled. "Thank you for the tour."

"Of course," he said, holding the heavy iron-clad wooden door for her. "What do you think?"

She peered up at the drizzling sky and stepped back under the porch. "It's beautiful."

"I agree."

"But I don't know if I find it beautiful because it is, or because it's new to me...or if there is an echo of home there."

"Are you homesick after only a day?" Tor asked, smiling.

"Weren't you?"

He settled his hat back on his head. "Of course. How long will you be in Bergen?"

"I'm not sure."

"May I call on you?"

"Oh," Oleanna said, stepping back.

"It's just—it's nice to talk with someone from the country," he shrugged.

"Oh, Tor. I'm afraid that won't be possible. Thank you for the tour, though. I'm sorry that I can't pay you."

"But—"

"Good day," she said.

With a rueful grin, he tipped his hat. "Good day." He wandered away and approached an English couple, walking up the path and peering between their guidebook and the great stone edifice.

Oleanna retraced her steps, back down to the harbor. She wove her way through the crowds, getting thoroughly turned around. With a huff of impatience, which served to hide her underlying fear, she headed toward the fishmarket where she'd spent the morning. As she did, she passed the slip for the Liverpool steamer, and the company's ticket office.

She slowed and turned back. The door was open, and inside she could see an excited young man standing at the counter. The ticket agent had a booming voice; she hovered just outside the door.

"Worth every kroner, young man, I assure you," the ticket agent said. "Oceans of wheat, is what they tell me. Oceans." The young man said something she could not hear and the ticket agent laughed, a short, sharp burst like a ferry's horn. "You'll get your sea legs in no time. You'll need it for the passage to America. Long and lonely, that, but worth it when you get to New York. At least, that's what they tell me."

The young man said something else and the ticket agent sobered. "No. I can't say that I do see anyone back here again. At least not in the thirty years I've been working here, though of course I've had thousands through my door. Can't keep track of everyone."

The young man nodded and, with a deep breath, took his ticket.

Oleanna backed away, heart thudding. Without a backward glance, she ran along the quay toward the sound of the fishwives' cries. What am I doing? she thought, dodging carts and fishermen. What have I done?

# CHAPTER SEVENTEEN

Bergen, Norway
June 1905

THE NEXT DAY, OLEANNA LOOKED UP from the book lying open in her lap as the library's ornate mantel clock struck 10.

"Is there somewhere you need to be?" her uncle said over the top of his newspaper.

"No," she said, taking a sip of lukewarm coffee.

"You didn't come to Bergen to sit quietly in my library. Or did you?"

She closed the book and set it on the table between them. "I was never much one for reading," she said quietly. After a few moments, she said, "There is so much life here."

He nodded.

"I'm tired," she laughed ruefully. "I thought I wanted to see the world, but all I want to do today is sit here and look out the window at the trees."

"The city can be exhausting."

"The noise…" she sighed.

"Yes," he said.

"There's a part of me that wishes I was back at the sæter, milking that terrible goat."

Her uncle folded his paper and set it in his lap. "I don't think I've ever stopped longing for the farm. Maybe it's naïve desire to shed the complexities and problems of life here, or maybe that love is ingrained so deeply in me I can never shake it. It's a kind of ghost, you know."

"Do you feel like you want to be in both places at once?"

"Yes."

"Why did you choose the city?"

"I'm a coward," he shrugged.

"That's what John said, before he left."

"Perhaps it's easier to leave home and avoid the ghosts than to exorcise them."

She nodded.

"Have you purchased your tickets for Monday's steamer?"

She sighed. "No."

"Are you going to stay here? In the city?"

She thought the energy and excitement of the harbor, how her sense of direction was turned around, how the young girls chattered with each other so differently, and yet so much the same, as the girls at the lake. She thought of Anders, returning to the farm in months or perhaps years, ready to collect her and start their life. "I don't know," she said finally.

"You've only been here for two days, and journeying longer than that, and grieving even longer. You don't need to decide anything right this moment."

"Thank you," she said, standing. "You've been so kind."

"You're Brita's daughter," he shrugged.

She nodded and walked out of the library, up the set of creaking wooden stairs to her small guest room. She pulled the door closed and, without taking off her shoes, lay down on the bed and fell deeply asleep.

Hours later, a shrill ringing startled her from her nap and she was immediately on her feet. She looked around for Torjus and Elisabeth, then half-laughed at herself. Still blinking sleep from her eyes, she stumbled out onto the landing. Katrine stood at the base of the stairs.

"What was that sound?" Oleanna asked.

Katrine looked up. "When?"

"Just now."

"That was the telephone."

"You have a telephone?"

"Yes," Katrine said, brows furrowed. "Have you never heard one?"

"No," Oleanna said, walking down the stairs despite herself. "There are no telephones at Jølster. Telegraph messages come over from Førde, with the newspapers." She reached the base of the stairs and looked around.

"It's in your uncle's office. He's speaking with one of his clients. Sleep well?" Katrine asked, walking toward the front foyer.

"Yes."

"Good. Now, are you going to stay here and moon around like your uncle?" Katrine asked, pulling on her coat.

"No, I—"

"Come with me to my suffrage meeting."

"I don't think—"

"That's not the problem. I think you think too much. Time for you to do something."

"But—"

"Gunnar, we're leaving," she called down the hallway.

"Supper is in the icebox?" he called back.

"Yes."

"Enjoy yourselves."

Katrine rolled her eyes and pushed open the door.

Oleanna, pulled into Katrine's wake, emerged into the street behind her. "Do I look presentable?"

"No more than you have," Katrine shrugged. She stuttered to a stop and grabbed Oleanna by the arm. "Wait here."

Oleanna looked up and down the street, the cool drizzle bracing, washing the sleep from her head. Before she had time to think or worry, Katrine returned with a simple black hat and coat. "Here," she said, helping Oleanna shrug into it. "Bend down a bit." She settled the hat on Oleanna's head and stepped back. "Better."

Oleanna touched the brim of the hat tentatively. "Thank you."

They hurried together down the steep hill, reaching out to steady each other as the cobbles slicked with the ever-present drizzle. "Where are we going?"

"The weekly meeting of our local suffrage society. We meet in the offices of the Labour Party."

"Why?"

"The Labour Party has done more for working men–and women–in the two years they've been in the Storthing than has been done in the last 100?"

It was not the answer she was seeking, but she allowed herself to be pulled down the street.

"Come on. Let's go open those eyes of yours," Katrine said, turning them down a narrow street off of Kong Oscarsgate. She ushered Oleanna through a low door and a dark hallway, which emptied into a small, high-ceilinged room, permeated with the smell of cigars and strongly floral perfume. A broad-shouldered woman in a burgundy dress and extravagantly adorned hat stood behind a battered wooden desk, talking with a small man in a checkered suit.

Katrine led Oleanna to two seats at the edge of the room. Other women filed in, a group of about 20 all told, women Oleanna's age and middle class, by their dress, and older women with rough hands and plain dresses.

"Look at the work on that bolero," she heard a woman behind her whisper.

"And the pleating," another said. "That dress would cost me a year's wages."

"And the hat," the first woman laughed. "It looks like she has a hydrangea growing out of her head."

"Are you joking?" Katrine said, turning around in her seat. "Those gloves could buy me dresses for the rest of my life"

Oleanna chuckled.

"Who's this?" one of the women asked.

Katrine poked Oleanna's arm, and she turned around. Behind them sat two women, about Katrine's age, wearing dark coats and hats, their faces lined and temples gray. "This is Oleanna. One of Gunnar's nieces."

"From Jølster!" the older of the two said, extending her hand. "Pleased to meet you. I'm Hanna. This is my sister, Marit."

"How do you do," Oleanna said, shaking their hands in turn. "How do you know—"

"Shh, we're getting started," Katrine said, nudging her.

"Welcome to—" the large woman began, and the chattering subsided, as latecomers settled, red-faced, in their seats. "Welcome to the National Association for Women's Suffrage, Bergen Chapter. The meeting will now come to order."

Oleanna was now wide awake, though she felt as though she was in a dream. How did she go from fast asleep to sitting in a women's suffrage meeting in the space of half an hour? Perhaps she was still dreaming…

The large woman looked around the room, and satisfied by what she saw, nodded. "Thank you. I see some new faces. Will you please stand and introduce yourselves."

Oleanna's heart jumped. She looked around the room, and was relieved to see another young woman in a fine checkered dress stand. "My name is Agnes Josok, and I am a student at the university."

"Thank you. And you?" the woman asked, looking at Oleanna.

Oleanna paused, then stood. "I am Oleanna Tollefsdatter Myklebost. I am—" she looked around, unsure. "I am visiting. From Jølster."

She looked Oleanna up and down. "Charming," the woman drawled. "You live on a farm, I presume?"

"I own a farm there, yes."

"Lovely. You may be seated."

She sat back down, cheeks burning.

Katrine leaned over. "Well done," she whispered.

"What?"

"She's an arrogant ass."

"I wasn't trying to—"

Katrine grinned.

"If there are no more newcomers, let us then begin." The woman opened a great leather-bound book and set it on the table before her. "For the benefit of our newcomers, let us have some introductions. I am Gina Nordness, President of this chapter. This is Mr. Rasmussen, our liaison with the Labour Party and staunch supporter of women's suffrage." The small man, jittery and bespectacled, inclined his head as the group applauded. "Katrine Johannesdatter Fiksdal is our Treasurer," she said, her tones clipped.

Katrine acknowledged the group with a wave, then pulled a small notebook and pencil from her bag.

"And Mrs. Moen is our secretary," Mrs. Nordness continued. "She was unable to join us this evening due to an unavoidable social conflict. I'm sure you all understand."

"I don't think she's doing the washing up at home, if that's what she means," Hanna whispered.

Katrine giggled, but continued to look forward.

"Mr. Rasmussen, would you please take a moment to summarize the minutes from our last meeting?"

As Mr. Rasmussen, in a surprisingly deep voice, read out the notes, Oleanna looked around the room. Large wooden desks, typewriters hulking on each, were pushed against the far wall to make room for the meeting, and in the corner not one, but two, telephones. Electric light bulbs illuminated the room, casting harsh shadows on the faces of the gathered women.

Oleanna's head began to spin and she closed her eyes. Is this what is true? she wondered. Are the northern lights and the sæter and the lake all a dream?

"What's the matter?" Katrine whispered.

Oleanna opened her eyes; Katrine's look of concern made her smile. "Nothing," she whispered. "Just tired."

"And that brings us to this evening's meeting," Mr. Rasmussen finished, closing his notebook.

"Thank you," Mrs. Nordness said. "Now for tonight's business. As we all know, the right to vote in municipal elections is not enough. Our goal is universal suffrage," she thundered, as the group of women nodded. "We must stay alert in the coming weeks. Norway is a free country now—"

The group clapped enthusiastically, though Oleanna did not join in. She looked around the room at the women, young and old, rich and poor, their faces shining with hope.

Finally, Mrs. Nordness held her hands out for quiet. "We are a free country in name only. A free country only for men."

"And what good is that?" Katrine called out.

"Were we not created by the same God?" Mrs. Nordness cried. "Are we not equal in mind, and spirit?"

The crowd nodded, some applauding again.

"Do we not have the honorable labor of raising children?"

"Yes," the crowd replied.

"Do we not work together, side by side, in the fields?"

"Yes."

Oleanna raised her eyebrows at this.

"Do we not toil in the factories and in the markets, just as men do?"

"Yes!"

"Do we not labor in the homes of men, in the cities and on the farms?"

"Yes!"

"Should we not, then, be as equal and free as every man in this country?"

"Yes!"

"Then now is the time," Mrs. Nordness bellowed, "now is the time to press our advantage. Now is the time, when our country is learning to be free again, for all of its citizens to share in that freedom that is our right from birth!"

The crowd began again to cheer, but Mrs. Nordness silenced them again with a wave of her hand. "We must look for every opportunity to press our point, to win our own independence. Mr. Rasmussen, please be kind enough to provide us with the details of the Labour Party's current stance on universal suffrage in the new, independent Norway."

Oleanna's face flushed. Her uncle's words came back to her: it is a new century. We can choose our lives. Can we? Can we really?

The next hour passed with speeches and reports, applause and fervent nodding of heads. But in the end, Oleanna realized, no plans or agreements were made as to what to do next.

"We will meet again next week, at the same time. Meeting adjourned," Mrs. Nordness said, tapping a small mahogany gavel on the scratched and worn desk.

The group of women stood, their chairs scraping on the wood floor, and broke into small groups to chat and exchange pleasantries. Katrine took Oleanna by the arm and led her out into the cool night air.

Oleanna wiped the damp from her forehead. "It got so close in there."

"Mostly thanks to Gina," Katrine laughed.

"She was inspiring."

"Yes, that is what she's good at. What she's not good at is organizing, but she refuses to give up any control. So we never get anywhere."

"Why do you keep coming?"

"It's a night out of the house," Katrine shrugged.

Oleanna narrowed her eyes. "It's more than that."

Katrine sighed. "I keep hoping that one of these times we might actually make a decision. That we might make a difference."

"Why don't you take control?"

Katrine laughed. "Because I'm a maid of all work, and she is the wife of a wealthy merchant."

"But—"

Hanna and Marit emerged laughing into the street, the cold air making their jackets steam. "Come with us to the pub," Hanna said, pulling at Katrine's sleeve. "Just this once."

"Yes, come with us," Marit echoed. "You haven't been in ages."

"Next time. I promise," Katrine said.

Oleanna saw her glance in her direction. "I can find my way back to uncle's house."

Hanna laughed. "Come with us."

"Yes, come with us."

"No, I don't want to intrude," Oleanna said.

"You're not intruding," Marit said. "We've just invited you."

"No, thank you. I think I'll go back and rest."

Katrine shrugged. "Suit yourself."

The three women walked away, disappearing down the street, their shapes illuminated, then shadowed, by the sputtering gas lamps lining the way. After a few moments, Oleanna called after them. "Wait for me!"

Fishermen lingered around the doors of the waterfront pub, done selling their catch and spending their wages as quickly as they were won. The women glanced at them but did not acknowledge their presence as they shouldered past.

She followed Katrine through the door and was assaulted by a wave of tobacco smoke and the stench of spilled beer and unwashed men. The rowdy conversations stumbled to a stop as she shut the door behind her. Katrine chose a small table by the lone window, greased and smoked over and letting in very little light.

Oleanna sat at the table, resting her hands on its surface until she realized it was sticky and pulled them off, wiping her hands on her skirt. Katrine, Hanna, and Marit laughed and chattered, taking off their coats.

"Ladies?" An older woman with frizzled gray hair and a soiled apron approached.

"Beer all around?" Marit asked.

They all assented and the barmaid nodded and bustled away.

Oleanna sat back and surveyed the room. Men gathered in clutches around tables, talking and laughing, most dirty and smelling of the sea. Fishermen's nets hung from the ceilings and lanterns lined the walls, and sawdust sprinkled the floor. In the farthest, darkest corner, a group of men sat hunched over a table, whispering urgently. Oleanna leaned forward, keen to catch a stray wisp of their words.

"Gina looked particularly smug tonight," Hanna said, looking at the others with a gleam in her eye.

Marit sat forward. "I hear she and her husband's valet-"

"Shhhh," Katrine said.

"Oh, you know it's true," Marit said. "Everyone knows. Besides, I heard it from her cook."

"Agnethe told you no such thing," Katrine said.

"Because it's not the valet," Hannah said with relish, "it's his business partner, Mr.—"

"Honestly," Katrine said, shaking her head and accepting a beer from the barmaid. "You two are terrible."

Oleanna sipped her beer and wrinkled her nose. She would always prefer the beer she brewed, the way her mother taught her. She sighed.

"What did you think of our meeting, then?" Marit asked.

"She thinks it was a lot of hot air," Katrine said.

Hannah laughed. "That's our Gina."

"Do you believe what she says?" Oleanna asked.

"What do you mean?" Katrine countered.

"Do you believe that getting the vote will give you freedom?"

Hanna and Marit shrugged, but Katrine nodded. "Yes. I do."

"The illusion of freedom," Oleanna said.

"I will have a say in what happens in my city, and in my country," Katrine said.

"But you'll still be a maid-of-all-work," Oleanna said. "You'll still have to rise at dawn to make sure my uncle has his breakfast right on time."

Hanna raised her eyebrows but said nothing.

"Yes. But don't you see, that's my choice. I am not required to be a maid. I could choose to return to Førde. I could choose to save my wages and take that steamer to America. I choose to stay in Bergen, with your uncle."

Marit and Hanna exchanged a look, then leaned forward; Katrine ignored them.

"So why do you care if we get the vote, if you can already choose your life?"

"It's the principle, Oleanna. Don't you see? Something larger than me, and my life. It is the right thing to do. And besides, you and I, and Hanna and Marit, we can choose. It is a new century."

"You've been talking to my uncle," Oleanna smiled. "Did he get that from you?"

"It is a new century, Oleanna. We can choose our own lives. Though not all women can, not yet, not really. So if we have the vote, perhaps we might one day have a woman in the Rigsdag-"

"Storthing," Hanna said. "It wouldn't be the Rigsdag anymore."

"Just so," Katrine nodded. "And we can help women, all over Norway." Her eyes glittered in the flickering light from the gas lamps.

"Katrine, I think you go too far," Marit said. "Isn't the vote enough?"

"No," Katrine said. "But it's a start."

"So why don't you start by taking over the suffrage meetings from Mrs. Nordness?" Oleanna asked.

Hanna finished her beer and slammed the glass on the table. "Yes!"

Marit giggled. "Shh, Hanna."

"Yes, that's what Katrine should do," she said, more quietly.

"Well then, maybe I will," Katrine said, lifting her chin.

"Marit and I will introduce a point of order at the next meeting," Hanna said.

Oleanna smiled.

"Do you have suffrage meetings, in Sunnfjord?" Marit asked.

Oleanna laughed. "No. We don't have time for things like that. We have crops to sow, and to bring in, and goats to milk-"

"And anyway," Katrine interrupted. "Oleanna is going to America."

"Are you really?" Marit asked, leaning forward.

"I—I haven't—"

"Her brother, John, asked her to come. To North Dakota," Katrine said, the name tangling on her tongue.

Oleanna glanced at her, surprised Katrine knew so much about her plans.

"When are you leaving?" Hanna asked.

"The steamer for Liverpool leaves on Monday."

"Have you bought your ticket?" Katrine asked.

Oleanna sighed heavily. "No."

Marit and Hanna sat back and, after a glance at Katrine, started chatting again about Mrs. Nordness and her supposed lover.

Katrine leaned over to Oleanna. "You could do a lot of good, here in Norway," Katrine said quietly. "Out in the fjordland, with the women there."

Oleanna smiled. "You think you've convinced me about the vote."

Katrine shrugged. "You'll come around."

Oleanna sipped her beer and looked around the crowded, dirty pub. "I don't know what I can do anymore. I don't know what I want. My heart is being pulled in so many directions."

"Your mind, you mean."

"What?"

"Your mind is being pulled in so many directions. Your heart knows."

Oleanna chewed her lip. "I don't feel like I have a choice."

"Oh, Oleanna, haven't you been listening? There's always a choice."

# CHAPTER EIGHTEEN

Bergen, Norway
June 1905

FOR THE THIRD MORNING IN A ROW, Oleanna was awake before the rest of the house, staring out the window not at the frenetic city, but the pine-clad hills beyond. Her thoughts raced around the same track that they had for the last day: stay or go? Go where? Home? America? Stay and find Anders? Or just stay?

It seemed easier not to make a decision, to wait, suspended in time, until her hand was forced yet again. She looked out the windows, she pretended to read in the library. But the indecision, the waiting for life to somehow again act upon her, made her jittery and ill-tempered. After half an hour standing at the window, watching the city but not really seeing it, Oleanna shook her head. "Enough of this," she muttered.

She got dressed and walked downstairs, directly into the kitchen. Katrine was not yet awake, so Oleanna made the coffee and cut herself a large chunk of dark bread, left over from the previous day's loaf. She took it, and a cup of coffee, and headed for the small garden beyond the library. The day's drizzle had not yet begun; the dawn spread pink and golden and the scent of pine and sea, for the moment, won out over the scent of coal fires and automobile exhaust.

Her dreams had been fractured, images of Midsummer bonfires and John's traveling trunk, long dark Bergen alleyways and women with vines sprouting from their heads. And always, Anders slipping by, his shape and shadow in the distance, or out of the corner of her eye.

She watched the dawn give way to a shining summer's day, the rumble of the city coming to life just beyond the confines of the small walled garden. She sat poised on the edge of her chair, ready to move but not yet sure what direction she'd take.

"I thought I'd find you out here." Katrine stood in the doorway, arms folded. "Thank you for making the coffee."

"Would you like some help with breakfast?"

"No."

"Please. I need to do something. Let me feel useful."

Katrine smiled. "Be careful what you ask for," she said, turning and walking back into the house.

They fixed breakfast together, chatting Oleanna's uncle, and life in Bergen. Oleanna felt more content than she had in many days, washing dishes and stirring rømmegrøt on the fancy stovetop. An hour later, they heard Gunnar's steps in the room above them and Katrine moved more quickly, setting cups and saucers on a tray. "Here, take these out. Hurry," she said, handing the tray to Oleanna.

Oleanna nodded but looked at Katrine askance.

"Go," Katrine said, distracted, setting plates and silverware on another tray.

Oleanna took the tray out to the small table in the garden. The beautiful morning held, and just as she turned to return to the kitchen, her uncle appeared at the door. "Good morning," he said, stepping out with the morning's paper under his arm. "You have brought the beautiful country weather with you."

"It's the least I can do to repay you for your hospitality."

"I believe we are even, in that case." He smiled and sat down at the table, shaking out the newspaper and burying his head in its pages.

Katrine bustled out moments later, laden tray in hand. She set the breakfast out without a word; Gunnar continued to read his newspaper and Oleanna hovered, attempting to look, or feel, useful.

"Thank you, Katrine," he said as she withdrew. "Please, Oleanna, have a seat."

"Katrine, are you joining us?" she asked, hesitating.

"Yes, yes, please join us again," Gunnar said, spreading his arms expansively.

Katrine nodded and disappeared back into the house.

"And what are your plans for today?" he asked. "Are you going to leave the house?"

She took a deep breath. Time to choose, she thought. "Yes. It's time," she said.

"Time?"

Katrine returned with a place setting for herself, and sat between them, rattling cups and silverware as she did.

"Time for what?" Gunnar prompted.

"Time to purchase my ticket. Time to go."

"Are you sure this is what you want?" Gunnar said.

"Leave her be," Katrine said. "She can make her own choices."

"I am aware—"

Oleanna put up her hand, and Gunnar and Katrine grew quiet. "Please. I appreciate your kindness, and your advice. But I'm so tired of talking about this, and thinking about this. I'm leaving tomorrow."

Gunnar set his newspaper on the table. After a pause, he said, "Are you going to try to find your—"

"Anders."

"Yes. Before you go?"

Oleanna sighed deeply. "No. And in any case, I don't know where I could find him, in this big, noisy—"

"You followed a man to Bergen?" Katrine interrupted, her face flushed. "Didn't you hear anything that was said at the meeting?"

Oleanna laughed. "I didn't know suffrage and love were mutually exclusive."

"Well, they're not, but—"

"No, I didn't follow him here. He left me, and I am leaving. Honestly, I don't think it is any of your concern," Oleanna said, voice rising, "why I'm here, and why I'm leaving, and where I'm going."

"Katrine, please," Gunnar said.

"And in any case," Oleanna said. "I don't think you are in any position to throw stones. Didn't you leave the country and follow a man to Bergen?"

"No," Katrine said, coloring. "How dare you?"

"No?" Oleanna said, looking between them.

"It was the other way around," Gunnar said, pushing his plate away and picking up his newspaper.

Oleanna looked between them, torn between embarrassment and amusement. "Oh. Well. I see," she trailed off.

Katrine stood abruptly and gathered the empty cups and plates and, then disappeared into the house without a backward look.

Oleanna paused, then said, "Why didn't you and Katrine—"

"Busy day," he said, shaking out his newspaper and folding it haphazardly. "Please excuse me." He stood and walked back into the house.

The morning had steadily darkened during their meal, and now gray clouds blanketed the sky. Raindrops plinked on the remaining dishes; Oleanna gathered them up, pushing the door open with her shoulder. In her uncle's office, she could just catch the sound of hushed, insistent voices, her uncle's low and slow, Katrine's rapid and rising. "Why are we discussing this, again?" she heard Katrine cry, and then again, her uncle's quiet voice, soothing.

Oleanna hurried to the kitchen and deposited the tray of dishes in the sink. The voices from the office grew louder, sharper, and when her uncle bellowed, "No!" Oleanna's eyebrows shot up in surprise. She hesitated, looking around at the mess in the kitchen, but when she heard Katrine crying, she hurried out, down the hall, to the foyer. She pulled on Katrine's extra coat and stepped out into the street, closing the door quietly behind her.

She wandered, lost, and lost in her thoughts, past St. Olaf's pockmarked cathedral and all the way to the noisy and stinking railway station. Oleanna slowed and looked up at the entrance. The hulking, hissing trains belched black smoke and white steam, obscuring even the clouds and drizzling rain. The great clock struck twelve.

She sank onto a bench and closed her eyes. The cacophony of traffic, animal and mechanical, in the street and the station, pressed in on her. The sæter came to her mind's eye, its windswept loneliness and beauty making her heart constrict. She stood and looked around, then approached a railway employee and tapped him on the shoulder. "Which way to the harbor from here?" she asked.

He pointed down a narrow, winding street. "Six or seven blocks. Can't miss it."

She nodded and walked quickly away, hands balled into fists. She hurried down the street, dodging businessmen and maids, tradesmen and upper class ladies with their fancy and ridiculous hats. She reached the harbor and weaved her way around and between fruit stands and their customers, jostling and being jostled. The crowds thinned as she reached the road fronting the water and the ramshackle buildings just beyond. Near the end of the quay stood the offices of the Liverpool steamer company.

She took a step forward, then paused again. Is running away going to change anything? she thought, closing her eyes and sighing. Is it running away? She kept moving forward, moving forward, the ghosts clutching at her ankles, her heart.

"Is it really you?"

She slowed to a stop, but did not turn to see who had called out to her.

"Oleanna?"

The harsh sounds of the streets disappeared, no more disturbing than snowmelt tumbling down the side of the mountain. The sun broke through, and sparkled merrily on the harbor. She turned slowly.

Anders, pale-faced, walked quickly toward her from across the road. He broke into a jog and she watched him approach as though in a dream. He stopped short, hesitating, then reached for her hand. She stepped back. "What happened?" he asked. "What are you doing here?"

Oleanna resisted, with some effort, the impulse to smack him, and then kiss him, right there in the middle of the street. She sighed. "You ghosts, following me everywhere I go."

He narrowed his eyes, then took her by the elbow and led her toward a bench overlooking the harbor. She shook his hand off, but followed him nonetheless.

"Is something wrong at the farm?"

"No."

"Good. Oleanna, I'm so pleased to see you. How long have you been here? Where are you staying?"

"I've been here three days. My uncle has been kind enough to let me stay with him."

"Did you come here to find me?"

She hesitated. "No."

"Then what are you doing here?"

She shook her head. "That's the only possible reason? To come find you? You are an arrogant ass, Anders Samuelsson."

His face clouded over. "Then what are you doing here?"

Oleanna lifted her chin. "I'm going to America."

He flinched, then closed his eyes. With some satisfaction, she saw he was shaking.

"John sent me money. I'm leaving tomorrow." She clenched her jaw.

Anders opened his eyes. After a moment, he said, "So John didn't trust me, either?"

"I don't know what John thought. It's my decision. Just as leaving me to come here was yours."

"I was coming back," he said, desperate. I swear—"

"You wanted me to wait for you, but you left me with all of those ghosts. You left me."

"Oleanna—"

"How does it feel?" she said quietly.

He recoiled as if he had been struck. "Are you doing this out of spite?" he said finally.

"No."

"What about Elisabeth, and Torjus?"

"They've got Jakob now."

"What do you mean?"

"They got married last Tuesday."

He stared at her. "You're joking."

"No. We had a small wedding, and he came to the farm the same day. He was already making changes to the planting schedule when I left."

"Oleanna," he said, reaching for her hand. She snatched her hand away; he pressed on. "You don't have to go to America because Jakob moved onto the farm."

"I know that. I'm not an idiot."

"No, you're not. All I'm saying, is you could live with me."

"Where?" she demanded. "When? You chose the world over me, remember? Well, I can choose too." She stood and started walking toward the ticket office.

After a few moments, he caught her by the arm and spun her around. "I love you," he hissed, squeezing her arm. "I love you. Don't do this."

"I'll do whatever I damn well please, and you can go to the devil."

"Oleanna—"

The chaotic sounds of the city came rushing back; the sun disappeared again behind its blanket of gray clouds. Oleanna took a deep breath. "You chose this dirty, smelly, noisy city over the farm," she said, her voice rising. "Over me."

He laughed mirthlessly. "What do you think America will be like, then?"

She shrugged.

He shook his head. "You'll hate it."

"I guess I'll find out soon enough."

"You stubborn ass," he said, shaking his head.

"No more than you."

He sighed. "Please don't do this. Please."

"Why not? You left me, Anders. You left me."

"You don't understand. I had to," He looked around; their argument was drawing a crowd.

"I doubt that."

"I had no choice. Please—"

"Then explain it to me. Or are you too busy with the nation's business?"

He folded his arms. "We're doing important work here."

"As you've said. Well, don't let me detain you. Good day, Anders Samuelsson."

Neither moved. They stood a foot apart, glaring and red-faced. Finally, he said, "Let's go somewhere quiet, and I can explain."

"I think we've talked enough."

"Please, Oleanna. Please."

He searched her face, then turned and walked away without a word, and she watched him go. After a few moments, teetering, she followed after him.

They walked, near though not touching, through the narrow streets along the waterfront until he took a sudden turn to the left and they climbed a small hill. He pushed open the door to a narrow, weather-beaten white wooden building on Strandgaten, with a painted sign: Pedersen Boarding House.

"Is that you, Samuelsson?" a woman's voice called from the parlor.

"Yes," he said, pausing on the first stair to the bedrooms.

A broad horse cart of a woman rounded the corner, wiping her hands on a soiled apron. "I am making stew for—" she said, stopping as she saw Oleanna. She narrowed her eyes. "I said no whores, Samuelsson."

Oleanna's eyes widened.

Anders choked back a laugh. "She's my sweetheart. From Sunnfjord."

The woman huffed. "Supper will be on the table at six," she said, turning and disappearing into the parlor without another word.

Anders squeezed Oleanna's hand and she followed him up the stairs, fuming. He pushed the door to a small, mean room and led her in.

"We couldn't have talked in a pub? In a park?" she asked, arms folded.

"No." He unfolded her arms and attempted to wrap them around his waist.

She stepped back. "What are we doing?"

"It's only been two weeks. Surely you haven't forgotten," he smiled.

"No. No, don't you dare. It's not that easy. You left me behind—"

"Are we going to go through this again?"

"Yes, you—"

"Oleanna, shut your mouth." He pulled her close.

"How dare—"

"I love you," he whispered on her lips. "I love you. I love you."


An hour later, they were twined together, and with the scratchy gray sheet, on his narrow bed. She drew figure-eights on his chest with the tip of her finger. "Do you spend much time in here?"

"No."

"It's very gray."

He shrugged. "It will do for now."

"I prefer your cabin."

He stilled and she could feel him shifting away. "Why did you leave the farm?" he asked. "Honestly?"

She rolled off of him and lay back, head pillowed on his arm. There are so many reasons, she thought. "I wanted to escape the ghosts once and for all," she whispered finally.

"You don't escape them by running away."

"How would you know?" she asked, sitting up and resting her back against the wall, her legs draped over Anders' legs.

He shrugged. "I just do."

"The ghosts are thick around the lake. And here, apparently."

"You can't outrun them."

"How would you know?" she asked again, climbing off of him, and the bed, and searching the floor for her chemise. He put his hands behind his head and watched her, silent. Once she was dressed, she stood next to the bed, hands on her hips. "I have to go," she said. "This doesn't change anything, Anders Samuelsson. You left me. You left me, and-"

"Do you know who Karl Nilsson is?" Anders interrupted.

"What?"

"Do you know who he is?"

"Only what you've told me."

"He is my brother-in-law."

Oleanna's stomach clenched. "He's your what?" she asked quietly.

"My wife's brother."

She breathed heavily through her nose, arms folded tight across her chest. "You're married."

"I was married."

"What do you mean?"

"She's dead."

Oleanna gasped. "What happened?"

After a deep breath, he said, "We were out in my little boat, my wife and I, rowing along the shoreline. It was five years ago."

Oleanna sat on the edge of the bed.

Every muscle in his body tensed. "There is a little inlet just east of Vik, with a Viking mound, and she had wanted to have a picnic. It was beautiful that day.

"I was rowing around a shoulder of land that juts out into fjord. The area was rocky, so I had to row out farther than I wanted to with her in the boat. I knew I should have said no, I knew we should have taken the hike over the mountain..."

Oleanna shivered. "Did she know how to swim?" she whispered.

"No."

"Did you?"

"No."

"Oh no."

"They didn't find her body for a few days. Karl was the one who told me she'd been found," he shuddered. "I didn't recognize her..."

Anders' shoulders began to shake. After a moment's pause, Oleanna squeezed his hand and climbed back into bed, resting her head on his chest. "Tell me about her," she whispered.

He was silent for what felt like an age. "She was lovely," he whispered finally. "Mathilde. The daughter of my mother's second cousin."

Oleanna swept her hand back and forth across his chest. "What else?"

"She was an excellent cook, but a terrible hand with tending the garden." Anders covered his eyes with his hand; Oleanna could feel his chest shaking. She reached up and kissed him on the cheek, then lay back down, holding her breath and resting her hand, a solid anchor, on his chest.

After a few minutes, Anders swallowed and wiped his eyes. "Karl is her only sibling. He never blamed me," he said, covering her hand with his. After a few moments, he said, "I hated him for that."

"You've been wandering ever since."

"Until I came to Jølster. I thought I had outrun the ghosts. When he contacted me, I told myself I came here for Norway. And I did, in a way. But," he shook his head, "I would do anything he asked. To repay my debt."

Oleanna sighed, laying down and burrowing next to him. He put his arm around her and they lay quietly together.

He rubbed circles onto her arms. "Do you believe me now?" he asked quietly.

"About?"

"About outrunning ghosts?"

"I don't know."

"They can't be outrun. They have to be exorcised. It is a skill I have not yet learned."

"If you exorcise them, you forget. Do you really want to forget her?" Oleanna waited, very still.

"No."

"I left the farm to escape the ghosts and they're right here in this room."

He sighed. "I don't have any answers. If I knew what to do, I don't think I'd be here in Bergen. I'd be at the cabin at your sæter, watching the light shift over the mountains with you."

"And my ghosts." After a few moments, she sat up on her elbow and looked at him. "When will it be enough?"

"What?"

"When will your debt be repaid?"

"I don't know."

"And so you'll be at Karl Nilsson's beck and call for the rest of your life? Leaving the things you say you love behind, every time he asks?"

"It's not like that."

She crawled over him; he tried to hold on to her, but she shook him off and stood. "You will be led around by your guilt for the rest of your life, then? Leaving at a moment's notice because Karl asks you to?"

"Oleanna. Please. You don't understand—"

"I understand perfectly well," she said, chewing her lip. "I understand better than you know. And that's why I'm leaving."

# CHAPTER NINETEEN

Bergen, Norway
June 1905

"OLEANNA, PLEASE DON'T DO THIS."

"Can you promise me that you can leave your ghosts behind?"

"No. Can you?"

"No." She sighed. "It's always leaving with us, isn't it?"

"I suppose so."

"I don't know what else to do anymore."

He buttoned up his trousers. "I don't have any answers for you."

"I know."

"You can't outrun them."

She shrugged.

"At least let me walk you back to your uncle's house."

"I know the way."

"Please."

They walked back toward the harbor in silence. Oleanna shivered, not from the drizzling rain and chilly wind, but the proximity of Anders, the pain and confusion and frustration coursing through her blood. She yearned to take his hand, to absolve him, and herself, to forget their ghosts. She reached out to take his hand, when a voice stopped Anders in his tracks.

"Samuelsson!"

Oleanna turned to see a man with dark curly hair, liberally shot with gray, hurrying up the street. His wide grin, pointed chin and teeth, and small dark blue eyes put Oleanna not in mind so much of a ferret but of an elf.

"Where in the devil have you been?" the man asked, looking between Anders and Oleanna.

"Karl Nilsson, this is Oleanna Tollefsdatter Myklebost."

Karl grinned, and shook Oleanna's hand vigorously. "The famous Oleanna! Well, it is a pleasure to finally meet you. Now Samuelsson can finally shut up about you," he said, slapping Anders on the back.

Anders winced.

"What are you doing in Bergen? Oh, wait—" he said as Oleanna opened her mouth to answer. "Come, let's get dinner and you can tell me all about it. Samuelsson, I wanted to talk to you about the next print run while we're at it."

"Thank you," Oleanna said, "but I have business to attend to."

"Oh, come along," Karl said, grinning. "We'll go to the Grand Café. My treat." Karl held his arm out for Oleanna with a flourish. "Samuelsson, come along. Don't be so sour."

Despite herself, she was intrigued by the infamous Karl Nilsson. With a brief glance up at Anders, who had folded his arms, she took Karl's arm.

Karl provided a running commentary on Bergen's fish market, and the state of labor and unions in the county, the history of the buildings ringing the harbor, and the current political gossip. She nodded and exclaimed at the right points, all the while feeling Anders' gaze on the back of her head.

As they were seated at their table in the Grand Café, she looked over at Anders, who stared out the broad windows at the mute pantomime of Bergen's street life.

"You're grim," Karl said, shaking out his napkin.

Anders shrugged.

The waiter appeared with menus. "Mr. Nilsson, a pleasure as always."

Karl nodded and gestured for Oleanna and Anders to peruse their menus.

She glanced at Anders, who continued to look out the window, the menu closed in front of him on the table.

"Sir?" the waiter said, standing still and attentive at Karl's side.

"The cod please, with peas and potatoes. A glass of claret as well. Samuelsson?"

"Duck, and vegetables."

"Oleanna?" Karl said.

"Oh," she said.

"Have the eel, it's fresh today," Karl suggested.

"I'll have the roast venison, thank you," she said to the waiter. "And a glass of beer, please."

The waiter glided away and Karl sat back in his chair. "You're quiet, Samuelsson."

Anders shrugged.

Oleanna looked between them, then sighed.

"When did you arrive in Bergen, then?" Karl asked.

"A few days ago. I've been staying with my uncle."

"What's his name?"

"Gunnar Johansson."

"The architect?"

"Yes. You know him?"

"No, not personally. He's well known."

"Oh," she said. "I had no idea."

"Has he been showing you around town?"

"No, he keeps to himself. And—I arrived without notice. He has been kind enough to let me stay with him."

"You've been keeping her to yourself all this time?" Karl said, smiling at Anders. "I don't blame you. No wonder you've been so distracted."

She looked at Anders, who finally turned to face her. "I—" she started, but was interrupted by the waiter, who set their drinks in front of them. Anders turned away again, glowering.

Karl shrugged. "Have you met anyone in town?" he said, pressing stoutly on.

"Yes, one or two people."

"I might know them. Who did you meet?"

"You know everyone in Bergen?" she laughed.

"The people who matter," he grinned.

"Do you know Gina Nordness?"

"Of course," he smiled. "I have business with her husband quite often. How do you know her?"

"I was at a suffrage meeting. She's the president of the group."

Anders turned around and raised his eyebrows.

"Were you really?" Karl asked, leaning forward.

"They didn't get much done, though," Oleanna said, taking a sip of her beer. "Gina talked a lot, and a man from Labour talked a lot, and then everyone felt very proud of themselves for making pretty speeches, and then we all went to the pub."

"If they were smart, they'd work with us."

"You can't guarantee women the right to vote," Oleanna said.

"We can do a sight more than the fellows in Labour."

"That's just more talk," Oleanna shrugged.

"What do you mean?"

"It's easy for you rich city men to talk a lot and make proclamations. Seems to me talking's a far cry from doing."

Karl sat back and smiled. "You remind me a little of Mathilde," he said, laughing suddenly.

Anders and Oleanna grew very still.

"Nilsson…"

Karl laughed. "What?"

"Leave it."

"I can't talk about my own sister?" Karl asked, leaning forward. "My God man, it's been five years."

Anders sat back, his face again closed and stony.

"You have this lovely woman sitting by your side, and you want to live in the past? Is that what this," he said pointing to them in turn, "is about?" When Anders did not reply, Karl sighed. "You're an idiot."

Anders folded his arms and Oleanna scowled.

"Oh. You're both idiots, then," he said, shaking his head.

Oleanna's eyes widened. "How dare you?"

"If you're not going to live now, why don't you step aside and give me a chance?" Karl said, reaching across to take Oleanna's hand.

She snatched it back and folded her hands in her lap.

"Stop it," Anders said quietly.

"You have a chance to be happy for the first time in a very long time."

"Apparently I don't have a say in the matter anymore," Anders said.

After a few moments, Karl sat back, throwing his napkin on the table. "I don't blame you."

"What?"

"I don't blame you for what happened to Mathilde. It was an accident."

Anders shook his head.

"I did, at first. I was furious."

"You should have been angry. You should still be angry."

Karl shook his head. "Anders. It was an accident. Leave it be."

"But I—"

"I'm done talking about this," Karl said, eyes narrowing. "I absolve you, my son," he said, suddenly laughing and making the sign of the cross.

"This isn't a joke," Anders said.

At that moment, the waiter arrived with their meal, setting the plates before each of them with a flourish. Karl thanked him, and the waiter withdrew without a word.

The smell of the roasted meat made her mouth water and, despite the tension twisting her stomach, Oleanna applied herself to her meal with gusto, while the men sat back, arms folded.

"You're an ass," Anders said after a few minutes.

"And you're a fool," Karl replied, shaking his head and finishing his glass of claret. "A damnable fool."

"Don't let this food go to waste," Oleanna said. "Eat."

Anders shook his head. "I'm not hungry."

"Suit yourself," she said, shrugging.

Karl leaned forward across the table, pointing at Anders. "Don't make me the reason you refuse to live," he said. "I won't have it."

"Nilsson," he whispered. "How can you—"

Karl pounded the table with his fist, making the delicate crystal, and Oleanna, jump. After a moment, he leaned forward and hissed, "Don't you dare set your grief and guilt at my feet." Karl sat back, glowering, and reapplied himself to his meal.

They ate in stony silence, Karl making valiant attempts at conversation, until he too gave up and fiddled silently with his silverware, casting looks of annoyance and exasperation at both Anders and Oleanna. When the bill came, he tossed a few notes on the table and stood quickly.

Oleanna and Anders looked up at him.

"I forgive you, Anders," he said. "Honestly, I do. Forgive yourself."

Anders looked down and sighed.

Karl took Oleanna's hand and kissed it. "It's been a pleasure, Oleanna Tollefsdatter."

"Thank you for the meal," Oleanna said quietly.

"Convince him to forgive himself, would you?" Karl said.

"I'll have to forgive him first."

Karl sighed. "You're both fools. Samuelsson, I'll see you at the printer's offices tomorrow at 10." He shrugged on his coat, but did not leave.

After a few moments, Anders said very quietly, "Oleanna?"

She looked at him, holding her breath.

"Please forgive me."

She considered him for long moments. How fond she was of his face, his moods and the gift of his sudden laughter, his kindness. She sighed. "I forgive you," she whispered.

He slumped in his chair and covered his face with his hands; his shoulders shook and Oleanna yearned to reach out and take his hands. Finally, after long moments, he dropped his hands and said, "Let's go home."

Oleanna's face flushed with indignation. "You want to go back to your rooms? Now?"

"No, no," he said. "To Jølster."

Oleanna stilled. "But I'm going to America."

Anders dropped his chin. "You're still leaving," he whispered.

A rush of anger spread through her. "How does it feel?"

He looked up at her sharply.

"Why shouldn't I go?"

Anders closed his eyes. "If that's what you've decided, I can't stop you."

Oleanna sat back and folded her arms. "You're an ass."

Karl cleared his throat. "Yes, he is. Excuse me for a moment," he said, disappearing into the depths of the dining room.

"Give me one reason why I shouldn't get on that boat tomorrow," she pleaded. "Give me one reason."

He opened his eyes. "Being here in Bergen," he said quietly, "all I could think about was being at the lake, with you. I hate it here," he said, glaring at the crowds passing by the window.

"But I thought—"

"I finally had some peace at the lake. Ironic, that."

Oleanna sighed. "When were you coming back?"

"Two more weeks."

"You were never coming back," she said quietly.

"You have to have some faith in me."

"Why?" she half-laughed. "Because you say so?"

"Oleanna."

"Have you earned it?"

"Please," he whispered. "Please, you need to believe me. Believe in me. Forgive me."

"Anders..." Her heart broke at his look of pain, yearning, desperation.

"I love you. I'm a ghost without you."

A sudden warmth spread through her, making her dizzy. After a few moments, she said in a rush, "If I'm not being a stubborn ass, which I think is rather rare—"

Anders chuckled.

"—I know, I just know, that I am a better version of myself when you're near. Well, usually," she said, and Anders chuckled again. "You push the ghosts back, you give me room to breathe. You might even make them disappear."

Anders grew very still. Oleanna looked out the window at the busy street and milling crowds. In the distance, she could see a great steamship making its slow way toward its slip at the end of the quay. Her heart began to thud. She thought of the farm, and the lake, the back-breaking work and the beautiful sunrises. She thought of her mother's grave and the wide-open sæter, and a tiny shoulder of land jutting into the dark lake on which Anders' tiny cottage perched, wreathed in painted leaves.

Finally, she said, "What am I going to tell John?"

Anders looked up at her and smiled. She grinned and took his hand.

Karl reappeared a few moments later, a bottle of akevitt in one hand and three tumblers in the other. Without a word, he poured out three shots and handed them around. "Cheers," he said.

Oleanna tipped her drink back.

Anders nodded. "Cheers."

"When are you leaving?" Karl asked.

"Tomorrow," Oleanna said. Anders raised his eyebrows, but shrugged in acquiescence.

"And where are you going to?" Karl asked, pouring himself another tumbler.

"Home. To Sunnfjord," Oleanna said.

"I'm sorry, Nilsson," Anders said. "But I have to go."

Karl waved the apology away. After a few moments, he said, "You know the Sogn and Sunnfjord country."

"Yes," both Anders and Oleanna said.

"Will you do something for me?"

Anders stilled. "Depends on what it is."

"We need people in the counties to organize and get the word out. We need the country folk to understand what they need to do when the referendum starts in August."

"In the fjordland," Anders said.

"Just around Sunnfjord. It's a paid position, Samuelsson. Go talk with the pastors, go talk with the farmers."

Anders looked at Oleanna. She took a shaky breath. "Will you come back to me?"

"Always."

Her smile widened into a grin. "You have a deal, Mr. Nilsson."

Karl laughed and took off his jacket. "Then let's give you a proper send off," he said, sitting down and pouring another round of akevitt.

Anders scooted his chair over and took Oleanna's hand, twining their fingers together. "You won't regret it," he whispered. "I promise."

"I hope you won't, either."

The next morning, the sun tried its valiant best to convince them to stay, sparkling off the waves in the harbor, covering Bergen in a warm glow. They walked, hand in hand, from the gray boardinghouse, past the pub, skirting the fish and fruit market, already bustling with activity.

They had parted with Karl in good humor, and a bottle of akevitt, with Karl late the previous night. Anders was more merry than she had ever seen him, his broad smile sunshine on the mountainside. A suggestion of that smile lingered, though the dark circles under his squinting eyes balanced the effect. "How are you feeling?" she asked in a stage whisper.

He shook his head, then winced. "How are you not miserable?"

Oleanna shrugged. "Practice."

Anders grinned and squeezed her hand, speeding them past the raucous fishermen and their early customers. His small suitcase bounced against his leg as they walked. They climbed the hill to her uncle's home in the wooded hills and Anders slowed.

"Don't tell me you're nervous," she smiled.

"It would be much easier if I didn't feel like my head was coming off of my shoulders."

Oleanna grinned. "Wait here." She walked the final steps to her uncle's door, and tried the handle. She pushed the door open and winced at the small creaks that echoed in the quiet morning.

She heard the swish of skirts and Katrine appeared in the hallway. Her eyes went wide, but then narrowed to slits. "Where have you been?" she hissed.

"I—"

"I was up half the night, worrying about you. If you stay here, you're under your uncle's care. How dare you—"

"Does he know?"

Katrine folded her arms. "No."

"Then don't worry."

"I'm the last person to question you about what you do," Katrine said. "But it's not like being in the country. It's dangerous."

Oleanna hovered in the doorway. "I can take care of myself."

"I'm sure you think you can, but—" she left off, and shook her head. "Well, come in then. You can help with breakfast to make it up to me." She turned and started walking back down the hallway toward the kitchen. "Where were you, anyway?"

"She's been with me."

Katrine spun around. "And who the devil are you?"

"This is Anders," Oleanna said, as he took her hand.

She glared at them. "A man," she said finally, turning and disappearing down the hallway.

Anders raised his eyebrows. "That went well?"

Oleanna shrugged. "Let's go help her with breakfast."

"You," Katrine said, pointing at Anders as they walked into the kitchen. "Roll up your sleeves. You're peeling potatoes."

Anders grinned, and did as he was told.

"You," Katrine said, pointing at Oleanna. "Watch the porridge and don't let it burn."

Oleanna and Anders chanced amused glances at each other across the kitchen as Katrine bustled, muttering under her breath. After nearly a half an hour of work, Katrine stopped and put her hands on her hips. "Are you worth it?" she asked Anders.

He swept the last of the potato peels into the bin and looked up. "I hope so."

At that moment, they heard movement in her uncle's room above. Katrine nodded at Oleanna, who poured the coffee into a porcelain jug and set it on a tray.

"Hurry," Katrine hissed.

The sound of her uncle's footsteps on the stairs spurred them into frenzied activity; Anders kept back, watching the ballet.

"Wait until he's done with his breakfast," Katrine said, pushing the door open with her foot.

The door swung shut and Anders walked over to Oleanna, hugging her tightly. From the library, they could hear her uncle's voice. "Where's Oleanna?"

"Having a lie-in, I expect."

A few moments later, Katrine reappeared, setting the tray back on the table. "You can help me clean up while you wait."

Half an hour later, as the final dish was washed, Katrine nodded. "Go on."

Oleanna wiped her hands on a towel and took a deep breath.

"Make sure you're worth it," Katrine said as Oleanna pushed open the door.

"He is," Oleanna said.

"I mean you," Katrine said.

Oleanna blinked. After a few moments, she nodded and they walked down the hallway into the library. Despite the bright golden sun illuminating the lonely back garden, Gunnar sat in the library, squinting at his newspaper. Oleanna stepped forward; when he didn't react, she cleared her throat. "Uncle?"

He nodded absently, then finally looked up. "Oh."

"Uncle, this is Anders Samuelsson."

Gunnar stood slowly, tucking the newspaper under his arm. He offered his hand. "Samuelsson."

"Sir."

They shook hands. After a few silent moments, searching first Anders' face, and then Oleanna's, Gunnar said, "She is very dear to me."

Oleanna blinked, looking between them.

"And to me," Anders said, his face grave and still.

"You should know that I am her only male relative still in Norway. If there are any problems, you'll answer to me."

"There will be no—"

"No," Oleanna interrupted. They both looked down at her, surprised. "If there are any problems, he'll answer to me. And maybe Elisabeth."

Gunnar smiled, and Anders laughed, a great bark of mirth. He grabbed Oleanna's hand and kissed the top. "Of course. Yes, you're right."

"And where are you going? America?"

"No," Oleanna said. "We're going back to Jølster. It's where my heart is."

Gunnar nodded, and squeezed her hand. "You are always welcome here. Both of you."

"Thank you, uncle." She reached up and kissed him on the cheek. Oleanna glanced at Anders. "We have to go," she said. "The ferry is leaving in an hour."

"Oh," Gunnar said, nodding vaguely. "Yes, of course. Of course."

"I'll go get my things," she said, squeezing Anders' hand. She turned and hurried up the steps to the guest room, strangely sad. She opened the door and found Katrine folding her few things and stowing them in her carpetbag.

"You're going back to the farm," Katrine said quietly.

"What's wrong with the farm?"

Katrine shrugged.

"The farm belongs to me. I'll work for myself, for my livelihood. I have no man telling me when I can leave and when I can drink akevitt—"

"The farm isn't yours anymore."

Oleanna raised her eyebrows.

"Gunnar told me."

"Elisabeth lives on it, but it is still half mine."

Katrine snapped the bag shut and handed it to Oleanna. "So what are you going to do?"

Oleanna shrugged. "Live in Anders' cabin, I suppose."

"Are you going to get married?"

"Oh. I don't know. I hadn't really thought about it."

Katrine turned away from Oleanna and looked out across the rooftops of Bergen. After a few moments, she said, "There is so much you can do here. We could use you at our meetings. The two of us, we could—"

Oleanna smiled and took Katrine's hand. "I'll miss you, too."

"I hope you'll be happy."

"I expect I will."

"Don't assume you will," Katrine said, squeezing Oleanna's hand and dropping it. "Make sure."

Oleanna nodded. "Thank you."

"You'd better get going."

Oleanna nodded and turned. She paused in the doorway and turned around. "They need you. In the suffrage group."

Katrine nodded. "I know."

"Goodbye." Oleanna turned and walked down the hall, down the stairs, and into the library, where Anders and Gunnar stood chatting.

"Oleanna," Anders said.

She set her shoulders. "I'm ready."

Anders again offered Gunnar his hand. "I'm sure we'll meet again."

"I hope that is so," Gunnar said.

"Thank you for your hospitality, and your kindness," Oleanna said.

"You're welcome here at any time."

"And you're welcome to come back to the country. It would do you good," she said.

"Good luck to you both," Gunnar said, turning away and looking out the tall windows to the back garden, hands clasped behind his back.

"Let's go," Oleanna whispered.

Anders took the bag from her hand and they left the library without a word.

The walk down to the harbor was quiet, but for a brief tussle in which Oleanna attempted to carry her own bag and Anders refused, a small smile on his lips. At the ferry-side, he purchased their tickets while she watched and listened as Bergen's engines rumbled to life, a cacophony of color and noise.

The great steamer for Liverpool sat at rest at the end of the quay. Oleanna's heart thudded. She reached into her bag and pulled out John's letter, and with it the letter she had started to Elisabeth. My grand adventure, only a week long, she thought, shaking her head. The steamer's horn blew; she was surprised to find that she was crying, watching it pull away from the docks.

Anders returned and quietly took her hand. "I'll make you happy. I promise."

"You can't promise something like that."

"I promise that I'll always love you."

She shrugged, wiping away the tears with the sleeve of her shirt. After a pause, she said, "I don't know if I like it here. But in a way, I hate leaving."

"I know," he said, putting an arm around her waist. She leaned into him and sighed.

A few minutes later, the great steam-driven ferry rumbled to life and they were roused from their reverie. "Ready?" he asked, picking up their things.

"Yes."

# CHAPTER TWENTY

Sognefjord, Norway
June 1905

THE FERRY SWAYED IN THE CROSS-CURRENTS from the pounding North Sea, jittering and straining as it made its turn eastward into the great Sognefjord.

Her heart swelled as she watched the Solund Islands disappear into the distance. The strange longing for the sea crept again into her heart, and she shook her head, both laughing and crying quietly.

Anders took her hand. "What is it?"

She laid her head on his shoulder. "The sea."

He squeezed her hand. "I know."

As the ferry steamed into the Sognefjord, its tall, stern mountains crashing directly into the deep blue water, the constriction of Oleanna's heart eased and she looked up at Anders and smiled. "It's beautiful, isn't it?"

He looked out the window, watching the tiny red- and white-painted fishing villages disappear as soon as they came within sight, nestling in the shoulder between the mountain's top and the water's edge. "Yes."

Sitting up, she turned to face him. She looked at him for a long time, chewing her cheek. "It's where I belong," she finally said, shrugging. "I don't know how else to explain it."

He took her hands and squeezed. "I know."

She glanced at him and grinned suddenly. "We're going to have to live in your cottage, you know. It will be very…cozy."

He leaned over and kissed her lightly on the cheek. He grinned and sat back, holding one of her hands tightly in his.

In the early afternoon, the ferry finally pulled into the tiny dock at Vadheim and, stretching and creaking, Oleanna and Anders stepped off the boat. She looked up, shielding her eyes from the sun. "At least we'll have light for the first part of the walk," she said.

"Do you want to rest first?"

"No," she said. "I need to walk."

They turned their back on the ferry and walked up the road, away from the tiny town, and into the green forest. She finally convinced him to let her carry her bag, and they walked together in silence, Oleanna taking deep gulping breaths.

"What's the matter?" Anders said.

"Nothing. The air is clean," she shrugged. "And it's quiet."

He smiled and squeezed her free hand.

After an hour's walk, she slowed to a stop. "Less than a week in the city and I've grown soft," she laughed, hands on her hips.

He put his hand out for quiet. "What's that?"

She straightened and looked around, hearing nothing. Then she smiled.

A rumbling cart appeared around the corner, heading inland from Vadheim. Anders waved his arm and the old farmer slowed his horse with a soft word.

"Afternoon," Anders said.

"Afternoon."

"We're headed to Myklebost on the lake."

"I'm stopping short of that, but you're welcome to ride as far as I'm going."

Anders smiled. "Thank you."

He handed Oleanna up into the back of the cart and settled in, bracing himself against wagon's sides.

The ride was bone-rattling and inconducive to talk, so they bounced along together, holding hands and smiling, until the farmer slowed his horse five hours later, well past Førde, this time beside a tiny turf-roofed farmhouse. "This is the end of my road," he said, jumping down and patting his horse on the flank.

"We're much obliged," Anders said, climbing down and helping Oleanna do the same.

"Thank you," Oleanna called. The farmer waved vaguely behind him and she turned back toward the road.

They walked together, growing more quiet the closer they came to the lake. After another hour, he stopped suddenly in the middle of the road and turned to her. "I have not kept my promises to you," he said, running a hand through his hair.

She raised her eyebrows.

"I swore I would never hurt you, and I would never leave you, and I did both."

Oleanna took a deep breath. "Yes, you did."

He looked up, stricken.

"Hounded by ghosts, the both of us," she said, walking over to stand before him. "I love you," she whispered. She took his hands and turned them over, kissing the palms and closing his hands.

"We're meant to be here," he said, nodding at the tiny wooded pathway that passed for a road.

"Yes," she said.

He pulled her into a crushing hug, kissing the top of her head. "I'm sorry."

"I'm sorry, too."

He leaned down and kissed her, setting her back moments later, breathless. She regained her bearings, then grinned. "I'm glad we're home."

"Me too," he laughed.

They walked the last quarter-mile, skirting the Sanddal farm and its boisterous boys, and came, all at once, upon the elves' wood and her mother and sister's graves. She slowed, and dropped her hand from his. He wandered off to the water's edge, kneeling down and letting the gently lapping waves wash over his hands.

Oleanna sat in the tall grass next to the graves of her mother and Anna. She picked the long blades and slowly wove them into a braided circlet. "It was so loud there, mama," she whispered finally.

"What did you think of it? Why didn't I ask while I still had you with me?" She settled the crown at the head of her mother's grave, then sat back. "I know it was an accident," she whispered after a few long moments. I wish—there's so many things that I wish, she thought.

Closing her eyes, she took a deep breath. "I miss you," she whispered. "I miss you so much." She covered her face as the broad, warm darkness of grief spread through her. Her shoulders shook and the tears came through gasping sobs. She could feel Anders kneeling nearby, and leaned into him.

He held her, rubbing her arms, rocking her, smoothing hair away from her face, until her tears were spent. "Does it ever get easier?" she whispered.

"The grief can come on you all at once," he said, sitting back and putting her head in his lap, stroking her hair. "You will be working outside, or walking to church, or looking up at the sky, and you'll remember something about them. The smell of lily of the valley makes me think of Mathilde and the day we were married."

Oleanna sniffled.

"It's as though I'm there again. I remember what I thought, and the sound of the sheep bleating out in the field, and the echo of the ferry blowing its horn at the far end of Aurlandsfjord. I can remember Karl and his ridiculous attempt at playing fiddle on the way back for the feast," he laughed.

Oleanna pushed herself up.

"When I remembered that day, in the months and years right after, I couldn't think for the rest of the day. It was like my mind had gone dark, the grief was so powerful. And the things that would make me remember were so strange."

"And now?"

"And now, I remember, but the waves of grief are gone, or less powerful. Like those waves," he said, pointing at the lake, "and not the sea. It was my guilt, not my grief, that bound me to Karl. Or so I thought."

Oleanna looked out at the water. After a few moments, she sighed. "I was so young when Severina died, I hardly remember what happened. And when father died—well," she shrugged.

He took her hand and stroked the back with his thumb. "We won't forget them," he said, nodding at the graves behind her. "But we can't carry them anymore. It's time to choose to set the burden aside."

Oleanna took a deep breath, nodding.

He stood and held a hand out to her. "Are you ready?"

She took his hand, and allowed herself to be helped up. She smiled. "Yes."

"Come on, then."

"I don't know what happens next."

"Neither do I. Frightened?"

"No," she smiled. "You?"

"No."


Though she had only been gone for less than a week, it felt like it had been years since Oleanna had seen the lake. It sparkled in the late afternoon sun, dazzling and lovely. Every wildflower seemed a brighter hue, the grass more soft, the birch trees whispered more gently, the pine trees more fragrant.

"I've missed it," she said, breaking the silence of their walk.

Anders took a deep breath. "Me too."

"It's so quiet."

They rounded the final corner and, just beyond the last stand of birch trees, heard Torjus squealing with delight.

"It was so quiet," she whispered, laughing quietly.

He chuckled.

"Jakob, come get your child," Elisabeth called; Oleanna could hear the amusement under the anger in her sister's voice. Oleanna peered more closely between the branches and saw Jakob stand and stretch, hands on his lower back, leaving aside the haying and sauntering down to the turf-roofed farmhouse.

"Welcome home," Anders whispered into her ear.

She squeezed his hand. "Welcome home."

# Author's Note

THIS STORY IS A WORK OF FICTION. Elisabeth and Oleanna's names are taken from my (presumably spinster) great-great-aunts who lived at Myklebost on the banks of lake Jølster. They were both weavers of some acclaim and significant skill, sisters to Johan, Anton, Severine, Bertil, and Anna, but that is where the resemblances in this story end.

I've always wondered about these women, who carried on living on the farm after everyone had died or left for America. What were their stories? What were their lives like? Who did they love? The genealogical record does not indicate much, but not everything is revealed by a countrywide census or a parish's records.

My mother visited them when she was in her early 20s, in 1963, and returned with the most beautiful weavings, which I'm proud to say are now in my home in California. Unfortunately, I did not ask mom about Elisabeth and Oleanna in detail before her own death in 2006; all I know is their names were uttered with reverence and love, especially around Syttende Mai (May 17, Constitution Day) and the holidays.

Elisabeth and Oleanna's brother John is based on my great-grandfather, Johan Elias Tollefson Myklebust, who emigrated to the United States in 1902 and was one of the first homesteaders of Ramsay County, North Dakota. He married Ingeborg Briesnes of Aurland (Sogn, Norway) and lived in Starkweather until his death at the age of 97 in 1978. He accompanied my mom on her trip to Norway; I visited the country in 2004 and hope to go back someday.

The split between Norway and Sweden in 1905 is definitely not fiction and I am indebted to a number of authors and resources, which I detail in the Acknowledgements.

The solitude of the western fjordlands is not fiction, either. Even the main city of the region, the historical power Bergen, was primarily accessible via the sea—the Bergen Line railroad connected over the Hardangervidda to Voss in 1883 as the narrow gauge Voss Line, but it wasn't until 1909 that the line extended all the way to Oslo.

If the main city of the region was hard to get to, imagine little farming communities high up in the mountains, next to glacial lakes. Down next to the network of fjords, residents could travel to church thanks to an all-day boat ride. But up in the mountains? Because the Myklebost farm is on a lake, high up in the shadow of Jostedalsbreen glacier, I like to think it was doubly isolated—getting down away from the lake took a day along rutted cart paths, and then from there the only options were boats of all sizes, including the Fylkesbaatane ferries (established in 1858).

The women's suffrage meeting and Mrs. Nordness were a fiction, but inspired by Mrs. Quam and her pioneering efforts to gain women respect and the right to vote.

When it comes to language, it can be a little thorny. The Nynorsk (New Norwegian) movement in the late 19th century was an attempt (like folk song and story collecting) to revive and reclaim "authentic" Norwegian culture and language. Danish had been the standard written language for 400 years, and the nationalist Nynorsk movement sought to reclaim a true Norwegian language, blending Old Norse and local dialects.

Norway continues, in its spoken language, to be a country of dialects, and I presume it would have been even more noticeable at the turn of the 20th century. My assumption in this story is that the dialects of Bergen and Sunnfjord were mutually intelligible, and that the people Oleanna encountered in Bergen would have found her speech completely comprehensible, if not charmingly outré.

And finally, a note on emigration. In 1825 the first organized emigration from Norway to America sailed from Stavanger to New York. Those first 52 people led the way, and eventually more than 800,000 Norwegians emigrated to American between 1825-1939. In 1884, the highest number of Norwegians in one year left for America—28,804 emigrants, with a similarly large spike again in 1903.

Years after I had begun this book, during the final stages of editing, I found the most delightful letter from my great-grandfather John to his daughter and granddaughter, my mom. I include it here as a tribute to him, to the stories of his life I never knew, and to the beautiful, poetic spirit beneath the quiet, solid, oh-so-Scandinavian homesteader's exterior. This letter is included here as I found it, in an old envelope of family photos.

Starkweather, Mar 22, 63

Dear Janis and Mom and Dad

Thank you Janis for the very wellcome Letter. It's good to know someone
is thinking of you and that someone really understand. Just eleven days
ago it was a year since Grandma was called to her rest, and the Events has
kept comming back to me like it was just happining this year. I don't think
I will ever forget or overcome the loss of Her. When grief and sorrow
wants to overwhelm me I have to drive out to the cemetery and spend a
few moments by Her grave-side, and a few tears seems to relieve the
pressure.

That sick spell I had some time ago has cleared upp in good shape so I
feel fairly well now.

The weather is just lovely here today - 58 - How is that for a spring day?
Soon the Robins and the middowlarks and the Geese and everything else
connected with Spring will be here, so you really must exuse me if I don't
come out to visit you this spring, no matter how much I would like to see
your new car and the new House (that I'm glad you got) But I will have to
be here and wellcome thos Robins when they come.

Lots of love to you all from Grandpa.


*Wellcome thos Robins when they come, indeed.*

# Acknowledgements

I'M VERY GRATEFUL to a number of authors for their very useful books, including: *Scandinavia: A Political History of Denmark, Norway and Sweden from 1513 to 1900* by R. Nisbet Bain, 1905; *Norwegian Folk Art: The Migration of a Tradition*, Abbeville Press (1995); *The Woven Coverlets of Norway*, by Katherine Larson (U of Washington Press) (2001); *Remedies and Rituals: Folk Medicine in Norway and the New Land*, by Kathleen Stokker, Minnesota Historical Society Press, 2007; and *A History of Modern Norway, 1814-1972*, by TK Derry (Clarendon Press) (1973).

Also incredibly helpful was the Sogn og Fjordane fylke (county) cultural website http://sognogfjordane.kulturnett.no and the Norway Heritage website http://www.norwayheritage.com. The 1903 Baedeker *Norway, Sweden, and Denmark Handbook for Travellers* was also invaluable, and made available for free online by the wonderful folks at http://archive.org.

I must make clear that any errors in this book are entirely mine.

I'd also like to thank the divine Trio Mediaeval for their inspiration during my writing. Their *Folk Songs* was on constant repeat during the writing, and I've used their translation of "I Mine

Kåte Ungdomsdagar" ("In My Reckless, Youthful Days" and "So Ro, Godt Barn" ("Rest Now, Sweet Child") in Chapter Ten.

This book was a long one in the writing. I began the story in November 2006, and completed the last draft in April 2011. Throughout, the support and kind words of dear friends and family kept me going. In particular, I would like to point out the support— both editorial and collegial—from Heather Domin, Anna Scott Graham, and Jeff Sypeck. You helped the book become what it always wanted to be, and I am grateful for your input, support, and friendship. I am also very grateful to Andrea Connell, who provided valuable feedback on the formatting of the first edition, which informed the design of this second edition. Again, any errors are entirely mine.

I am very indebted to Jane; she knows why, and I am forever grateful.

And there is always, always Craig, who is patient and loving, and believes in me even when I don't.

*Oleanna* would never have been written had it not been for my mother's interest in, and passion for, Norway. She passed those qualities along to me, for which I am deeply grateful. It is an essential part of who I am.

I began writing this book a few months after mom died, and it is a great sadness in my life that she will never read these words.

Julie K. Rose writes historical and contemporary fiction. She lives in the Bay Area with her husband and cat, and loves reading, watching episodes of Doctor Who, and enjoying the amazing natural beauty of Northern California. She is also the author of *The Pilgrim Glass*. Learn more at www.juliekrose.com.

Made in the USA
San Bernardino, CA
22 June 2019